SALVATORE

A DARK MAFIA ROMANCE

NATASHA KNIGHT

Copyright © 2016 by Natasha Knight

All rights reserved.

No part of this book may be reproduced in any form or by any electronic or mechanical means, including information storage and retrieval systems, without written permission from the author, except for the use of brief quotations in a book review.

Cover by CoverLuv

Editing by Ann Curtis

Photographer Michelle Lancaster @lanefotograf

Click here to sign up for my newsletter to receive new release news and updates!

PROLOGUE
SALVATORE

I signed the contract before me, pressing so hard that the track of my signature left a groove on the sheet of paper. I set the pen down and slid the pages across the table to her.

Lucia.

I could barely meet her gaze as she raised big, innocent, frightened eyes to mine.

She looked at it, at the collected, official documents that would bind her to me. That would make her mine. I wasn't sure if she was reading or simply staring, trying to make sense of what had just happened. What had been decided for her. For both of us.

She turned reddened eyes to her father. I didn't miss the questions I saw inside them. The plea. The disbelief.

But DeMarco kept his eyes lowered, his head bent in defeat. He couldn't look at his daughter, not after what he'd been made to watch.

I understood that, and I hated my own father more for making him do it.

Lucia sucked in a ragged breath. Could everyone hear it or just me? I saw the rapid pulse beating in her neck. Her hand trembled when she picked up the pen. She met my gaze once more. One final plea? I watched her struggle against the tears that threatened to spill on her already stained cheeks.

I didn't know what I felt upon seeing them. Hell, I didn't know what I felt about anything at all anymore.

"Sign."

My father's command made her turn. I watched their gazes collide.

"We don't have all day."

To call him domineering was an understatement. He was someone who made grown men tremble.

But she didn't shy away.

"Sign, Lucia," her father said quietly.

She didn't look at anyone after that. Instead, she put pen to paper and signed her name—Lucia Annalisa DeMarco—on the dotted line adjacent to mine. My family's attorney applied the seal to the sheets as soon as she finished, quickly taking them and leaving the room.

I guess it was all official, then. Decided. Done.

My father stood, gave me his signature look of displeasure, and walked out of the room. Two of his men followed.

"Do you need a minute?" I asked her. Did she want to say good-bye to her father?

"No."

She refused to look at him or at me. Instead, she pushed her chair back and stood, the now-wrinkled white skirt falling over her thighs. She fisted her hands at her sides.

"I'm ready."

I rose and gestured to one of the waiting men. She walked ahead of him as if he walked her to her execution. I glanced at her father, then at the cold examining table with the leather restraints now hanging open, useless, their victim released. The image of what had happened there just moments earlier shamed me.

But it could have been so much worse for her.

It could have gone the way my father wanted. *His* cruelty knew no bounds.

She had me to thank for saving her from that.

So why did I still feel like a monster? A beast? A pathetic, spineless puppet?

I owned Lucia DeMarco, but the thought only made me sick. She was the token, the living, breathing trophy of my family's triumph over hers.

I walked out of the room and rode the elevator

down to the lobby, emptying my eyes of emotion. That was one thing I did well.

I walked out onto the stifling, noisy Manhattan sidewalk and climbed into the backseat of my waiting car. The driver knew where to take me, and twenty minutes later, I walked into the whorehouse, to a room in the back, the image of Lucia lying on that examining table, bound, struggling, her face turned away as the doctor probed her before declaring her intact, burned into my memory forever.

I'd stood beside her. I hadn't looked. Did that absolve me? Surely that meant something?

But why was my cock hard, then?

She'd cried quietly. I'd watched her tears slip off her face and fall to the floor and willed myself to be anywhere but there. Willed myself not to hear the sounds, my father's degrading words, her quiet breaths as she struggled to remain silent.

All while I'd stood by.

I was a coward. A monster. Because when I did finally meet those burning amber eyes, when I dared shift my gaze to hers, our eyes had locked, and I saw the quiet plea inside them. A silent cry for help.

In desperation, she'd sought *my* help.

And I'd looked away.

Her father's face had gone white when he'd realized the full cost he'd agreed to; the payment of the debt he'd set upon her shoulders.

Her life for his. For all of theirs.

Fucking selfish bastard didn't deserve to live. He should have died to protect her. He should never—ever—have allowed this to happen.

I sucked in a breath, heavy and wet, drowning me.

I poured myself a drink, slammed it back, and repeated. Whiskey was good. Whiskey dulled the scene replaying in my head. But it did nothing to wipe out the image of her eyes on mine. Her terrified, desperate eyes.

I threw the glass, smashing it in the corner. One of the whores came to me, knelt between my spread legs, and took my cock out of my pants. Her lips moved, saying something I didn't hear over the war raging inside my head, and fucked up as fucked up can be, she took my already hard cock into her mouth.

I gripped a handful of the bitch's hair and closed my eyes, letting her do her work, taking me deep into her throat. But I didn't want gentle, not now. I needed more. I stood, squeezed my eyes shut against the image of Lucia on that table, and fucked the whore's face until she choked and tears streamed down her cheeks. Until I finally came, emptying down her throat, the sexual release, like the whiskey, gave me nothing. There wasn't enough sex or alcohol in the world to burn that particular image of Lucia out of my mind, but maybe I deserved it.

Deserved the guilt. I should man up and own it. I allowed it all to happen, after all. I stood by and did nothing.

And now, she was mine, and I was hers.

Her very own monster.

1

LUCIA

Five Years Later
Calabria, Italy

The last time I walked down the aisle of this cathedral had been my confirmation day. I'd been a child. I'd worn a beautiful white dress, and my mother had wound a rosary through my fingers, binding my hands in prayer.

I hadn't prayed, though. Instead, I'd thought of how I looked in my dress. How it was the prettiest of all the girls. How I was the prettiest.

Today, I wore black. And I no longer cared who was the prettiest. Today, I followed my father's casket to the front of the church.

Black lace hid my face, so I could take in the audience without them seeing me. The pews stood empty until we reached the front rows, where ten were occupied. Fifteen mourners on the right—my family's side. Double that on the left. Did soldiers count as mourners, though? Because that's what the Benedetti's had brought.

I ignored them and looked at each of the fifteen faces who had dared show up on my side. My father did not have many friends. In fact, of the fifteen, two were his brothers, my uncles, and one, his sister. The other twelve made up their families. Only the women sat in the pews, though. My male cousins carried my father's coffin.

As the procession neared the front pew, I prepared myself for the moment I would see *his* face. The face of the man who had, five years ago, sat across from me in a cold, sterile room and signed a contract, declaring his ownership of me. A vow, like a marriage vow, perhaps. But the words *cherish* and *love* had been absent from the pages; *take* and *keep* having taken their place.

No, we had a different sort of contract. My life to spare my family. Me as the sacrifice, the payer of the debt. Me to show anyone in the DeMarco family who had any fight left that the Benedetti's owned their daughter. The Benedetti's owned the DeMarco princess.

I hate the Benedetti family. I hate every single one of them.

The procession halted. My sister, Isabella, stood close enough behind me that I felt her there. At least she wasn't crying. At least she knew not to show weakness. In fact, no sound came from her at all.

Seeing her today, it had surprised me.

Seeing my niece, Effie, for the first time, it twisted my heart, reminding me of yet another thing that had been taken from me.

Six pallbearers laid my father's coffin down on the table arranged to receive it. It would be a closed-casket funeral. No viewing. He'd blown half his head off when he'd shot himself in the mouth.

My cousins turned to me. Luke, who was the adopted son of my uncle, looked just beyond me, though. Beyond me and to my sister. His eyes, a soft, pale blue I remembered from childhood, had hardened to steel. I watched, wishing I could turn back and look at my sister, see what her eyes said. But then his gaze shifted to me. He looked very different from the boy I'd grown up with. But he *was* very different or had become so over the last five years. We all had. Through the lace shielding my face, I met his eyes. Could he see the rage simmering inside me? He gave me a quick, short nod. An acknowledgment. I wondered if anyone saw it. He could be killed for it. The Benedetti's took no prisoners. Well, apart from me. But a woman. What could a woman do?

They would see.

A man moved into my periphery and cleared his throat. I knew who it was. Standing up straighter, steeling myself, I forced my heart to stop its frantic pounding and turned to face him.

Salvatore Benedetti.

I swallowed as my gaze traveled from the black silk tie he wore upward. I remembered him. I remembered him clearly. But the suit seemed to stretch tighter over muscle now, his chest broader, his arms thicker. I forced my gaze higher, pausing at his neck, willing myself to slow my breathing.

I could not show weakness. I could not show fear. But that day, when they'd forced me onto that table—I still shuddered at how cold it had felt against my naked thighs—he hadn't spoken. Not a single word. He had looked at me, watched my struggle, watched me bite my tongue as they shamed me.

But I also remembered something else, and that gave me the courage to raise my eyes to his. He'd turned away first. Was it that he hadn't been able to look at me? To witness my degradation? Or could he not stand the thought of me *seeing* him for what he was?

Our families had decided. I'd had little choice. I wondered for a moment what choice he'd had, but I wouldn't consider that. It didn't matter. Salvatore

Benedetti would one day rule the Benedetti family. He would be boss. He would become what I vowed to destroy five years ago.

I masked any emotion as I turned my gaze up to his. I'd learned to hide my feelings well over the last few years.

My heart stopped for a single moment. Everything seemed to still, as if waiting. Something fluttered inside my belly as cobalt-blue eyes met mine.

Not steely but soft.

I remembered how I'd thought that five years ago too. How, for just the briefest moment on that terrible day, I'd thought there was hope. That he'd stop what was happening. But I'd been wrong. Any perceived softness, it only deceived. It hid behind it a coldhearted monster, ready to take.

And what happened in that magical garden a year ago, when before I'd seen who he was, I'd placed my hand inside his. Danced with him.

No. I couldn't think about that night now or ever again. I would need to remember that. To not to allow myself the luxury of being fooled.

Salvatore blinked and stepped aside, gesturing for me to enter the pew. His father and brother stood watching me, his father's expression screaming victory. He gave me a cruel grin and held out his hand to the space beside him. I moved, my legs somehow carrying me even as I trembled inside.

I would turn my fear to hate. I would make it burn hot.

Because I would need it to survive what lay in store for me. I'd been sixteen when I'd been made to sign that contract. I knew well the true terror of what it meant was only about to begin.

I took my place beside his father. Salvatore resumed his seat to my right. I had the feeling he took as much care not to touch me as I did not to touch either him or his father. I didn't turn to look at my sister when she was ushered into a pew across the aisle. I paid no attention to the Benedetti soldiers lining the perimeter of the church just as I hadn't paid any to the army the Benedetti's had assembled outside. Instead, I watched Father Samson. He'd been old when I'd been confirmed. Now he looked ancient.

He blessed my father, even though he had taken his own life. He prayed for his soul. After all this time, I didn't think I cared anymore. But that kindness, it gave me some small comfort.

No one cried. How strange that no one would cry at a funeral. That fact impressed itself upon me, and it felt wrong.

The service ended one hour later. My cousins once again circled the casket and lifted it. Once it passed us, Salvatore stepped out of the pew. He waited for me to go ahead, and I did, stiffening when I felt the slight touch of his hand at my lower back. He must have felt me stiffen because he removed his hand. We emerged from the darkness inside the church out onto the square, the bright Italian sun momentarily blinding. My father would be buried in Calabria. It was his wish, to be returned to his place of birth. Both the Benedetti and the DeMarco families were well-known here, and for once, I was grateful for the soldiers holding the press at bay, even as camera's clicked in quick succession, capturing everything from a distance.

I stood to the side and watched as they set the casket inside the waiting hearse. The Benedetti men flanked me with Salvatore standing too close for my comfort. Some commotion caught my attention, and I watched as four-year-old Effie escaped from her nanny's grip and ran toward her mother, my sister, and wrapped her arms around Isabella's legs. All of us turned, in fact, and I took that moment to break away from the Benedetti men and walked toward them, toward my family.

"Lucia."

Isabella greeted me, her eyes reddened, her cheeks dry. She looked different than the last time I'd seen her. She looked harder. Older than her twenty-two years.

She took a moment to look at me, to take in how five years had made the difference between the sixteen-year-old girl she had known and the woman who stood before her now. She then surprised me by pulling me in for a tight hug.

"I missed you so much."

I let out some sound, and for a moment, allowed my body to give over to her embrace. We'd been so close for so long, but then she'd left. She'd turned her back on me and walked away. I knew why. I even understood. But it hurt all the same, and my anger over everything wrapped even her up into this neat little world of hate I'd created for myself.

The thought that it should have been her, that it would have been her, blared inside me, even though I wanted it to go away. It wasn't her fault. None of this was her fault. In fact, she was the only one not to blame.

"Mama," came Effie's voice.

Isabella released me from her embrace but squeezed my arms as if willing upon me strength. Did she see my weakness in that moment? Could they all see my fear?

"Mama," Effie repeated with the impatience of a child, tugging at Isabella's skirt. Isabella picked her up.

"Why did you come back?" I asked, my voice sounding foreign. Cold. "Why now?" It was that or falling apart, and I would not allow the latter.

She looked taken aback. Her little girl watched me while I tried not to look at her. It was impossible, though. Pretty, blue-gray eyes watched me, seeming to bore right through me. I wondered if they'd come from her father, but Isabella had always refused to tell anyone who that was.

"This is Effie," Isabella said, choosing to ignore my question. "Effie, this is your Aunt Lucia."

Effie studied me for a long moment, then gave me a quick smile, a small dimple forming in her right cheek when she did.

"Hi, Effie," I said, touching her caramel-colored curly hair.

"Hi."

"Why are you back?" I asked again. I felt so much anger, and I wanted to burn everyone up with it. Everyone who had abandoned me. Who had so easily given me up.

"Because I should never have left. Forgive me." She glanced at the hearse. "Life is too short."

I knew she'd not had a choice. When my father had found out she was pregnant, he'd freaked. First-born daughter to the boss of the DeMarco family pregnant out of wedlock. As modern as my family was, there were some things that did not change. I still wonder if my father regretted his decisions. It had cost him two daughters.

But then again, we seemed to be easy to give away. If he'd had a son, perhaps things would have been different.

"I'll come see you next week."

"Why? Why bother now?"

She lifted her chin, a stubborn gesture I remembered from when we were little.

The sound of a car backfiring made us all jump. The soldiers circling the square all drew weapons until we all realized there was no threat. Before I turned back to her, though, I noticed Salvatore, who stood by his car, tuck the shiny metal of a pistol back into its holster beneath his jacket.

These were violent men. Men to whom killing was part of life. Part of business. Even having grown up in their world, it still made me shudder.

Salvatore shifted his gaze to me. From this distance, I couldn't see his eyes, but he watched me while standing beside the sedan ready to drive us to the cemetery. "I have to go."

"Lucia," my sister started, this time taking my hand. Hers felt warm, soft. It made me want to cry for all we'd lost.

"What?" I snapped. I could not cry. I would not. Not here.

"Be strong. You're not alone."

"Really?" I tugged my hand free. "That would be a first."

Anger flashed through her eyes. Did she want to slap me, I wondered? Would she? Would Salvatore allow it? For a moment, I thought of him coming to my rescue, of him punishing my sister for laying a hand on me. But then, I remembered who I was. Who he was. *What* I was to him.

"I have to go." I took a step back.

Isabella's eyes filled with tears, sadness replacing the momentary anger, and I turned away.

Show no weakness. Not an ounce of it.

I faced Salvatore, the man who owned me. Surely the contract we'd signed wouldn't hold up in any court of law. But it wasn't the contract that dictated my life. I knew what would happen if I didn't do as I was told. I knew who would pay.

I glanced at Isabella and her daughter again. At my uncles and aunts and cousins.

No, they wouldn't need a court of law to ensure I cooperated. The contract was simply another means of humiliation, like the examination had been.

No. Block that memory. I would not have it.

Salvatore straightened to his full height, standing nearly a foot taller than me at six feet four, and opened the sedan door. Even from across the square, I could see he waited patiently, and I thought he might be trying to be civilized, polite. For the sake of the gathered reporters? Surely not for my benefit. I wondered for a moment if he wanted this. If he wanted *me* like this, knowing it was not my will.

But then again, *owning* another person? That had to be the ultimate high.

I glanced back once more at Isabella. I couldn't help it. For the last five years, I'd been shut away at school. I'd lived at St. Mary's and received private tutoring to earn my high-school degree before attending the small college there, studying, free—to a point. But now, it was time to enter the den of the wolf. My schooling was complete, and it was time for me to assume my place as Salvatore Benedetti's *possession*. For one moment, I tried to imagine that it wasn't true. That it was all a dream, a nightmare. That I could look at my big sister and know she'd make it all okay, like she always did. Just one moment, then I'd be able to do this. To go to my enemy, to enter into his house, knowing I would be an outsider forever. Hated. My presence like a living trophy of their victory over my father, my family.

What would Salvatore expect of me?

I steeled myself and faced him, determined to hold his gaze as I crossed the square. Eyes burned into my back, and the crowd hushed, watching me go to him. He didn't smile as I neared. Nothing changed. His face seemed to be set in stone. I reached him and stopped just inches from him, our eyes locked on each other.

"Lucia."

Salvatore said my name, his voice low and dark, making me shudder.

I didn't know what to say, even though I'd practiced this moment in my mind for months. Years. Now, I simply stood like a mute thing.

But then his father, Franco Benedetti, head of the family and a man I thoroughly despised, approached. He didn't even try to hide his enjoyment of the situation.

I cleared my throat, finally finding my voice. "Why are you here? You have no right." I heard my question, knew it was the same one I'd asked my sister.

"I came to give you my condolences."

Franco leaned in, looking around as if we were somehow coconspirators.

"Actually," he started, his tone lower, "I wouldn't miss it for the world."

I didn't think. I didn't do anything but feel the anger, the hot rage as it bubbled over inside me. My hands clenched into fists, and I spat at his shoe. Except he moved at the last moment, and I missed. When I looked up, Salvatore's face showed his shock, and Franco's was quickly reddening, showing his fury. Although I stood my ground, my heart jackhammered against my chest. I wasn't sure he wouldn't hit me. Hell, between this and my comment to Isabella, maybe that's what I was going for.

Salvatore gripped my arm. "Apologize."

"No," I replied, my eyes locked on his father's black gaze.

Dominic, Salvatore's brother, who'd stood watching from a few feet away, approached. He had a smile on his face as he put his arm around his father's shoulders. Salvatore tensed beside me.

"We're getting some attention. Come on, Paps. Let's go."

I met Dominic's gaze, and I would have sworn he was enjoying the spectacle.

"Apologize." Salvatore's grip tightened around my arm.

I cocked my head to the side. "I'm sorry I missed," I said, a grin spreading across my face.

Dominic's eyebrows shot up, and Salvatore muttered a curse under his breath.

"Let's go," Dominic said just when I thought his father would explode.

"In." Salvatore's other hand gripped my waist as he pushed me into the sedan.

"Get your hands off me," I said, trying to force him off.

He climbed in beside me and pulled the car door shut. The driver started the engine. Salvatore transferred his grip to my knee, his eyes burning a hole through me. "That was a very stupid thing to do." His fingers bit into my flesh.

I had nothing to say. In fact, all I could do was shake violently. I wrapped my arms around myself.

"Turn down the air conditioning," he told the driver, his gaze still locked on mine.

I wished it were the cold that had me shivering.

"Yes, sir," the driver said.

Being so close, seeing him again, it was too

much, too intense. It brought too many memories back and foretold a future I did not want.

"You're hurting me."

Salvatore blinked, as if processing each word I spoke one at a time. He shifted his gaze to where his hand gripped my knee. I held my breath, feeling powerless, knowing I was entirely at his mercy.

Knowing this was only the beginning of my hell.

2

SALVATORE

I looked down to where I held her, how hard my fingers were squeezing her. It took some effort, but I released her and sat back in the seat, my gaze still on her, on this rebellious, courageous stranger.

Courageous. Lucia was courageous.

She was also a stranger.

I knew nothing about her. Only her name and her face. Her signature on a stupid piece of paper.

I had never seen a woman stand up to my father like that. I'd never seen a man do it either—or, I should say, when I had, it had been the last time I'd seen that man alive.

I looked out the front window. "Don't antagonize my father. He always wins."

"Everyone loses sometime." She turned away

and folded her arms across her chest, watching the streets pass by as we drove to the cemetery.

The black veil of her hat had shielded her face from me in the church, but her whiskey-colored eyes had shone through, bright, strong, angry. Very angry. I refused to let the image of how those eyes had looked at me the last time occupy my mind. I would know only this new, angry Lucia.

The one I needed to control.

Her interaction with her sister had been stiff. I'd seen it even from the distance in the courtyard. I knew she hadn't seen either her sister or her father—even once—in the last five years. The day she'd signed the contract, she'd been sent away to finish her schooling. A year-round, all-girls Catholic school chosen by my father. A small institution hidden away in the suburbs of Philadelphia, where she'd lived comfortably but was under strict supervision. Her movements had been monitored, and at least one bodyguard had accompanied her wherever she went. For the most part, at least. Apart from our surprise meeting at Hollister's gala. I had monthly updates on her comings and goings, and not once had her family come to visit her. Well, her father had tried, but she'd refused to see him. She'd chosen to spend the holidays at school.

I glanced at her, wondering if she regretted that now.

"I'm sorry for your loss."

Her body stiffened, and the only sign that she might be crying was when she moved her hand toward her face, pretending to scratch her cheek after swiping it under her eye.

"Are you?" she asked, her voice strained, her face still turned toward the window.

"I know what it's like to lose someone you're close to." I knew firsthand, in fact. My brother, Sergio, had been my best friend. It had never once, not even in the world we lived in, occurred to me that he could die. My mother had died soon after him. Her death, thankfully, not as violent as Sergio's. Although cancer brought its own sort of violence, snuffing out a human life as efficiently as a bullet did.

She turned to me and lifted her veil, tucking it behind the small hat fitted on top of her head. She was stunning. When I'd first met her in person, she'd been sixteen. She'd been pretty, but now, she was no longer a child. Her features had sharpened, her lips fuller, her cheekbones even more prominent. Her eyes...even more accusing.

She studied me, a slow, steady perusal from head to toe. When her gaze met mine, I swallowed, uncertain. Uncertainty was not new to me. I lived with it daily. But this? This was new, this was something—someone—I knew not at all.

The day we'd signed the contract, the day I'd stood by and allowed her to be humiliated, something had happened to me, some obligation had formed, some bond between us. Maybe it was the disgust I felt for myself for standing by and letting it happen. At the time, I told myself, I'd had no choice, but I tried not to lie to myself. Not anymore. After that day, something had changed. I owed her something. What that thing was, I did not know. An apology? Seemed stupid, a waste. My protection? She would have that, she already did. But she was my enemy and the spoils of war. My father had tried very hard to drill that into my head, but he hadn't seen that look in her eyes that day—the desperate, terrified plea inside them—nor did he see it every time he lay his head down to sleep.

I wondered if my father lost sleep over anything at all, actually.

You were twenty-four. What could you have done?

No, not good enough. Not anymore.

"You know what it's like to lose someone close?" Her tone dripped sarcasm. "My father and I weren't close."

I studied her, feeling my face tighten, my eyes narrow infinitesimally.

I did not speak.

"But let me ask you something. Do you know what it's like to watch people you love killed before your very eyes?"

I did, but still, I remained silent.

"To have everyone taken away from you? To become the *property* of your enemy?"

Oh yes. Yes, I did.

"To be sent to live on your own among strangers with not a friend in the world? Under constant watch. I don't think you know those things, Salvatore, because if you did, you would *feel*. You would have some compassion. Be human." She gave me another once-over. "But there is one thing you do know, isn't there? You know how to stand by and do nothing at all."

My hands clenched into fists, and a sudden, hot anger burned inside me. I saw the driver's eyes flash back at us in the rearview mirror, but he kept driving, slowing down as we passed through the cemetery gates.

"Be careful," I warned, my tone low and quiet. But it was true, wasn't it? What she said was true.

Lucia's eyes narrowed, and she tilted her head to the side, one corner of her mouth rising into a smirk. "Did Daddy give you his seal of approval that day? Did he pat you on the back later? Call you a 'good boy?'" she taunted.

My fingernails dug into my palms, and I made it a point of looking out the window as the driver parked the car.

"Is that it, Salvatore?"

She misunderstood my silence, mistaking it for weakness.

The driver killed the engine. "Give us a minute," I said. He stepped out of the car and closed the door, standing just outside.

I turned back to her.

"Are you Daddy's little puppet?" she asked.

Her eyes spewed hate. Did she know she toed a very dangerous line? That she broached a truth that had kept me in a state of constant struggle these past few years?

I gave a little snort and relaxed my body, smiling, leaning just a little closer. I could see the pulse at her neck working, telling me her heart pounded hard, telling me that on the inside, she wasn't so sure.

"Lucia." I said softly, raising my hand.

Her gaze shifted to it, then back to my eyes.

I touched her face with the backs of my fingers, caressing that soft, creamy skin. "So pretty," I said, my eyes on her lips when I gripped her chin. "But such a big mouth."

She swallowed, her eyes widening.

I leaned in close enough to smell her perfume, something soft and light and somehow, even now, erotic. I inhaled deeply before drawing her to me, my eyes still on those lips. She held her breath. "So, so pretty." My other hand traveled to her chest, to the soft swell of one breast, coming to rest on her pounding heart. She knew I knew I affected her.

I turned her face to the side, rubbing the scruff of my jaw against it before bringing my mouth to her ear. "Be careful," I whispered, feeling her shudder when I ran my tongue over the ridge of her ear before sliding it inside.

She gasped. Her hands came up to my chest, but she didn't push.

"When you try to bite the wolf," I said, "he just might bite back."

To make my point, I took her earlobe into my mouth and gently drew my teeth over it, drawing it out. Beneath the hand that rested against her heart, her nipple hardened.

A moment later, I released her and sat back, victorious. I tapped my ring against the window, absently glancing at the family crest. The driver opened the door.

"Let's go put your father in the ground," I said, climbing out. She emerged a moment later, the net of her hat back in place. I buttoned my coat jacket. "Fucking stifling here." I gestured for her to go ahead. She did, refusing to meet my gaze or make a comment. I smiled, putting one tick on my side of the column marking my win for this round.

We stayed in my family's home in Calabria, sharing a suite of rooms—a bedroom for each of us and a common sitting room. Our flight to New Jersey left the next day. Lucia would move into my home tomorrow. She'd finished her studies, graduated with honors, and now that she'd turned twenty-one, it was time for me to take possession of her.

A knock at the door announced the delivery of dinner. As a kindness, I'd ordered our meal in our room rather than making her eat with my family. A girl I didn't know set the table in the living area and left. The scent of the food made my stomach rumble. I knocked on Lucia's bedroom door. I wouldn't force her to share my bed. Not just yet.

"Dinner's ready," I said through the door.

"I'm not hungry," she replied. "I already told you that."

"Well, you need to eat. You haven't eaten anything all day."

"What are you, my mother?"

"Open the door, Lucia."

"Go away, Salvatore."

"I'm only asking once."

"Then what? You'll huff and you'll puff and you'll break my door down? Isn't that what the big bad *wolf* does?"

I smiled. Clever.

But I was cleverer.

I slid my key into the lock and pushed the door open. She gasped, turning from where she sat at the vanity.

"No need to exert myself huffing and puffing. I

have the key. It's my house." I held it out for her to see before tucking it into my pocket.

Even air-conditioned, the rooms felt sticky, and her bedroom more so. I'd taken off the heavy jacket and tie I'd worn earlier, and now I unbuttoned the top few buttons of my shirt.

"You mean your father's house," she goaded. She already knew the buttons to push.

I forced a grin and went to her suitcase, flipping it open. After rifling through her things, I found a pair of lace panties and lifted them out.

"Don't touch my things! Get out!" She lunged to take the underwear out of my hand.

I raised it above my head and out of her reach, really smiling now. "Dinner's ready."

"You are one stubborn son of a bitch!"

She jumped to reach the lacy slip. I stepped back and lowered it, inspecting the little pink thing. "Pretty."

"Screw you!"

I allowed her to grab it this time, and she shoved it into her suitcase and attempted to zip it. With a snort, I took her by the arms and turned her, holding her so I could look at her and she at me.

"Let me go!"

She had already changed into a nightie, a simple, long, almost sheer white cotton dress that reached to just above her knees. She wore no bra, and her small, round breasts swelled beneath the fine fabric, her dark nipples pressing against it.

"You're finished with school, and you're twenty-one now, Lucia. You know the contract. You will come live with me. You belong to me, like it or not, and you will do as I say."

"Oh!" She made an incredulous face. "Oh! I will *do as you say*?"

"Yes."

"Or what?"

She attempted to free herself from my grip, but I shook her once, holding her tighter. Her fingers curled around the fabric of my shirt.

"So many options," I said, slowly dropping my gaze to her breasts while I brushed a thick strand of hair over her shoulder. "So many possibilities."

Before I'd even turned my gaze up to hers, she raised her free arm in an attempt to slap me. My grip hardened, and I tossed her onto the bed. Before she could right herself, I climbed on top of her and grabbed her wrists. They were small and delicate and vulnerable. I dragged them out to either side of her, pinning her with my weight, my gaze traveling down over the mounds of her breasts to where her nightie rode up her thigh, exposing white lace panties.

She liked lace.

I liked lace.

In fact, I'd like to lick her cunt through that lace.

My cock stiffened. Lucia stilled, her eyes wide on the crotch of my pants for a moment before they met mine.

The fun was suddenly out of it for me. I released her.

"Don't make this harder than it already is," I said, climbing off the bed, turning my back to her momentarily until I adjusted the crotch of my pants.

"How is it hard for you? I'm the one whose father we just put in the fucking ground. I'm the one who's lost everything. I'm the one who pays when I didn't have anything to do with anything!"

Her hand shook as she wiped away the tears that streamed down her face. She looked at me with puffy, red eyes, and I realized she'd probably been in here crying.

Fuck.

She turned away and, pulling two tissues out of the box on the nightstand, wiped her face clean.

"How is this hard for you?" she asked again, her voice quivering as her chest heaved with a heavy breath.

The way she looked at me—did she think I wanted this?

I raked my hand through my hair, feeling like an asshole. "I meant it earlier, when I said I know what it's like to lose someone you love."

She remained silent, watching me.

"Even if you weren't close with your father, he was your father."

I knew on the one hand that I needed to control this, control her. I knew how my father would do that. Knew he'd call me weak if he saw me now. But I couldn't do it. Not yet. Not today.

"Look, it's been a really long day. A long fucking week. We're both tired. Just eat something. I'll leave you alone."

I left her room without looking back and walked out the door of the suite, trying to shake off the image of her anguished face. It was impossible.

"You look like shit, boss," Marco said as I walked out into the hall.

Marco was my private bodyguard and my friend. One of the very few in the world. Maybe the only one I had left.

"I feel like shit. Make sure she doesn't go anywhere, okay?"

Marco nodded.

I headed for the stairs. The house had four floors, of which my room took up half of the third. My father's rooms were on the top floor, and Dominic's were down the hall from mine. The second floor housed more guest rooms, but we didn't have any other overnight guests apart from Lucia tonight.

Before reaching the first-floor landing, I heard the loud voices of men talking. I followed the sound into the dining room, where a large group had gathered around the table, my father at its head. He looked at me, his gaze flat. I wondered what he thought of me right at that moment. If he was surprised to see me downstairs. Dominic, my younger brother, sat beside him with that stupid grin he always wore. The one that made me want to smack the living shit out of him.

I didn't miss the fact he sat to my father's right. My seat.

He didn't make a move to rise. Instead, my uncle and family advisor, Roman, who sat to my father's left, got up. He was my mother's brother, and one of the few men my father trusted.

"Salvatore."

He offered me his seat. I thanked him and sat down.

Dominic picked up his beer and leaned toward me. "Thought you'd be busy with your shiny new plaything."

"She just buried her father, asshole." I signaled for a beer, which the waiter brought a moment later. They were all jumpy, eager to serve. Probably more eager to get us the hell out of there. I hadn't been back in a few years but knew when we were in town, the house became a target. The Benedetti family was a sort of legend here. We owned southern Italy and were moving in on the Sicilian territory. Another war brewed, one we'd win, like we'd won over the

DeMarcos. Wherever we went, violence followed. The girl upstairs was testament to that.

Her words played back in my ears.

"I'm the one who pays when I didn't have anything to do with anything."

She was right. She was an innocent; her fate decided when she hadn't been more than a child. Her sister's pregnancy had placed Lucia at the heart of a decades-old war.

"She is a sweet little thing," Dominic continued, sipping his beer. "Nice piece of—"

"Shut the fuck up, Dominic," I said, my hands fisting.

"Salvatore's right. Girl just buried her father," my father admonished my brother, his gaze locked on me.

I didn't trust this, didn't trust him. My father had always been better at cutting me down. Certainly not defending me.

"You just make sure she knows who the boss is, son. I don't ever want to see another incident like this afternoon again, you understand?"

Ah, there they were, my father's true colors.

I nodded without looking at him, swallowing half of my drink.

"Good. Let's eat."

3

LUCIA

Salvatore surprised me. I expected violence. I'd prepared myself for it. But this, this kindness? His attempt to understand? Was that what it was? I didn't like it. And I didn't like how my body reacted to having him so close.

When I heard him leave, I went to the outer room. My stomach growled. I hadn't eaten all day, and as appealing as a hunger strike seemed, when you were actually hungry, it lost some of its appeal.

I took the lid off one of the two dishes to find a thick steak, potatoes, and mixed grilled vegetables. I swallowed, salivating already, and sat down. Picking up the knife and fork, I glanced at the door before I dug in. If he returned, I'd be ashamed at having given in. Even if he kept his word and stayed away, when he saw I'd eaten, wouldn't it just be a second victory to him?

I placed a piece of the meat in my mouth. So buttery and delicious, it melted on my tongue. God, that made me not care what he thought. I took a second bite, then tasted the grilled potatoes spiced with rosemary and more butter. A bottle of wine stood open on the table. I poured myself a glass, sipping it before returning to the meat. I finished nearly my entire plate and took the wine with me to my room, locking the door behind me even though I knew he had a key. Of course he had a key. It was his house.

I sat on the bed and poured myself another glass. That comment had gotten to him, just like what I'd said in the car had. I didn't know much about Salvatore's relationship with his father, Franco, but I had felt Salvatore tense when Franco approached us at the church. I'd been guessing when I taunted Salvatore with my comment about being his father's puppet but didn't realize I'd hit the nail on the head. When I'd said it was his father's house, not his, I'd seen it again, that I'd gotten under his skin. I would learn more, watch their interactions, find and exploit their weaknesses. Maybe it was a matter of pitting son against father.

Then there was Dominic, his younger brother. I knew his relationship with Salvatore was strained, and I didn't like the way Dominic looked at me, but maybe I could use that too.

Salvatore had mentioned knowing how it felt to

lose someone close. I knew he'd lost his older brother, Sergio, and his mother, both within a year of each other. I assumed they were who he meant. I felt like a jerk for a minute. I picked up my glass, drained it, and poured some more. Was he trying to connect with me over our shared pain or something? Why? What would be the point?

I lay my head back on the headboard and closed my eyes. I was tired, overwhelmed with emotion, jet-lagged, and exhausted. I'd cried over my father after the funeral once I'd been left alone here. Why hadn't I talked to him when he'd called? Why had I refused to see him when he'd come to the school? I knew he regretted what he'd done, selling me to buy his and our family's lives, but what choice had he had? I was a peace offering, in a way. An olive branch. The white flag of surrender to keep everyone else safe—my sister, my niece, my cousins, aunts, and uncles. It was the deal: no more bloodshed. We surrender. You own us.

I just happened to be the sacrifice.

Whose idea was it, I wondered, my father's or Franco's?

I swallowed two sleeping pills and finished the second glass of wine. Setting it on the nightstand, I pulled back the sheets and climbed into bed. I wanted to sleep, to stop thinking about everything.

Darkness fell when I switched off the lamp, and I closed my eyes. My thoughts moved from Salvatore and Franco and my father to Izzy. The pregnancy had saved her, or she'd be the one here in this bed right now. They'd wanted her, the firstborn. I'd heard my father and my sister arguing, yelling like I had never heard him yell before. Not at us, anyway. That's how I'd found out she was pregnant. That was when Izzy had run away, leaving me to a fate that should have been hers.

I couldn't blame her, though, not when I thought of Effie. She was protecting her baby. But it didn't absolve her for leaving me without a good-bye. Without telling me the truth herself. She knew what would happen to me.

Those few words we exchanged at the funeral were the first we'd traded in the last five years. Maybe it was time to forgive her. I needed at least one ally, didn't I?

My head hurt the next morning. Probably a combination of too much crying, too much fighting, and too much wine.

A knock came on the door just as I zipped my suitcase.

"Come in," I said, expecting Salvatore but finding someone else.

"Car is ready," the man said. He was the same one who'd stood at the door after accompanying us up here yesterday. He moved toward my suitcase. I'd only packed one. It was a brief trip, and we'd be going back to the US today. I'd be going to my new home—Salvatore's home—in New Jersey.

"Where is Salvatore?"

"He was called to a meeting, left earlier this morning."

"What's your name?"

"Marco."

"What meeting, Marco?" I asked, my curiosity piqued.

The man simply looked at me, letting me know he chose not to answer.

"Fine."

I walked out the door carrying my purse, leaving him behind to follow me with the suitcase. I went downstairs with my head held high, hoping most of all I wouldn't run into Franco Benedetti. As much as I hated to admit it, he scared me.

The front doors stood open, letting in the bright sunshine and already too hot temperatures. I refused to glance around and kept my eyes on the car waiting outside, the driver standing beside it. Marco's footsteps followed.

I was almost out the door when I heard a small clicking sound and instinctively turned my head. There stood Dominic, leaning against the doorway to another room. He watched me, and I took a moment to look at him, to *see* him. He and Salvatore couldn't be more different in appearance. Salvatore was big and thickly muscled, whereas Dominic stood maybe an inch taller but not as wide, his build leaner. Salvatore had dark hair and olive skin. Dominic was blond and lighter skinned. His eyes, though, were a piercing, steely blue-gray so cold, they chilled me through.

But then he smiled a big smile. The change in his features became suddenly disarming.

Marco cleared his throat behind me.

I glanced back to find Marco's eyes locked on Dominic. Dominic only shook his head and disappeared back into the room he'd come from. I walked out the door and got into the backseat of the car. After loading my suitcase in the trunk, Marco climbed into the front passenger seat, and the driver started the engine. I glanced up at the mansion as we drove off, irritated that Salvatore hadn't come with me, wondering if I was being sent away again on my own, hating knowing I was a prisoner to his will.

I had a hundred questions but refused to ask Marco. I wouldn't let them know I felt unsure, uncertain. Instead, I sat in the backseat of the car and watched the small Italian villages roll by on the hour-long drive to Lamezia Terme International Airport. I would connect through Rome, and the combined flights would take over fifteen hours to get back to the US. Getting to Calabria was a pain in the ass. I remembered hating the flights when we'd come here as kids, and that hadn't change. I still hated the long trip. At least Salvatore wouldn't be on the flight with me. Although would Marco then accompany me?

At the airport, Marco opened my door, and I climbed out, the heat coming off the asphalt stifling after the air-conditioned car. The driver unloaded my suitcase. Marco gestured for me to go ahead, guiding me toward the check-in counter. The man seemed to know Marco. I noticed their small exchange when he handed over my passport and ticket, neither of which I'd been allowed to hold on to, as if I'd skip out on my own father's funeral and fly home. The desk agent took my bag and handed my passport and ticket back to Marco.

"This way," Marco said.

"You didn't check-in. You won't be allowed past security," I said.

Marco smiled. "I will hand you over to one of my...colleagues in a few moments."

Marco's Italian accent was distinct. Raised in the US, although I spoke fluent Italian, I had no accent. Neither did Salvatore.

"He will travel with you."

I would have been surprised if they let me go alone, honestly.

Used to having guards nearby since I was a little girl, I went along, ignoring Marco and the other man, whom Marco introduced me to and whose name I instantly forgot. We boarded our flight within the next half hour, and I settled in. I read the coverage of my father's funeral in the newspaper reports, saw my face in the photos along with Salvatore's and numerous others plastered across page after page of both local newspapers I'd picked up. We made big news here. The reining Mafia family, coming to bury their biggest rival. The daughter of the fallen man, now on the arm of the opposing family's son. Most of the articles actually told the story of how we'd met and fallen in love. That would be Franco Benedetti's work. It wouldn't look good to tell the public the truth.

I folded the paper and tucked it into the pocket of the seat in front of me. I closed my eyes. I felt my bodyguard's gaze on me, but I ignored him as best as I could.

With a three-hour delay in Rome, by the time we arrived in New Jersey and then drove the hour and a half to Salvatore's home in Saddle River, I was exhausted. Evening fell, and it took an effort to keep my eyes open, to take in the surroundings of my new home. I was grateful it was Salvatore's house and not the Benedetti family home.

Salvatore's estate was large and very private. Tall iron gates opened upon our arrival. Only moonlight illuminated most of the grounds, until we drew closer to the house, and I got my first glimpse of the mansion with its huge garage, outbuildings, and extensive and various types of landscaping lights. The grounds, from what I could make out, were expansive, with woods circling most of the property. It seemed to me that the driveway was at least a mile long before it finally circled at the main entrance to the residence. A woman came outside and waited for us. As soon as the car stopped, I climbed out on my own, needing to stretch my legs after so many hours of sitting. I'd grown up surrounded by wealth, but I'd never lived in a house this grand. It seemed pretentious of Salvatore, maybe another weakness. I walked toward the woman.

"Ma'am."

"Just Lucia," I answered, attempting to give her a warm smile. I'd need allies. I didn't want to be hated.

The woman smiled back and nodded. I turned to the guard who'd flown with me. He looked as tired as I felt.

"When will Salvatore arrive?" I asked, wanting information.

"I'm not sure."

"Come inside," the woman said.

I followed her in, looking around the house—my new home—for the first time. The large circular foyer led off in several directions, one of which had to be the kitchen, considering the delicious smell coming from that direction. I could see the living room through a large archway. At the far end stood a wall of glass, and large doors led to a patio. Dim, colorful lights shone off the glass-like surface of the swimming pool, inviting even now. The rest of the interior doors stood closed. I turned my attention to the large marble staircase leading to the upper floor.

"Are you hungry?"

I shook my head, stifling a yawn. "I'm just very tired."

She nodded. "I'll take you to your room."

I touched her elbow to stop her before she turned. "What's your name?"

"Rainey."

"Rainey. That's a pretty name."

"Thank you."

I figured her to be in her early forties. It felt strange to have her wait on me. I'd always hated that, actually. I felt uncomfortable and awkward even with servants. I didn't mind a housekeeper or cook, but a servant felt different.

I followed Rainey up the stairs and toward the double doors at the end of the hall. I assumed that was the master bedroom. My heart thudded as we approached, knowing he'd expect to have me in his bed. Of course he would. Why not? What sense would it make for him to *take possession* of me but not fuck me?

But before we reached the foreboding doors at the end, we turned to the right, where Rainey opened a single door.

"This one's yours," she said, switching on a light and gesturing for me to enter.

The room was huge and richly decorated with heavy dark curtains draped from each of the windows. Exposed brick made the space appear darker and gave it a masculine flair, but I liked it, especially the large fireplace I wouldn't have need for just yet. Rainey pointed out the bathroom, which I barely glanced at, because my gaze had fallen on the large, four-post, king-size bed in the room with a thick duvet and overstuffed pillows at the head.

"Shall I help you unpack? We've already moved your other things into the closet."

"Other things? Oh." I'd forgotten. Salvatore had had my things packed up and brought here a few days ago. I didn't have much, hadn't needed much at a Catholic school, but what I had was neatly organized in the open walk-in closet Rainey stood at the entrance of. "I'm actually tired. If you don't mind, I think I'll just have a shower and go to bed."

"Of course."

She closed the closet doors and moved over to turn down the bed—another thing I didn't like. I could turn down my own bed.

"Thank you, Rainey," I said, dismissing her.

Once she left, I went over and peeked inside the closet. Huge. The racks were full and contained my clothes as well as items that did not belong to me. I checked the size of a dress. Four. He'd probably bought them for me. Or had them bought. I couldn't see Salvatore Benedetti shopping.

Apart from the bathroom, there stood another door Rainey hadn't pointed out. I walked over to it, but when I tried to open it, I found it was locked. I'd ask about it tomorrow.

I went into the bathroom and saw the separate shower as well as a bathtub set in the middle of the large space. It was old-fashioned, one with copper feet and fixtures. All surfaces were sparkling clean, and on one of the shelves stood several of my favorite brands of shampoos and body washes. Even bubble bath. I hadn't had a bubble bath in years. I decided I'd have one instead of a shower.

I turned the taps on in the bath, checked the temperature, and poured in the soap, watching as champagne-pink bubbles began to appear almost instantly. I found a hairclip in one of the sink drawers and piled my hair up on top of my head. The deep auburn mass would fall to the middle of my back when I let it down. As I undressed, I checked out the rest of the space. Everything was high-end, from the gold-veined marble on the floor and countertops to the copper fixtures on the taps. A stack of towels stood on a shelf. I touched them. Soft and luxurious. Brand-new.

The bath filled. I turned the water off and dipped a toe inside. I caught my reflection in one of the two mirrors. I'd lost a few pounds in the last two weeks. I ran almost daily, and at 5 feet five and 120 pounds, I was healthy with long, lean muscle, small but pert breasts, and a bubble butt. That was the yoga. The sisters at the college actually allowed a woman to teach classes three evenings a week, and I never missed a single one. It was that and the running that kept me sane, that kept me from tearing my hair out in frustration at how life had turned out for me.

I sank slowly into the bath. Steam rose off it, but the warmth felt good compared to the relative coolness inside the house. They must have had the air conditioner cranking, since it was July and the heat outside was stifling, with the evenings offering only the slightest relief. I wadded up a small towel and lay my head back against it, closing my eyes. Between the heat and my exhaustion, I must have dozed off, because the sound of someone clearing his throat startled me awake.

My eyelids flew open, and I caught my breath when I saw Salvatore standing just inside the bathroom, watching me.

"Jesus!" I sat up, instinctively covering myself, although it wasn't necessary. The bubbles created a barrier between us. "You scared the crap out of me!"

"I knocked, but there was no answer."

He wore dress slacks and a button-down shirt he'd undone to where I could see the gold chain circling his neck. A small cross hung from it. It took me back five years, seeing that. I remembered noticing it, concentrating on it when I couldn't bear to look him in the eye.

I flushed and glanced away.

"I fell asleep, I guess."

"It's dangerous to do in the bathtub."

"Yeah." I pulled my knees up, making sure the bubbles still hid me. When Rainey had told me this was my room, I'd assumed we weren't sharing it. I'd assumed the double doors had led to the master. Had I misunderstood? "What do you want?" I tried to keep my voice friendly. Salvatore seemed to process the question slowly. He looked like he had a thousand things on his mind. Was it the meeting he'd been called to?

He opened his mouth to speak, but instead shook his head and ran a hand through his thick, dark hair. It made me think of his brother, of how different they looked, and thinking about his brother made the water suddenly feel cold.

"I wanted to check on you, see if you needed anything," Salvatore finally answered.

"I'm fine." I wanted to ask if we were sharing the bedroom, if it was his, but couldn't bring myself to just yet. "Where were you? Marco said you had a meeting."

"I did."

A wealth of information.

"How close are you to your cousins, Lucia?" he asked, coming a little farther inside the bathroom and leaning back against the counter, ignoring my question entirely.

"Odd question. Why?"

"I'm curious."

"I don't know. Not particularly, at least not in the last five years." I wasn't going to tell him that Luke had been keeping me in the loop with the goings-on of my family while I was at school. Besides, it wasn't like he told me anything Salvatore would be interested in.

"So you didn't talk to Luke once a month over the last five years?"

"Am I being interrogated?"

He folded his arms across his chest and studied me closely. "Do you need to be?"

"What are you talking about? Luke is my cousin, we talked, so what?"

"You didn't talk to any other member of your family, not even your sister."

"Christ, you were keeping tabs?"

"I was keeping an eye on my property, yes."

"Oh, right, your *property*." I glared at him. "You do know I'm a human being, right? That we typically aren't referred to as property."

"I don't think there's anything typical about our relationship."

He stepped over to the tub, and I leaned back, covering my breasts. He didn't touch me, though.

Instead, he sat on the edge and dipped a hand in the water.

"You and Luke good friends? I saw the way he looked at you at the church."

"He's my cousin."

"Not by blood."

"What are you implying? What, are you jealous?" The moment I said it, I knew there was truth to the statement. I saw it in the slight shift of Salvatore's eyes. In his momentary hesitation before answering.

"I want to be sure you realize you're as good as a Benedetti now. Want to be sure your loyalties are where they belong."

"Just because I was forced to sign that stupid contract doesn't mean my loyalties suddenly shifted. I am not a Benedetti."

He snorted, shaking his head. "Water's cooling." He rose to stand. He wiped his hand on a towel. "Get out of the tub," he said, without looking at me.

"I'm not getting out with you here."

"I want to have a look at what I own." He said the words purposefully and unfolded one of the plush bath towels. He held it out before him but remained several feet away, so that I'd have to walk toward him to reach it, giving him a full view.

"What exactly is this? What do you want, Salvatore?"

"Just what I said. I want to see you. Naked."

"You want a look at what you can't have?" Flimsy words, and I knew it. He could take whatever he wanted. I just, for reasons that had no basis in reality, didn't think he would. And I was determined not to give him this particular power over me. My heart pounded against my chest as I slowly rose, suds clinging to me as I stood. "You want to see?" I asked again, seeing how his eyes darkened as they raked over me before returning to mine. His attraction to me, mine to him, this cruel sort of push-pull between us, I would use it. I would be stronger than it, and I would use it. I climbed out onto the bath mat and stood before him. "Have a look, then. Get your fill," I bit out.

Salvatore's throat worked as he swallowed. Without a word, he stepped toward me, held my gaze, and wrapped the towel around me. His hungry eyes held mine, meeting my challenge, posing his own as he dried me, his handling of me rough, the soft towel now scratching at my breasts, my sex. Once he finished, he stepped back, letting the towel drop to the floor.

"Now I can have a proper look."

He did, gaze pausing at breasts and belly, hovering at my naked sex. Again, he swallowed, then met my eyes once more.

I stood still, watching him. Watching his eyes. They burned, the blue darker now, sparkling like blackest onyx. Something raged behind them, inside them. Something that screamed for release even while it reduced me to flesh alone, to a thing, an object possessed.

Was this some sort of contest, some game? If it was, I lost, because I blinked first, looking away, unable to maintain the contact.

"Go to bed." He turned to leave the bathroom but stopped at the door.

I swooped down to grab the discarded towel and held it against myself, shielding my body from his view.

"And Lucia," he said, turning to look at me and taking a step back inside, back toward me. "Don't do anything stupid."

He rubbed his hand across his mouth, that rage behind his eyes burning now.

"I *will* punish you if you betray me."

He turned on his heel and walked out the door.

I sat down on the edge of the tub, trembling.

4

SALVATORE

My cock throbbed. I'd had to force myself to leave her room. Fuck, she was so beautiful. Her anger, her hate, it only made her all the more appealing. I wanted her. Wanted to take her. Have her.

The monster inside me screamed to possess her.

My cell phone rang. I tugged it from my pocket and checked the screen. It was Dominic.

Prick. I rejected the call, almost running Rainey over in the hallway on my way to the study.

"Mr. Benedetti! I'm sorry," she apologized, although I was the one not paying attention.

"No, it's fine. It was my fault."

I raked a hand through my hair. What the hell was that upstairs? Why had I gone in there when I'd seen her in the tub? I should have walked away.

"Would you like to eat dinner, sir? Miss...Lucia... wasn't hungry, but—"

It's dangerous to fall asleep in the tub? Christ, what did I think she was, a kid? No. Not with that body. She was certainly no kid.

"No, it's fine. I'm..." I walked into the study, looked around, then walked back out. "You know what, I'm tired. I'm just going to go to bed."

"Oh. All right."

I went back up to my room. It connected to Lucia's, but I doubted she knew that. Once inside, I stripped, headed into the bathroom and turned on the shower.

I didn't understand Lucia. Hell, I didn't understand myself around her. The meeting earlier, it had been last minute and required both myself and my father to be present. Dominic had been pissed to be left out, but that was too bad. I knew what Dominic wanted: anything I had. Including becoming our father's successor. But it didn't work that way. It would have been Sergio, firstborn, as the successor, but he'd been killed, so I was next in line. As little as I wanted to be the boss of the Benedetti family, Dominic taking on the role I wanted even less. My little brother had a mean streak, a violence inside him that when unleashed was terrifying to witness. Some days, I wasn't sure I knew him at all, wasn't sure I wanted to know the depths of his darkness.

I stepped into the shower, the water so hot, it scalded me. I turned it down.

My father, Roman, and I had been the only three of the Benedetti's at today's meeting. There was talk about a new group forming. Luke DeMarco was a problem. Or he could become one. Was it vengeance that fueled him or a lust for power? I'd bet the latter. Given that one DeMarco daughter wanted nothing to do with the family business and the other belonged to the enemy, Luke stood to gain a whole lot if he were able to gather enough support and rouse them to war. Which was exactly what he was attempting to do. And he'd come farther than any of us had expected. He'd gained supporters from the Pagani family, our fiercest opponent of the two Sicilian families.

Was Lucia in any way involved? I'd seen the look exchanged between Luke and Lucia at the church, but that had fueled a different sort of burn. One of jealousy. Why did I feel so possessive of her? Why did I care? I could have any woman I wanted, as many as I wanted. Our contract bound her to me with no restrictions on me. My father had orchestrated it, enjoying the idea of having a living trophy under his thumb he could torture as he pleased.

Thoughts of my father made my stomach turn. I switched off the shower and grabbed a towel. My eyes locked on the door connecting my room to Lucia's. I bypassed it, climbed into bed, and laid there with the sheet tossed aside. I closed my eyes and gripped my cock, the image of her standing before me, naked, suds sliding off her creamy skin, her hard little nipples, her shaved cunt. I wanted to see all of her, to take my time. To lay her out and open her. Smell her, taste her. Sink my cock inside her.

Her eyes flashed into my mind, accusing and hard. I pumped faster, imagining her here, watching me, sucking me, squatting over my face while she took my cock in her mouth and fed me her pussy. *Fuck.*

I bit my lip when I came, ropes of cum landing on my chest, my cock throbbing against my palm as I squeezed out the last of it with a groan, knowing it would not be enough, knowing this would not sate me, knowing however many women I fucked, none would give me the release I needed, the one only *she* could give.

I WOKE a few minutes past five. It was a long, deep sleep, considering my usual two- to three-hour stints. I lay there for a few minutes, hoping if I kept my eyes closed, I could sleep again. Less hours to get through in the day if I could just sleep them off. But that wasn't happening.

My cell phone buzzed on the nightstand. I

picked it up. Dominic. A quick glance told me he was still pissed about the meeting. I decided to delete Dominic's message without bothering to read the rest.

I tossed the covers back, got out of bed, and pulled the curtain aside to look outside. Dawn. The sun would rise soon.

Finding clean running clothes, I put them and my Nikes on, glanced once at the connecting door, and walked out of my bedroom and down the stairs. I used the door in the kitchen, which opened onto a large terrace. I jogged out, crossing it and the swimming pool area, and headed into the woods, running to meet the sun. It only took me a few minutes to realize I wasn't alone.

Gates protected the grounds, and cameras recorded all movement. The sound came from a short distance away: branches cracked underfoot, and I could hear the crunching of pine needles and leaves. Too heavy for a squirrel or bird. Deer sometimes jumped the fence, but it was rare. As I stalked closer, I heard the sounds of shortened breath. My intruder on my morning ritual run was human.

A few moments later, I caught sight of Lucia. She didn't see me. I slowed to her pace, watching her, lean muscle working as she leaped over a tree stump and avoided a moss-covered boulder. She'd bound her long hair in a ponytail that bounced from side to side, and sweat glistened on her bare shoulders. She wore a sports bra and shorts, the white fabric bright against her lightly tanned skin. Earbuds connected to an iPhone secured on her arm told me why I was able to get so close without her hearing me.

I caught up, startling her. She stopped, clutching her chest.

"Stop doing that!" she said, pulling the earbuds from her ears.

"I was behind you for the last five minutes. You should be more aware of your surroundings." The music was loud enough that I could clearly make out the song. Mumford and Sons. "You don't need that anyway, not when you run in the woods." I loved the stillness of this place, the peace I found as soon as I disappeared into the cover of the trees.

She looked me over. "You're running?"

I nodded. "You're up early."

"Couldn't sleep."

"Me either." I glanced up toward the place I ran to, a clearing on a hill that gave the best view of the sunrise. "Come on. I'll show you something."

I turned and ran. It took her a moment, and I imagined her mind working up some snarky comment, but then she followed. I slowed my pace so she could keep up, and we ran in silence for the next twenty minutes, climbing up the slope. Lucia slowed, her breathing coming shorter but her condition obviously good. Used to running.

"Wow."

I heard the awe in her voice as we reached the top of the hill. The sun had just broken through the clouds, and the sky was a wash of orange and pink and red.

"This is...amazing."

She walked a bit farther. I watched, finding myself smiling.

"Beautiful," she muttered.

"It's the one good thing about being an insomniac. I never miss the sunrises."

She glanced back at me, and I realized how easily I'd given away that piece of myself. I imagined the staff at the house knew I slept little, but no one else.

Lucia returned her gaze to the sky. I watched her framed by this show of lights.

"How long have you been like that? Unable to sleep, I mean."

"As long as I can remember." I was twenty-nine now so maybe fifteen years.

We watched the sunrise in silence. When the sun had crested, she turned to me, her whiskey eyes shining bright, the accusations of last night absent this morning, although her gaze remained cautious.

"I don't know what I'm supposed to do," she finally said, her arms folded across her chest, defensive and closed.

"That makes two of us."

She scrunched up her forehead. "I don't understand."

"I'm not a monster, Lucia, but I am my father's son. I am obligated, just as you are." She studied me. "You choose how hard you want to make this on yourself. There are worse things than being in my care."

"In your *care*?"

"Yes, my care. It could have been my brother. Or my father. Where do you think you'd be if it had been either of them instead of me?"

"I don't see the difference."

Her words got to me. "Fine, let me simplify this for you. You're to be obedient."

"I don't even know what that means. Do you expect me to just..." She glanced away, a blush creeping up her neck to her cheeks. "What do you want?" she finally asked, straightening, obviously forcing herself to look at me.

"Your obedience."

She opened her mouth to speak, but I stepped closer to her and placed my finger over her lips.

"Hear my words, Lucia. I *expect* your obedience. I didn't say want. I own you, no matter how you feel about that. I can make this good for you." I couldn't keep my gaze from wandering to the soft swell of her breasts before they returned to hers. "Or I can make it bad. It's up to you how this goes."

"It was supposed to be my sister," she said, a sheen of tears obscuring her eyes.

Looking at her, helpless, alone—and she was alone—only made me want to comfort and reassure her. So opposite what I was supposed to do.

"But she got herself pregnant." She turned her back to me and wiped one hand across her eyes before turning and looking at me again. "I don't know what I'm supposed to do here. Are you..." she floundered again. "Do you... Fuck. Never mind."

Without warning, she bolted back toward the house, her pace faster now. I followed easily, keeping a short distance between us, unsure how to answer her questions, not knowing myself what the hell I wanted from her. Her obedience, what the hell did that mean? That she sit when I say sit and fetch when I say fetch? It was so much more than that. A woman like Lucia DeMarco didn't simply give her submission. A man would have to earn it.

Or break her to take it.

"Lucia," I called out when we drew near the back entrance to the house, the large sliding glass doors of the dining room standing open.

She glanced back but ran into the house. I followed, seeing the blur of a maid setting the table for breakfast.

"Lucia!" I was only a few steps behind her, and when she stumbled over the last stair to the second floor, I caught her around the waist and lifted her, holding her to me. I saw then why she'd run. Tears stained her cheeks, and her eyes were puffy again, her face flushed.

For a moment, I faltered.

For one moment, I was human.

But then I looked down at her. I watched her struggle uselessly as I held her tight.

"Lucia," I whispered this time, snaking a hand up her back, the feel of her body moving against mine making me forget everything else.

I gripped her ponytail and tugged her head back.

"Stop," she said, her voice quiet.

I held her like that, my gaze drifting to her lips, soft and pink, her mouth slightly open, and I kissed her. I just…kissed her. It was our first kiss.

She made some sound, but my mouth muffled it. I walked her backward until her back was against the wall, and I leaned down to kiss her harder, tasting her, her mouth so soft, so inviting, even as she protested, or tried to. But her body gave me this, and she opened, her hands relaxing against my chest, even curling a little over my biceps. I dipped my tongue inside her mouth, the moan coming from me now as my cock stiffened against her belly. It felt like a mutual want heated our kiss. Lucia's fingertips touched my shoulders, drawing me closer, her tongue meeting mine. Hands wrapped around the back of my neck and pulled me in. I relaxed my hold, feeling her surrender, but as soon as I did, she struck. She rammed her knee so hard between my legs that she knocked the wind out of me.

I doubled over, sucking in a loud breath as she stumbled backward, smiling.

"You want my obedience?" she taunted. "You want me to be a good little thing, do as I'm told? Fuck you when I'm told?"

I made some sound, more animal than human as fury fired me from the inside. Lucia backed away, a moment of uncertainty crossing her features before she reached her door down the hall, placing her hand on the doorknob.

"You've got another thing coming, Salvatore." She turned the knob and pushed it open. "If obedience was what you wanted, you chose the wrong woman to fuck with."

She ran into her room and slammed the door shut. I straightened, my balls fucking killing me, and reached for the key on top of the door frame. I'd installed the special lock on her bedroom door before her arrival for exactly this reason. She would not lock me out. Not in my own house. I imagined her in there right now, frantic when she discovered the missing key. I slid it into the lock and turned it, locking her in from the outside.

"Obedience is what I'll have," I said. "I don't mind teaching it to you. Remember what I said last night?"

She tried the door, jiggling the handle.

I smiled at her muttered curse.

"If you betray me, I'll punish you. This will be your first punishment."

I LEFT her to stew while I showered. She'd fooled me with that kiss. I'd thought she felt it too, thought she liked it. I think she had, at first. But then, maybe her own sense of duty made her attack.

Regardless, I grinned as I pulled on a pair of jeans. The thought of punishing her aroused me.

Drying my hair roughly with a towel, I went to the door between our rooms and turned the key in the lock on my side. Lucia sat on her bed, her hair wet from a shower, dressed in a pair of shorts and a silk tank, her knees tucked against her chest, a letter opener in her hand held like a knife. The look on her face told me of her shock to see me enter from this door. I locked the door behind me and pocketed the keys.

Her eyes raked over me, from the top of my wet head to my bare feet. I wore only a pair of jeans, wanting her to see what she was up against. I stood a foot taller than her and outweighed her by probably seventy-five pounds. I wouldn't hurt her, but I wasn't above a little intimidation. It would be good for her to learn her place and learn it fast.

When I stepped toward her, she got up on her

knees in the middle of the bed and pointed the letter opener at me.

"Put that down."

She shook her head. "What are you going to do?"

I stalked closer. "I said put it down." I didn't give her a choice this time. Instead, when she scrambled backward on the bed, I placed one knee on top of it and caught her wrist, dragging her down on her belly until I relieved her of her weapon, tossing it away. I released her. She climbed back up on her knees and glared at me.

"Get undressed, Lucia."

"No."

"Come on. I've seen it all before. You showed me last night, remember?"

She jumped off the other side of the bed. I liked this. Always liked cat and mouse.

"Go away, Salvatore."

"Strip, Lucia."

She'd cornered herself by now, but I gave her space to bolt, just because I didn't like the game to end too quickly. She ducked under my arm and did just as I knew she would. I turned, watching her try the door.

"Leave me alone!"

"Where are you going to go?" I asked, following her as she ran to retrieve the letter opener. I have to admit, she was faster than I thought, but I caught her around the middle and squeezed her wrist, taking the weapon from her a second time.

"Please leave me alone. Please."

"What would be the fun in that?"

"I hate you! I hate you!"

With her back to me, she shoved against me, but I had her locked in my embrace. She was trapped. We both knew it. "I'll tell you how this is going to go. I'm going to release you, and you're going to do as you're told and strip. Once you're naked, I'll take it from there."

"I'm sorry, okay?"

I shook my head. "No, not okay." I grinned a wicked grin, my cock hard already at her back, growing harder with anticipation.

"What are you going to do?"

"I haven't decided yet."

She glanced back at me, and I knew she felt me pressing against her back. She couldn't not feel my hardness.

"I'm not going to fuck you." From the look on her face, I surprised both of us with that. But it needed to be said. Hell, she had every right to be afraid of me.

I eased up, giving her a little space. "Do as you're told, and I'll go easy on you, but if you make me strip you, your punishment will be worse, understand?"

After a moment, she nodded.

I released her, this time tucking the letter opener

into a nightstand drawer. I took a seat on the chair at her desk and watched while she stripped off her clothes layer by layer, first her blouse, then the white shorts. She wore a matching set of white lace panties and bra beneath.

"Go on, Lucia."

She unhooked her bra and let it fall to the floor, that look of innocence now replaced by the same thing I'd seen last night: defiance.

That was good. I preferred defiant.

I'd work that out of her. Slowly, though. No sense in rushing the fun.

I waited for her to slide off her panties. Then she stood before me naked, her hands fisted at her sides.

"Come here."

Reluctantly, she walked over to me. I took her hips in my hands and looked her over, my gaze on her breasts, those nipples hardening beneath my perusal, the slight hint of arousal making the air musky.

I swallowed and rose to my feet, my hands moving up to her waist. She remained where she stood, turning her face up to keep her eyes on mine.

I walked her to the bed, sitting her on it when the backs of her knees hit it. "Lie back, and open your legs."

She stared up at me, and I worked my knees between hers, widening them a little, keeping my gaze locked on hers.

"I told you I'm not going to fuck you. I just want to see. Now lie back, Lucia."

She did, slowly, watching me as I took her in. I knelt between her legs. She let me spread them and presented me with the beautiful sight of her pussy opening to me, the pink lips glistening, gaping, her clit swollen.

She was aroused.

I inhaled deeply, my cock ready to tear free from my jeans. I pressed one hand against her chest, covering a breast with my palm so I could hold her down as well as play with the nipple. I brought my mouth to her, felt her gaze on the top of my head as I dragged my tongue along her length, the sound of her sucking in a breath music to my ears. Her hands came to my head, and she pushed then pulled.

I looked up. "Spread your arms out to the sides."

She obeyed, and I dipped my head back down to her pussy. She tasted as good as I imagined. Better. Fuck. She thrust herself against me, her cunt dripping as I sucked her clit, then licked her length, dipping my tongue inside her.

She moaned, twisting her body. I looked at her face while I worked the tight little nub. She squeezed her eyes shut and bit her lip. I circled my tongue around the clit, and she opened her eyes, her face flushing pink when our gazes locked. I took her clit in my mouth, watching her, making her watch me until I brought her to orgasm, holding her thighs wide as she bucked beneath me, her hands on the back of my head now, pulling me tight to her until she was spent and begging me to stop, to release her.

"Too much."

I grinned. "This is the punishment part," I said, holding her down and eating her pussy again, making her come twice more, hearing her beg me to go on, plead with me to stop, all while I sucked that clit and licked every drop of juice from her cunt until I couldn't take any more.

I rose to stand over her, my legs still between hers to keep them spread.

I looked down at her, her hair a tangled wet mess all around her, her face flushed, her limbs limp. I unzipped my jeans. When I did, her eyes went wide, and she startled, scooting backward. I caught her thigh and placed one knee on the bed.

"Stay."

She made a sound, her forehead furrowing.

"I'm not going to fuck you," I said again, knowing what she feared. But as I pushed my jeans down and off and began to rub the length of my cock, she stilled, swallowing, her gaze darting from my cock, away, then back. "Watch, Lucia." She wanted to, I could see it on her face, and somehow, the thought of corrupting her innocence made me harder.

I fucked my fist while she watched, her eyes riveted on my hand working my cock. It turned me the fuck on to have her watch me, and I leaned into her, just touching the head of my cock to her folds, making her gasp and bite her lip.

"Fuck," I said. "I love how you look at me, Lucia. And I love how you taste. How you come on my tongue."

"Salvatore," she started, trying to sit up.

I shook my head. "Lie back."

She did, and I pumped harder, my cock swelling, the scent of her, of me, filling the room with sex.

"Have you ever seen a man come, Lucia?" I asked, close now.

She met my gaze and shook her head.

"Have you ever had a man's tongue on your cunt?"

She flushed red and blinked twice before looking away.

"Answer me."

She held her lower lip between her teeth. "No. I've never..." She stopped.

"I'm going to come all over you," I said, pumping faster, gripping harder. "I'm going to cover you in my cum, and you're going to wear it all day long, so you know you belong to me." I jerked, moments away now. "Fuck."

I blew then, my orgasm coming hard and fast, making me grip one of the posts of her bed to keep upright as I emptied on her, covering her in my cum, watching her face, her eyes, as she took it. And when I finished, I leaned down and rubbed it into her skin, her chest and neck, her belly, her cunt. I then straightened, wiped my hand on her thigh, and pulled my jeans back on. Lucia sat up and looked down at herself for a moment.

"Get dressed," I said, buttoning my jeans. "Breakfast is ready."

"I need a shower."

I shook my head. "Like I said, you'll wear it all day." I slapped her hip twice. "Let's go. I'm suddenly ravenous."

5

LUCIA

I hated him.

Salvatore sat across from me with a huge grin on his face, chomping on a piece of sausage. I tore my bread into pieces and glared at him. He was gloating. Fucking gloating.

"I hate you."

I hated myself more. How could I have done what he said? How in hell had I enjoyed it? He'd made me come three times. Three times! I'd felt... Fuck, what had I felt for him? The man had made me come, that was all. Any feelings were physical. Sexual.

"You liked me just fine a little while ago." He bit into a piece of Nutella-smeared toast, a little of the chocolate paste sticking to the side of his mouth. He wiped it with his thumb then made a show of licking it off his finger.

Frustrated, I grabbed an apple out of the bowl of fruit and threw it at him. He caught it like a baseball and bit into it.

"Thanks."

I fisted my hands at my sides at this infuriating man. Rainey came by with a pot of coffee.

"More, ma'am?"

"No," I said, tacking on a "thank you," as I folded my napkin. I forced myself to take a deep breath. "I'm done."

She stepped away, nodding, and I made to rise.

"I'll have more, Rainey," Salvatore said.

I shoved my chair back, scraping the legs along the hardwood floor.

"Sit, Lucia," Salvatore said as Rainey poured. She avoided looking at either of us.

"I'm done." I set my napkin on my plate.

"I said sit."

His tone made me meet his gaze. He wiped his mouth and pushed his plate back, all joking gone from his expression. For a moment, we battled in silence, me standing, willing my legs to move, the limbs refusing. Him watching me, intently waiting to see what I'd do.

Rainey, who had left with the coffeepot, returned, saw us, and disappeared back into the kitchen. You could slice the tension in the dining room.

Salvatore raised an eyebrow and gestured for me

to sit. I thought about my options. I was in his house, in a town I did not know, miles from the next house, without a vehicle.

I sat, folded my arms across my chest, and jutted my chin out.

"Your sister does that."

"What?"

He stuck his chin out to show me. "Stubborn. I guess it runs in the family."

I adjusted my position, sitting up straighter, lowering my stupid chin. He was observant, I had to give him that. He must have seen it at my father's funeral.

"She and I are very different people."

He raised an eyebrow but apparently decided not to pursue it. He shifted his position, pushing his chair back and folding one leg over the other. He took up a lot of space. Too much.

"Let's go over the rules of the house now that you're finally here."

I waited in silence. I'd hear him out first. Tell him to go fuck himself after.

That thought took me back to an hour earlier, to him standing over me, his big naked body, his thick cock in his hand pumping, pumping...

I shook my head, forcing the image away, and looked at the floor littered with the bread I'd torn up throughout breakfast. I'd made work for Rainey in my anger at Salvatore. I'd pick it up when we were done.

"First rule, you are not to leave the grounds without my permission, and you are never to go anywhere alone."

I snorted. "As if."

"As if what?"

He leaned forward, his expression questioning but also consequential, calling me on my bullshit because he and I both knew I couldn't leave without A) having a car, and B) knowing the code to open the gate.

"I won't be treated like a prisoner." I almost added *in my own home*, but this wasn't my home.

"It's not a prison, Lucia. I want you to be safe. I have enemies, like your father did. They may think getting to me is best accomplished through you. I don't want to see you get hurt."

He sounded almost genuine. He sure looked it. But then again, he'd seemed different earlier too, before he'd used my body's surrender against me.

"You're free to wander the grounds. There are several acres of woods, so take care you don't get lost. The house as well, only my study and my bedroom are off-limits. I'll show you around once we're done. If you need or want anything, all you have to do is ask. You'll have a monthly allowance—"

"I don't need your money." I had my own. My family was not poor, even after the Benedetti's destroyed us. I'd inherited everything but the house after my father died. Although without credit cards, with no way to access that money as long as I was locked away here, I was still at Salvatore's mercy.

"Well, you'll have it anyway."

"I don't want it," I muttered.

"What are you doing, Lucia? What exactly is going through your mind right now?"

"I'm trying to wrap my brain around my new prison. First, you send me away to the fucking nuns for five years—"

"It was part of the agreement—"

"I may as well have been behind bars, and you know it!"

He just shrugged a shoulder.

"Now I'm sitting here in *your* house, where I'm supposed to live as your—what? Plaything?—and I'm being told the rules like I'm a child!"

"Aren't you? Look at how you talk to me. I'm not an unreasonable man, Lucia, but I will be obeyed."

"Obeyed? You want me to bow down to you? You've got another thing coming."

"I think I have a pretty good idea of what I have coming."

"Are we done?"

"No."

I bit my lip, waiting.

"I have a cell phone arriving for you today—"

"I have my own."

His jaw tightened, and he took a minute before responding. "Well, you'll have a new one. When you want your family or a friend to visit, you'll let me know first."

"I don't need to see my family, and I don't have any friends, so I'm well and truly yours. I guess that makes you happy."

"It doesn't, actually."

Why did he have to seem so fucking genuine?

It was my turn to shrug a shoulder and, needing to break eye contact, I leaned down to pick up a few pieces of the bread I'd inadvertently scattered.

"Leave it. Rainey will clean it up."

I shook my head, feeling tears building, refusing to let him see.

"Leave it, Lucia. When I'm talking to you, I expect your undivided attention."

I snorted, wiping my face, angry again. I faced him. "You expect so many things. Maybe what you need to do is check those expectations. You're less likely to be disappointed then."

His eyes narrowed, and his chest heaved as he took a deep breath in.

"Am I irritating you, Salvatore? Because you know what's irritating me? Your...stuff...drying on my skin," I said through clenched teeth. I stood so fast, I knocked the chair over behind me. "You've told me your rules. Well, fine. I have just one of my own. Leave. Me. Alone!" I turned on my heel to march off.

"Sit back down," he hissed. "Now."

"*Fuck. You.* I'm going to take a shower."

I heard his chair scrape back, and I started to run for the stairs, all the while wondering what the hell I was doing. Where I was going. He had the key to the lock. It's not like I could hide. What was I doing?

Salvatore caught up with me. I didn't even really fight him when he took my arm and dragged me up the stairs with him.

"You want a shower? Fine," he said through clenched teeth. "I'll take you to have that fucking shower if my *stuff* is so *irritating*."

"Let me go."

He hauled me to my bedroom and into the bathroom. There he released me. I backed into a corner, his fury suddenly frightening.

"Get in the shower," he said, reaching for the collar of my blouse and tearing it down the middle.

I screamed, trying to push him back, knowing it was impossible.

"You wanted a shower."

"I'll do it," I said as he popped the buttons off my shorts and yanked the zipper down. "Please. Just—"

"In the shower!"

He shoved me into the shower, even though I still wore my bra and panties.

"Let me go. I'll do it, I promise." He stopped and brought his face within an inch from mine.

"You don't have to promise. I know you'll do it."

He switched on the water, and I recoiled from the cool spray that hit one side of my arm.

Tears burned my eyes, and I cursed the drops that fell.

"Take off your bra and panties," he said, pushing his hand through his hair as he stepped back.

"I will. Just go, okay. I'm sorry. I shouldn't have pushed you."

His breath was audible, his lips tight, the look on his face telling me he was trying hard to get himself under control.

"I have to pee. Let me pee." I tried, hoping that would convince him to leave. Using that moment to reason with him. "I'm sorry, okay?"

Some battle raged behind his eyes, and next thing I knew, he had me shoved against the shower wall, one hand wrapped around my throat. I grabbed his forearm, trying to pull him off. He reached over and switched off the water, drenching one side of his T-shirt in the process.

"Piss."

"Wh...what?"

With his wet hand, he pushed my panties down to midthigh. "Piss."

"Salvatore..."

"Fucking. Piss. You want me to leave you alone? I

will. But first, you piss."

We stood staring at each other, his eyes dark with anger, mine, maybe the look of a deer caught in the headlights of an oncoming Mack truck? I didn't know what to do, whether or not to try to reason with him. I didn't know him. That fact well and truly hit me for the first time, right here, right now. He was the son of a mafia boss next in line to succeed him. I'd seen he was armed at my father's funeral. This man knew violence, it was his world. What horrors had his eyes seen? What atrocities had his hands committed?

In this moment, he was truly and utterly terrifying.

I let my arms fall to my sides, no longer fighting against tears, and I did what he said. I pissed. He glanced down for a second, then returned his gaze to mine. As warmth trailed down my legs, he released his hold around my throat and stepped back, blinking as if coming out of a stupor, shaking his head. I slid down and sat on the shower floor, watching him as he looked at me, the rage all but dissipated now, as if evaporated into thin air, replaced by...remorse?

Salvatore walked out of the bathroom, and I heard the bedroom door close. I rose and started the shower, stripped off the rest of my clothes, and stood under the warm flow, weeping, a sense of loss so all encompassing, so whole, it physically hurt.

6

SALVATORE

I left.

I walked out of the house and to the six-car garage, a building separate from the main house. Taking the keys from the locked box by the door, I chose the Bugatti and climbed inside. I turned the key, the engine crisp and sharp in the early morning quiet. The gates opened, and the tires squealed as I left the property and drove onto the lonely single-lane road. I opened it up then, enjoying the rush as my body pressed back into the seat, the car's powerful engine roaring, taking the turns tightly, my foot pressing harder and harder on the accelerator.

Who the fuck was I? What in hell had I just done, humiliating Lucia like that? Hurting her. Christ. Fuck.

I was a monster.

I inhaled and exhaled short, audible breaths, my stomach tight, the muscles of my arms clenched as I fisted the steering wheel hard.

She got under my skin. This barely twenty-one-year-old woman whom *I fucking owned* got under my fucking skin every single fucking time. I needed to control her for so many reasons. But I couldn't do it this way. Fuck. I'd scared the piss out of her, literally. Her eyes—they hadn't accused me. No. They'd been terrified of me.

"Fuck!" I punched the side of my fist against the steering wheel.

A car turned a blind corner, surprising me, his horn honking, waking me from wherever the fuck I was. I jerked the steering wheel, and the Bugatti swerved onto the side of the road, missing the car by inches.

"Shit!"

The man in the other vehicle flipped me off.

"Fuck you!" Not that he heard me. My windows were up. My cell phone vibrated in my pocket as I slowed to a full stop. The display on the Bluetooth said it was Roman. I got out, rubbed my face with both hands, and pressed the heels of my hands into my eyes. The phone stopped, then started again. I dug into my pocket and fished it out.

"Roman," I said after sliding the Talk button. I walked a few steps away to look over the deserted road, the dewy grass sparkling in the sun, the morning quiet apart from the birds chirping in the trees.

"Morning, Salvatore."

"You're calling early."

"I wanted to talk to you. I tried to call last night but couldn't catch you."

"What is it, Roman?" Was this about the meeting? Luke DeMarco?

"Your father wants to be sure you'll be attending his birthday dinner."

"You're calling me about that?" It was at the end of the following week, and of course I'd be there. There was no way for me not to be. Unless I wanted to give Dominic ammunition.

"He wanted to invite you and Lucia to spend the night."

"That won't be necessary. We'll drive home."

"He insists."

I took a deep breath. The party was going to be held at the house in the Adirondacks, but I'd have driven four hours each way rather than spend more time in that house with him.

"Of course," I said, understanding.

"Listen, there's one more thing."

I waited.

"Your brother."

He paused, and I could hear him measuring his words.

"I just thought you should know he met with your father late last night."

My father had gone back to the house in Calabria after I'd left for New Jersey. "So?" I asked, not surprised. He'd been pissed to have been left out of our meeting.

"He's stirring the pot, Salvatore."

"What's new with that?" I'd known my uncle all my life. He was an intelligent man. He was also a businessman. He knew what would happen if Dominic, rather than I, took over the family. And he somehow had a calming effect on my father. Sergio had trusted him. And I trusted Sergio.

"Nothing is new, but now that you're... distracted...with your houseguest, he's suggesting he take care of the DeMarco problem."

"Take care of it how?"

"Take out Luke DeMarco. Make an example."

I shook my head, although Roman couldn't see. "Fucking typical. This is my problem to deal with. Not his."

"He's got your father's ear."

"That's not news."

"It's different this time, Salvatore," he said heavily.

"When are they flying home?"

"Late afternoon. I'm flying with them."

Silence again, but I could tell he had something to say.

"Franco won't give the word just yet, but you need to know what's going on."

"Thank you, Uncle."

I hung up and pocketed my phone. I didn't want to deal with Dominic's jealous aggressions right now. I had other things on my mind. I needed to get back. Talk to her. Explain that I wasn't a fucking monster.

She'd said she had no friends and refused to see her family. Well, we had more in common than she knew. She'd learned to hate my family over the last five years. Learned to hate everyone, maybe. I just, stupidly enough, didn't want her to hate me.

I got back into the car, started the engine, and drove an hour to the cemetery. I came here more often than I probably should. Parking close to the family plot, I got out. The heat and humidity seemed to want to suffocate me after the air-conditioned drive. I stopped and picked up a dozen white Calla lilies from the flower store a block away, my mom's favorite, and headed up the small hill. The ground beneath my feet felt soft here, damp and covered in moss. A small gate surrounded the plot of land housing many of the Benedetti family. I walked my usual path, reading off the names of the dead in my head, noting the number of years each had lived. Too many damn lives cut short.

But this was what we did. We killed. We died. And for what?

I reached the spot where my mother's and brother's headstones stood side by side. I tossed the dying flowers, the ones I'd brought the last time I'd come, and replaced them with fresh ones. I pulled out some weeds and scraped dirt off the inscriptions on both their tombstones, noting the year of birth and death on Sergio's grave. He'd been a year older than I was now. Married. His wife pregnant when he died. It wasn't fucking fair.

When it had happened, I'd been broken. He was my one ally, my friend. He'd known how to become boss. Our father loved him and yet, Sergio wasn't like him. Not at all. He'd been gunned down at a gas station. A stupid, cowardly drive-by. He'd deserved a better death than that. And he'd deserved a life first.

My father had retaliated, but something didn't sit right with me. In fact, the whole thing stank. They'd blamed a smaller family from Philadelphia, one that was supposed to have been loyal to us. Somehow, evidence had turned up incriminating them. But it didn't make sense, not then, not now. My father had been crazed, though. He'd loved Sergio, and he'd simply reacted, killed off the boss's sons. Effectively ending the family.

I was supposed to have been with Sergio at the meeting he was coming home from, but I'd been sick. In a way, it felt like I'd cheated death, but then, if I had been there, maybe Sergio wouldn't have died. Maybe things would have gone differently.

I never said much when I came to the cemetery

and never stayed long. Just showed up. Wanted them to know I hadn't forgotten them. I got back in the car and headed toward Natalie's house. Natalie was Sergio's wife. Apart from her friendship with me, she'd cut off ties with the family after his and my mother's deaths. She hated my father and brother. She hated the life. But she had loved my brother, knowing the cost of that love.

My father hadn't really allowed her to walk away, though. Not with her bringing his first grandchild into the world. Jacob Sergio Benedetti was born six months after Sergio's murder. Natalie had purposely not given him an Italian first name, which had pissed off my father. Jacob was one and a half years old now. I knew she worried about what demands my father would put on her as Jacob grew older, but she kept those mostly to herself. My father supported them financially. As much as I knew Natalie hated it, she needed the money. And as long as she took it, Franco gave her the space she wanted. I guess he figured he owned her anyway.

I dialed Natalie's number on my cell phone. She answered after the fourth ring.

"Hello?"

"Natalie, it's me, Salvatore."

"Hey, Salvatore. How are you?"

"Okay." Not really. "How are you doing?"

"I'm fine. Just playing with Jacob."

"Can I drop by?"

"Are you sure you're okay?"

"Yeah," I said quickly, then added, "you know." Natalie was the one person who knew me for who I really was. I trusted Marco, my bodyguard, but he didn't know this side of me. I didn't trust anyone enough to share this vulnerability. Too many people ready and waiting for weakness.

"Come on over."

"Thanks. See you in twenty minutes."

I drove to her house, a two-story brick home about forty-five minutes from mine. Her parents lived nearby, and she'd moved here specifically to be close to them. When I rang the doorbell, Natalie answered with Jacob perched on her hip. He still wore his pajamas and held the stuffed animal I'd given him on his first birthday. He gave me a huge gummy smile. He only had three teeth, although I could see the fourth one was working its way in.

"Wow, haven't you grown." I took Jacob from Natalie's arms. He wrapped his arms around my neck and planted a wet kiss on my face.

"Nice," Natalie said. "You look...not so good."

She gave me a hug and a kiss on the cheek after wiping off the mark Jacob had left.

"Come in."

I put Jacob down on the floor among his toys, which seemed to be everywhere.

"Espresso?"

"Please." I took a seat on the couch and watched

Jacob play while Natalie made espresso and then joined me in the living room.

"How was the funeral?"

"Shitty." I took a sip of the espresso she handed me, dark and rich and bitter as hell, just the way I liked it. "He's got Sergio's eyes," I said, taking the toy Jacob held out to me.

Natalie stroked the little boy's hair. "And his stubborn streak."

"I don't know. I think you may both be responsible for that one."

She smiled. "You could be right on that. What's up, Salvatore?"

"Lucia's home with me."

Natalie nodded, knowing the situation. "How's that going?"

"Well, she's been there less than twenty-four hours, and I think I've fucked it up pretty well." I drank the last sip of espresso.

"Want to talk about it?"

What could I tell her? What could I tell her that wouldn't make me sound like a monster? Like my father. Hell, he would have been proud of me this morning.

"She hates me, as expected. She is battling me at every turn. Stubborn as hell."

"She's only been with you since the funeral?"

I nodded.

"Then you must really be pissing her off." She

winked. "Just give her some space. It's a huge change for her, and her father just died. Suicide, right?"

"Looked that way."

"You don't believe it?"

"I don't believe anything unless I see it with my own two eyes."

She studied me but dropped it. "What's she like?"

"Pretty. Young. Scared. She spit on my father at the funeral. Or tried to but missed." I chuckled.

"Tough too, then. I like her already."

"And full of hate for us. Rightfully so. I guess that's where I'm torn. She can't get out of this. Neither of us can." I paused. "Until death do us part."

"That's not too creepy." Natalie looked away for a moment.

"That's the wording in the contract. Like a marriage contract, but different. And if I die before her, Dominic inherits her. Like she's a fucking thing. My father has a sick sense of humor, as you know."

Her lip curled at the mention of his name. "Do you want to get out of it?"

Her question startled me. I answered without hesitation. "No."

"You like her."

I studied Natalie and felt the need to correct what she said. Whether that correction was for my benefit or hers, I wasn't sure. "I feel some obligation to her."

She snorted.

"Besides, even if I wanted to, I couldn't get out of it. And she certainly couldn't. I don't want her to hate me."

"Give her some space and some time, Salvatore," Natalie said, touching my hand. "She just needs to really see you, like I do. She only sees the Benedetti name right now. The Benedetti family, the one that destroyed hers."

She was right.

"Maybe you could…"

Natalie shook her head. "I'm sorry, I can't. I can't be a part of that anymore." Tears welled in her eyes.

"I understand. It's okay. I just think she needs some friends or something."

"I'm sorry, I just—"

I touched her shoulder. "I shouldn't have asked."

An awkward silence hung between us.

"Do you need anything?" I finally asked.

She shook her head. "No, we're fine. We're good."

"You'll call me if you do, right?"

"I promise."

"I miss Sergio." My eyes felt hot.

"Me too." Natalie wiped hers before leaning against my chest. I hugged her, rubbing her back.

"Hey, I'm going to take Jacob to the beach a little later. Why don't you come with us?"

I nodded, not really having to think about it. I didn't want to go home. I'd bury my head in the sand for a little bit longer. "I'd like that."

"Good."

Jacob stood then, holding out two of the farm animals he was playing with. Both were a little wet from drool, but I took them. He stood leaning against my legs, babbling.

"That so?" I asked, not really understanding a word he said.

Natalie chuckled and stood. "More coffee?"

"Sure."

"Hey, Jacob, Uncle Salvatore's going to come with us to the beach. What do you think of that, honey?

Jacob leaned his face into my leg and smiled, still "talking." I made out the word beach then something sounding like uncle in there before he gave me a cuddle. I cuddled him back.

I'd spend the day here. It would be good for me. And I'd think about what Natalie said about giving Lucia time and space. I could do that. It would help me get my thoughts figured out.

7

LUCIA

I was a prisoner here.

I spent the day in my bedroom. I slept a little, then read and slept some more. Rainey brought me a tray at lunchtime when I told her I wasn't feeling well, and then another at dinnertime. I didn't ask where Salvatore was or what he was doing. Didn't know if he'd just come barging in here and demand things from me. Punish me. Humiliate me. But he never did. When Rainey came to clear my dinner tray, I finally got up the nerve to ask.

"Is Salvatore home?"

"No, ma'am. He called a little while ago to say he wouldn't be home tonight."

So was he spending the night somewhere else? Where? With whom? And why did I care? At least he wouldn't hurt me, not if he wasn't here.

But Salvatore didn't come home the next night

either. Unable to hide in my room any longer, I finally left it late the following morning and gave myself a tour of the house, looking around in the corners, behind plants, for cameras. I wouldn't be surprised to find them. He'd said I had free rein of the house apart from his study and bedroom. Of course, the first thing I did was try his study door but found it locked. The bedroom, too, was locked, but when I saw the maid slip out of the room, I tried the door. She'd forgotten to lock it behind her.

I looked around to make sure no one was watching and slipped inside, closing the door quietly behind me. I spent a long moment with my back against it, trying to calm my breathing, knowing if he found out I was in here, that I'd disobeyed, he'd punish me. And yet I felt like a triumphant, defiant kid who'd taken the piece of candy she wasn't allowed to have.

I pushed away from the door and looked around. The room was about twice as large as mine, and the furnishings were all dark wood or metal, the carpet and drapes shades of blue to match his eyes in all his moods. Leather panels covered the whole of the wall behind the four steel frames of the bed, which was perfectly made, all corners tucked neatly in, since he'd not slept here for two nights now.

The connecting door to my room had a key in the lock. Figured it'd be on his side. Another door led to a bathroom similar to mine, just larger, this one containing black towels and bath accessories, nothing feminine about the space.

The final door opened to a closet. I stepped into it, chuckling at the inch of space between each of the black velvet hangers that contained suits, jackets, and pants on one side, dress shirts sorted by color along another wall, and more casual wear, again, grouped by color and perfectly spaced along the final one. Three dozen pairs of shoes filled the neat little show racks, and two shelves contained belts. Ties were rolled on their own cushions, the color coding continuing even there. The drawers held underwear and socks. Everyday items. Things I for some reason could not associate with the man who owned the house.

I ran a hand over the suits, then dragged them a little, messing up the OCD spacing, thinking it funny for a moment. But then I found myself inhaling deeply. I shook my head and walked back into the bedroom.

It smelled like him in here.

I tentatively touched one of the cool steel posts of the bed as I thought about what I was doing, not feeling quite good about it. I perched myself on the edge of the bed and told myself I needed to do this. To break his rules and invade his privacy like he had mine. To take back some of the power he'd taken from me when he'd made me do what he did.

The surface of the nightstand had just been

dusted. I ran a finger over it before opening the drawer and peeking inside. It was empty.

I walked to the other side of the bed. The book lying beside the lamp told me this was the side he slept on. I sat on the edge of the bed and pulled the drawer open less cautiously this time. This one wasn't empty. I reached in and took out a bottle of what I thought was hand cream, but when I read the label, I quickly set it back down. It was a half-empty container of lubricant. Digging deeper, I found a row of condoms and behind that, a set of handcuffs.

Voices outside the door had me quickly shoving the things back inside the drawer, and when the door opened, I dropped to the floor and slid underneath the bed.

The women spoke, and I saw the one come inside to pick up the bucket she'd left in the bathroom before walking back out the door. This time, she didn't forget to lock it behind her.

"Shit!"

I made my way out from under the bed. That was when I saw the leather restraint that hung off the post. Curious, I sat up and pulled it out from behind the cover. I then walked over to the post at the foot and found a similar one, and two more on the other posts.

I grinned. This was a side of Salvatore I hadn't considered, and I wasn't sure how I felt about it.

But now wasn't the time to think about that. I

had a bigger problem. I had to get out of his bedroom.

IT TOOK me thirty-five minutes to finally pick the lock and get into my own bedroom. Feeling like some sort of thief, I picked up my cell phone, which I'd been charging since it had run down completely. It showed six missed calls. All from Isabella. No texts, but voice mails after each one.

"*Hey, Luce. Call me when you get this.*"

"*Checking in, Luce. You there?*"

"*Um, I'm feeling like a stalker. You can't still be mad at me. Hell, you can be whatever you want. Shit, I'd be pissed. Okay, please don't be mad at me.*"

"*Fuck.*" Effie's voice in the background, then my sister again. "*No, honey, mommy didn't say a bad word.*"

I smiled.

"*Lucia, if you don't call me back right now, I'm getting in my car and driving over there!*"

"*Fuck. I'm on my way!*"

I checked the time of the messages. The last one was from about an hour and a half ago. Which meant she'd be here any minute.

I pocketed the phone and ran out the door. On my way down the stairs, I heard a voice I recognized as Marco's. I paused on the stairs, listening.

"She's got a visitor."

He must have been talking into a phone because I didn't hear another voice. He mumbled, "Okay, boss," and hung up.

When I heard his footsteps, I headed down the stairs, noting the room he'd come from. He looked up at me.

"Good afternoon."

Marco was always around, but at least he stayed out of my way. "Afternoon."

I heard a car door close and turned toward the front door. From the side window, I spotted my sister taking in the mansion before opening the back door to help Effie out.

"Your sister's here," Marco said, reaching the front door ahead of me.

"I can see that."

"Mr. Benedetti has given his permission for you to see her." He opened the door, but his comment made me stop and turn to him.

"Really? He's given his permission?" Asshole.

Marco faced me and was about to say something, but Isabella spoke first.

"Well, it is remote and it is protected," she said. "I wasn't sure they were going to open the gates for a minute there." She came right to me, looked me over from head to toe, and pulled me in for a hug.

I yielded right away, her warmth something I'd

missed, something I cherished. It made me feel protected.

"Izzy." I used the name I used to call her when I was little and couldn't say her full name. It had stuck. I was the only person who called her that.

She pulled back and looked at me. I wiped at my eyes but apparently not quickly enough because I saw the concern in hers. She glanced at Marco, who stood stupidly watching us.

I hated him.

"Mommy." Effie tugged on her mom's skirt. "The gift."

Her high-pitched voice made me smile. She held up a box. I could see from the torn wrapping that it contained chocolates.

"Why don't you give it to Aunt Lucia, and explain why the wrapping's been torn."

Effie turned to me and offered up the box. "I started to open it for you to help you."

"Is that really why?" Izzy asked.

I gave Izzy a look. So did Effie.

I bent down to take the box from her, trying to keep a straight face. "Is this what I think it is? My favorite chocolates?" I asked, picking up an end of the wrapping and peeking inside the torn paper. "Maybe you can help me get the rest of the wrapping off." She happily took the box and tore off the gift wrap.

"Yep. They're my favorite too." She reluctantly held the box out to me.

"You hold on to it. We should probably eat some, though. What do you think?"

"I definitely think we should eat some!"

I straightened and looked around, noticing how Marco hovered. "Let's go into the living room."

With a hand on the top of Effie's head, I followed him to the spacious room adjoining the dining room. The sun shone bright, and the swimming pool glistened blue just beyond the large patio.

"God, it's beautiful, isn't it?" Izzy asked.

"It is."

"Did you bring my swimsuit, Mommy?" Effie asked, her attention focused on the pool.

I looked at my sister, who rolled her eyes.

"I didn't know they had a pool, so no."

Effie gave her a look, which made me cover my mouth to hide the chuckle.

"How would I know? It's my first time here," Izzy protested.

"How about something to drink," I asked just as Rainey walked in. She smiled warmly, and I introduced everyone.

"What would you like? I have some homemade lemonade maybe for the little one?"

"Actually, for me too," Izzy said.

"Homemade?"

Rainey nodded.

"Make it three then, please," I said. Rainey had been my only point of contact over the last couple of days. My world had always been small, but now, it had become miniscule.

Rainey nodded and returned to the kitchen. Marco remained in the room with us. Izzy and I both eyed him while Effie worked on getting the plastic off the box of chocolates.

"Are you just going to stand there?" I asked him.

He looked at me with raised eyebrows.

"I want to have a visit with my sister. Surely you don't have to monitor every word I say. I promise, it won't be that interesting."

Before he could answer, footsteps echoed on the marble floors. We all turned as Salvatore entered the room. He wore a T-shirt and jeans, the V-neck clinging to his sculpted body. His cobalt-blue eyes locked on mine, and my heartbeat quickened, my body suddenly tingling, nipples tightening, every hair standing on end.

A moment later, he released me from his gaze, his posture relaxing as he nodded to my sister and smiled at Effie struggling with the plastic.

"Thanks, Marco. You can go," he said.

Marco nodded and left the room. Salvatore walked over to Izzy.

"I don't think I've met Lucia's sister officially. I'm Salvatore Benedetti."

She took his hand. "Isabella DeMarco."

"Good to meet you. And this is?"

Effie looked up. "Got it!" She held up the plastic triumphantly, then checked out Salvatore. "I'm Effie," she said, rising to her feet from the floor and holding out her hand.

Salvatore took it. "Nice to meet you, Effie."

Rainey walked in with a tray and set the glasses of lemonade down on the coffee table. We stood awkwardly.

"I'll let you and your sister have some privacy," Salvatore finally said, his tone casual, his gaze wavering. "I'm going to take a shower."

He waited. My body still did that vibrating, tingling thing as the air crackled between us.

"Thank you," I finally said.

He nodded and left the room. We watched him go. Only when he was out of the room did either of us breathe. My thoughts wandered to what I'd found in his room. I wondered if he'd think he'd forgotten to lock the door between our bedrooms, or if he'd know I'd broken in.

"Wow. He's intense."

I exhaled. "Yeah." I couldn't tell Izzy about what he'd done. What I'd done. Hell, I wasn't sure myself what it all meant or how I felt about it.

"Effie, it's polite to offer chocolates to others first before you dig in."

My sister tried to sound strict, but I saw the proud smile she worked to hide.

Effie turned her big, pale blue eyes to her mom, her mouth working on a second piece of chocolate. She rose to her feet and walked over to us.

"Would you like a chocolate?" she asked, turning to me first.

"I'd love one." I chose a dark chocolate and thanked her. Izzy declined, and Effie shrugged a shoulder and helped herself to a third.

"How are you doing? You didn't answer any of my messages. I thought he wasn't letting you use the phone!"

I shook my head with a weak smile. "No, it was just drained. I only checked the messages a few minutes before you got here, actually."

"Well, you're going to have to answer next time. I got worried."

I nodded.

"You okay?" she asked quietly.

I shrugged a shoulder. "I don't know. I don't want to cry." As I said it, the first tears wet my lashes.

"Shh." Izzy dug for a tissue in her bag.

Rainey walked out of the kitchen and toward us just then. I turned my face away.

"I'm getting ready to bake cookies in the kitchen. Maybe Effie would like to help?" she asked Izzy.

Effie's eyebrows rose, and she bounced up to stand. "Oh, can I, Mommy?"

"You sure?" Izzy asked Rainey.

After a glance and a small smile at me, she nodded.

"Sure," Izzy said. "Thank you."

Effie took Rainey's hand easily, and they walked off.

"That was nice," Izzy said.

"I haven't yet figured her out."

Izzy took my hands. "Are we okay, Lucia? This is important. I know we haven't talked about it, about me leaving. I was wrong to just take off. I know that. I'm back now, though, and I'm not abandoning you again, okay? You're not alone, even though it may feel that way right now."

I smiled. More tears fell. "We're okay, Izzy." It felt good to say that. Felt good to have my sister back, actually.

She hugged me tight to her, then whispered into my ear. "Are there cameras? Listening devices?"

Her question surprised me. "I don't know," I whispered back. "I haven't seen any but can't say for sure there aren't."

She pulled back and looked at me. "The pool looks amazing."

I knew what she wanted. "Let's go check it out."

We walked outside and away from the house toward the swimming pool.

"How is he? When no one's around, I mean?"

"Bossy." I couldn't tell her about earlier. About

any of it. "And gone, mostly. He just got back from wherever he was, actually."

"He looks at you like he wants to eat you alive."

He scared me, but I didn't want to say that out loud, and not to Izzy. "I can't figure him out. He's horrible one second, then nice. Almost…caring. Like he gives a shit what I feel or think." I picked a single dandelion growing in the otherwise immaculate lawn. "But then he's a jerk again, and then he disappears."

"Is he making you…" she hesitated.

"Sleep with him?" I thought of what I'd found in his bedroom and felt my face heat up.

She nodded.

"Not yet."

"Good. Are you able to come and go?"

"I don't know. Not on my own, I think."

"Okay, that's fine. I'll just come get you. If he wants to send someone to follow us, we'll deal."

"It doesn't matter, Izzy. I'm stuck here."

"Luke and I…We're not going to sit back and let them have everything. Let them have you."

"Luke?"

"Just because we lost one war, doesn't mean we can't start another."

"Izzy." Even in the heat of the day, a shudder ran through me. "You can't. We lost once, and we had an army to back us."

"We don't need an army. We've got access now."

"What?"

Izzy suddenly laughed out loud as if I'd told a joke. It was then that I saw Salvatore standing in the window of his study, watching us. "By access, you mean me."

"It's what you want, isn't it?"

"Well, yes." It was all I'd thought of for the last five years and for good reason. "I want my freedom. And I want Franco Benedetti to pay for what he did to us. For what he made Papa do." I remembered the last time I'd seen my father. It was in that horrible room when I'd signed the contract. Why had I refused to talk to him all these years? He'd tried. He'd come to the college once every month. He'd call once a week. But I blamed him for my fate. And he *was* to blame, but I also understood he had no choice.

I should have been more understanding of the strain he was under.

"And what about him?" she asked, cocking her head in the direction of Salvatore, who'd turned away from the window.

"I want my freedom."

"Well, that's a start. Let's go inside, before he gets suspicious."

"Cookies are ready!" Effie called out as soon as we got into the house.

"They smell amazing," I said.

She watched proudly as Rainey carried a plateful

of freshly baked chocolate chip cookies into the living room.

"I'm packing up the house," Izzy said. "Effie and I are moving in."

"You are?" I was surprised. Papa had still lived in the house we'd grown up in. I didn't think she'd want the house but was glad she wasn't talking about selling it. I wasn't ready for that yet. The thought—it was just too final. I wasn't ready to say good-bye to it, ending that chapter of my life so permanently.

Izzy nodded. "I should have come back sooner than this. I should have forgiven him."

"I didn't."

"It should have been me here in your place," she said, her eyes downcast.

"I don't want to think about that."

"If it weren't for me getting pregnant…"

"Do you keep in touch with the father?" I wanted to know who he was. It didn't matter anymore, not now that Papa was gone, and even if he had found out, it couldn't have mattered then either.

Salvatore chose that moment to walk into the living room. "I could smell the cookies from the study." His eyes met mine first, his expression guarded, almost cautious.

"I baked them. Rainey helped," Effie proudly said.

"Did you now? May I?"

She smiled, nodding.

He picked one up and took a bite. "Well, you did a good job. They're the best cookies I've ever had."

Effie gave him a big smile. "They are?"

"Yep. And Rainey's a good cook, so that says something."

Izzy checked her watch. "We should get going."

"You can't stay longer?" I didn't want her to go. I didn't want to be alone with him.

"I've got people coming to help with the house, and we'll be back with bathing suits soon. Maybe you can come help? I'm packing up some things and moving them to the attic, getting rid of some things. Maybe you want to do your room?

I glanced at Salvatore, hating that I had to ask his permission. Ask him for a ride. Ask him for everything.

"When?" he asked.

Izzy shrugged her shoulder. "Tomorrow or the next day."

"I think we can manage that."

I felt like I went from my father's house, to the nuns, to Salvatore Benedetti's. I was powerless to decide anything for myself.

"Luce?" Izzy asked.

I nodded, adjusting my expression. "My calendar is free," I said, giving Salvatore a smirk.

He didn't react.

"Great, we'll see you then. Come on, Effie, time to go back home."

"Ugh. Home is so boring," she said, her shoulders slumping.

"No, it's not. We've just got to find your box of toys. Maybe you can pack up a couple of those cookies for home."

I picked up a napkin, tucked the remaining cookies into it, and handed it to Effie.

"Here you go, honey. Don't forget your bathing suit the next time you come, by the way."

"I won't, Aunt Lucia."

She gave me a hug. Again came the thought that I'd missed out on the first years of my niece's life. I didn't know her. I hardly knew Izzy anymore. Or Luke.

Were Luke and Izzy really planning an attack on the Benedetti family? What did that mean for Salvatore?

Salvatore walked with us to the door. Once they had driven off and were out of view, he closed it. We stood in the foyer.

"I'm sorry," he said. "I shouldn't have done what I did."

Shit. An apology was the last thing I'd expected. If he'd locked me in a room, been a beast to me, it would make more sense. I could hate him. But an apology? Him offering to take me to my sister's?

"I hope we can forget it and start again," he added.

I think both of us found it hard to hold each other's gaze, and the last thing I wanted to do was talk about what happened, so I nodded. "Okay."

He smiled a small smile. "Thank you."

"If you ever do something like that again, Salvatore, I will kill you."

His eyes narrowed, and apologetic Salvatore was instantly gone. "You don't have to threaten me with murder. I said I was sorry."

He held my gaze until I blinked and nodded, looking down, my attention absorbed by an invisible piece of lint on my blouse.

"Are you really going to take me to help my sister?"

"You're not a prisoner, contrary to what you think, Lucia. This contract between us, the circumstances of our families, those things bind us, and although I have expectations of you and won't tolerate misplaced loyalty, I'm not interested in keeping a prisoner. Neither you nor I can get out of this, even if we wanted to. We have to find some way to live with it."

Even if we wanted to. Did that mean he didn't want to? And what did I want?

"I feel like a prisoner. I'm constantly watched. I couldn't visit with my sister without Marco standing by. I have nothing to do here. You have a cook, people who clean…"

He looked confused. "You're neither a cook nor a cleaner."

"But I am your property. You said so yourself. I have a degree, I want to work, but—"

His mouth tightened, and he looked away for a moment. "Come into my study, Lucia."

"Why?" I didn't trust him. And as much as I hated to admit it, he scared me.

"So we can talk. That's all."

I didn't move.

"I promise."

After a moment, I nodded. He gestured for me to go ahead and followed close behind me, opening the door to the study once we reached it and letting me inside. Once he'd closed the door, he moved behind his large desk. I looked around the room. The walls were painted a dark shade of gray, and two windows overlooked the backyard and the forest beyond. The furnishings were made of a dark, heavy wood, and his desk, the focal point, must have been an antique. Directly before it stood a leather sofa, and the shelves along two of the walls contained floor-to-ceiling books. Set apart from the desk and sofa was an armchair, the leather well-worn, with a matching ottoman at its foot. The reading lamp behind the chair was on, and although it was sunny outside, this room remained darker.

Masculine. Even the scent here was different, all man.

"Sit down."

I realized he'd been watching me take it all in. I lowered myself to the couch and faced him, the desk looming between us, him sitting behind it, making me feel small. I smoothed the skirt of my sundress down, unsure what to do with my hands.

Salvatore got up and walked around his desk. Surprising me, he joined me on the couch.

It only made me more uncomfortable, though. If only he'd act like I expected him to...

"What do you know about me?"

I studied him, drawn to him, to his eyes. I remembered for a moment how the blue had turned nearly black when he'd been aroused. Remembered how he'd looked at me when I'd lain before him. How he'd taken me in. How he'd gripped his cock...

Then the image of what I'd found in his bedroom flashed across the screen of my memory.

I cleared my throat and focused on the firm set of his jaw instead of his eyes. The scruff along the chiseled line told me he'd probably not shaved in the two days he'd been gone, and it didn't help my wandering mind. I lowered my gaze to his neck, to the exposed flesh there, the T-shirt hugging his powerful chest.

Shit. This wasn't working. I was attracted to this man I wanted to hate. In spite of what he'd done, the physical attraction was like an energy between us, a living, breathing, scorching thing.

I closed my eyes and willed myself to focus. Opening them again, I forced myself to meet his eyes. But when I did, I saw what he saw. He knew his power over me.

"Were you with a woman the last two nights?" I blurted out.

He chuckled, apparently surprised. "Not like you think."

So that was a yes?

"I felt ashamed of what I'd done. What I'd made you do."

My neck and face heated.

"That's why I left. I wasn't with another woman. I wouldn't be. We have a contract."

"That binds me to you." Nothing in the contract spoke of any obligation on his part, certainly not one to be celibate or faithful. It was not a marriage contract, after all.

"And me to you."

Now I was confused. Salvatore leaned back and crossed his ankle over his knee.

"Let me ask you again, Lucia. What do you know about me? Or perhaps the better question is, what do you *think* you know?"

"I know you're Franco Benedetti's son." I stuck my chin out. "That's all I need to know."

"I think you're smarter than that."

"I know your hand shook when you signed the contract."

He paused, his gaze faltering momentarily. "I'm not firstborn. I was never intended to be in the position I'm in."

"You mean, being your father's successor?"

"Yes."

"So you're stuck with me? If your brother were alive, I'd be his."

"I mean I am obligated to do many things, which I would not choose to do and do not condone."

"Me, you mean. You wouldn't choose me?"

"Stop putting words in my mouth."

"Isn't that what you're saying?"

"Why don't you try listening for a change and remember not everything is about you, Lucia."

Too shocked to retort, I unwittingly did as he said.

"I'm saying I wouldn't have created that contract in the first place. But to be fair, your father agreed. Remember that."

"My father didn't have a choice."

"He should have been willing to die..." he paused and leaned forward, anger marking his words, an anger I did not expect. "He should have been willing to die rather than see you go through what you did."

That last part made me stop.

"He did die." But Salvatore was right. And that was why I'd been so angry with my father all these years. Why I refused to see him. He'd given me up without a fight. Salvatore was right. How could he stand by and watch what they did? How could he have offered his daughter to the Benedetti beasts?

"I don't want to upset you, Lucia."

I wiped the back of my hand across my face, catching the single tear that had slipped from my eye. I shook my head, not wanting to speak for fear I would weep. It would be easier if he were unkind. Damn him, it would be easier.

"All I'm saying is I wouldn't have done what my father did. I would not have required the innocent daughter of my enemy as payment."

Fuck.

I swallowed back tears, knowing he saw right through me all along.

"But we're here now. You and I are both here, and bound to one another. I don't want a prisoner. I don't want someone who fears or hates me in my own house."

"Then I don't understand. Why do you care what I think? I'm your enemy, and you've won. My presence here is proof of that. To your power over me and my family."

"I'm not a monster, whether you believe it or not."

"What do you want from me, then?"

"I've already told you: your obedience. You give me that, and I'll make this easier."

Obedience. I hated that fucking word. "And if I don't, you'll punish me like you did before."

"I'll be creative in my punishments, yes," he said with a wicked gleam in his eye.

Goose bumps made the hairs on my arms stand on end, and my mind wandered to the restraints attached to the posts of his bed. Would he use those? Was that getting *creative*?

Salvatore reached out to softly touch my knee. My mind screamed for me to pull away, but instead, I looked from his eyes to his hand. I swallowed as he stroked the inside of my knee, then my thigh, pushing the dress up as he did so.

"I think you enjoyed at least part of your punishment."

I shook my head, just a small "no," but kept my eyes on his hand, on his fingers as they drew small circles on too sensitive flesh.

He slid toward me, making me look up, forcing me to meet his gaze.

"And it doesn't always have to be punishment."

His fingers left my thigh and touched the top button of my blouse. I watched in silence, unable to speak. He slowly undid the buttons and pulled my top open.

"Look at me."

I did, my breath hitching when I met those cobalt eyes. With both hands, he slid the blouse from my shoulders, leaving it at my elbows. He then explored my exposed chest, my nipples tightening just from his gaze upon them, barely hidden behind the white lace.

Bringing his face to mine, he inhaled, his mouth close to mine, so close, but not touching. He kissed my cheek softly, making my stomach flutter, his breath on my face making my sex throb.

"I can make this good," he whispered by my ear. "I want to make this good for you."

When his fingers traced the border of my bra, I licked my lips, wanting him to kiss me, preparing for him to kiss me. He could make this so good. I knew. I knew how good he could make it.

His fingers slid inside my bra as his mouth neared mine again. This time, I tilted my face upward to meet his and reached a trembling hand to touch the naked muscle of his arm. His kiss was soft, slow, tender almost as his fingers tickled my nipple. But then it changed, building in heat and intensity as one hand cradled the back of my head, and my mouth opened to his tongue, my entire body arching up to meet him, wanting—needing—something more.

"But only good girls are rewarded," he said, his mouth at my ear again, me breathless, blinking up at him as he pulled back. "Bad girls are punished. Have you been bad, Lucia?"

His eyes seemed to dance, and I knew in that instant he knew.

I straightened, trying to tug my shirt up to cover myself.

Salvatore shook his head and smiled, cocking his head to the side. "Tell me, have you?"

"No," I said, my voice cracking.

He reached over, and I gasped when he pushed the cups of my bra beneath my breasts.

"Wh...what are you doing?" I moved to cover them.

"No," he said, taking my wrists and pulling them behind my back.

"Salvatore?"

That smile still plastered on his face, he dragged me forward and laid me facedown over his lap. He kept my wrists at my back while the fingers of his other hand tickled the inside of my thighs as they dragged my skirt up.

"Have you been snooping?" he asked outright once he'd stuffed my skirt beneath my wrists at my waist.

"What? No!"

He smacked my right cheek. I think I was more surprised than pained. "What the..."

"Have you been snooping?" he repeated.

I craned my neck. "What are you doing?"

Smack.

"Ow! Stop!"

"Have you been snooping?"

I shook my head, squeezed my legs together, and

wriggled to get free, which was impossible, considering his size and strength.

"No?"

His fingers found the waistband of my panties and tickled the flesh there. "What are you doing? Let me up!"

I knew he heard me, he just was enjoying this. When he began to drag my panties down, I wildly kicked my legs only to have them trapped between Salvatore's hard thighs. The swoosh of his belt made me stop struggling, and he laughed at what I was sure was my deer in the headlights expression.

"Don't worry." He wrapped the belt around my wrists and secured them behind my back. "I'm just planning on using my hand this first time."

"What?"

But he began, smacking one cheek then the next, each slap screaming at my brain that this was really happening. That I was naked from the waist down being spanked!

"Stop! It fucking hurts!"

A few moments later, he did, rubbing circles over my punished cheeks.

"Let me up," I said, wiping my wet face on his jeans.

"Were you snooping?" he asked again. This time, there was no teasing in his tone.

"Yes!" He knew it anyway; why he had to humiliate me like this to get me to admit it was beyond me.

"Good girl," he said, his touch sliding between my thighs. "Bad girls get punished, but good girls get rewarded."

Then, without any warning, his fingers found my sex, and I sucked in a breath.

I tensed, squeezing everything tight, but Salvatore tickled and stroked until I relaxed my legs and let them fall open, my back arching of its own accord as he smeared my own arousal over and around my clit, rubbing soft, then hard, pinching, making me cry out.

"What did you find in my bedroom?" he asked, still rubbing.

When a moan escaped me, I hung my head, wanting to disappear. How could I be enjoying this? Enjoying this humiliation?

"No..."

"Remember, good girls are rewarded, bad girls punished. Lying would make you a bad girl."

"I hate you," I said, not believing it myself.

"No, you don't. You just feel powerless and are acting out in response."

"I'm not a child."

"I know that. Tell me what you found."

He started on my clit again, rubbing harder, faster. "God."

He chuckled. "God would be a first."

"I'm..."

"Focus, Lucia," he said, the fingers of his free hand taking one of my breasts.

"Restraints," I said, my eyes about to roll to the back of my head when he kneaded my nipple.

"And how did it make you feel to find them?"

He eased off my clit, and I groaned, arching back again, wanting to—needing to—come.

"I...I don't know."

He struck my pussy, and I gasped.

"What did you feel?"

He rubbed again, and I melted into him. "Curious."

Was it possible to hear a smile? Because I did. And then, I came. I came hard in his hand, the sounds I made foreign to my own ears, my body going limp over his thighs, my eyes closing, sleepy. When it was over, I felt him unbind my wrists and lift me, cradling me in his arms and leaning back against the sofa.

"Lucia, Lucia, Lucia. You surprise me."

"You'll still take me to my sister?" I asked, burrowing into his body, my eyes half-open.

"I told you I would. And we need to go shopping to find you a dress."

"A dress? For what?"

"My father's birthday party."

8
LUCIA

Being locked away with the nuns for five years had been easier than this. I didn't have to face anything. I could think about it. I could get angry about it. I could blame everyone and everything, but I didn't have to face them. Now I sat beside Salvatore in his car as he drove me to what should have been considered home to me. Thing was, I didn't know what was home anymore. I didn't know where I belonged, who I was. Who I was meant to be.

I looked at Salvatore, at his profile. At a glance, the set of his jaw told of power, of strength, while his eyes betrayed a depth beneath this outermost layer. Gave a glimpse into the darkness there. He kept his attention on the road while I studied him, wondering who this man was. What was expected of him.

Wondering what the hell had happened between us yesterday.

They'd examined me on the day of the signing. His father had wanted to be certain I was *intact*. A virgin. Was it only to humiliate me? To break my father to the point he could no longer be repaired?

I shook my head, trying to erase the memory of my father's face when I'd finally been able to look at him. How his hands had been fisted, his shoulders slumped. He'd been made to stand by and watch his daughter's degradation. Why?

Yesterday, Salvatore hadn't forced himself on me. He hadn't tried, and he'd had the opportunity. Multiple opportunities. And, he might argue, the right. He *owned* me. But he hadn't taken anything I hadn't given up. And I'd given it. I'd lain there and let him bring me to orgasm. I'd felt his cock pressing against me throughout both the punishment and the reward, but he hadn't taken his pleasure from me.

I fumbled to turn up the AC, feeling too hot suddenly. Our fingers touched when Salvatore adjusted it for me, and it was like a bolt of electricity. Our gazes locked, but I quickly blinked and turned away.

"If you get off at this exit, I can show you a shortcut."

He made his way over. Once we were off the exit, I gave him directions. We weaved our way through the narrow streets near my childhood home.

"Want to get a cup of coffee first?" I asked when we neared my favorite bakery, wanting to put off our inevitable arrival. Afraid Isabella would see right through me. Would I be a traitor then?

He seemed surprised by my offer. "Sure."

"Right here, you can park at the curb. The parking lot is usually full." And I wanted to walk through the streets, see the houses and neighborhood I didn't realize I'd missed. "You don't mind walking a few blocks, do you?" I asked once we climbed out.

"No, it's fine." Salvatore pushed a button to lock the car and looked around. "I'm curious where you grew up. This is very different from what I imagined."

Wayne, Pennsylvania, was a pretty suburb. Quiet. Wealthy. And, apart from the mob family living there, safe.

I slung my purse over my shoulder and glanced up at the sky. Clouds collected thick and heavy with moisture. It had to be ninety degrees already. As much as I hated rain, I'd welcome it today to cool things down.

Salvatore came to my side, his attention still on the surroundings. He wore a navy T-shirt and jeans, and I had no idea how he wasn't sweating his ass off. My tank top and shorts seemed stuck to me.

"What did you imagine?" I asked as I led the way,

liking the fact that most of the houses looked just like they had five years ago.

Salvatore turned his blue eyes my way. Would I always become breathless when he looked at me?

"I don't know. A castle with a moat."

I chuckled. "That's your family. We were more… low-key." I thought about it. "My father kept us out of things. He wasn't meant to rule the family, my uncle was. But when my grandfather and uncle were killed, he was forced to take over. I remember it happening. Well, remember all the meetings, all the people who were suddenly in our house all the time. I was maybe ten." They'd told my sister and me that they'd had a car accident, but I knew better. I'd snuck into my father's study and had seen the photos of the bullet-riddled car. Of them inside it. I shuddered. Some things you couldn't un-see, no matter how much you wanted to. "I remember not being allowed to play in the front yard or bike through the neighborhood anymore."

"Your father didn't have control of the family."

I stopped.

Salvatore turned to me.

"He's dead. Isn't that enough? I thought that would have satisfied you, but I guess I was wrong." Tears burned my eyes, but I didn't feel sad. Confused and remorseful, yes, the need to defend my father fierce. The desperation to understand my muddled loyalties even more so.

Salvatore ran a hand through his thick, dark hair and glanced away. He nodded but didn't speak.

"Why don't you just drop me off at the house?" I asked, feeling betrayed after yesterday. But what did I expect? What did I think, that we were building a relationship?

"Which way to the coffee shop?" he asked, ignoring my request.

I pointed and walked just ahead of him. The coffee shop was small and exactly as I remembered it. And it was full.

The entire place quieted when we walked in. I looked around at the faces, not really recognizing anyone, but knowing they must recognize me. Or, more likely, Salvatore. Benedetti were not welcomed in this neighborhood for a long time. That hadn't changed, even though now, they owned it.

"Let's get a table," Salvatore said when I walked up to the counter.

"We can just get a cup to go." I hadn't thought about how people might react to him. To me with him.

"No."

He made a point of meeting every eye in the place, and I was sure he felt it too.

"There's a couple leaving. We can take their table."

I looked to where he pointed, and sure enough,

the pair at the table left money on the check, gathered up their things, and walked out.

"We don't have to stay," I whispered, not sure if it was more for him or me. People would know who I was. They'd know either because of my father and the photos of the family after his death in the local paper or because of Salvatore.

"We'll stay."

He pulled out one of the chairs and waited for me to have a seat before he took the chair opposite. I saw how he'd chosen the seat where he could watch the whole of the café, especially the door. It was a subtle reminder of who he was. Who I was.

A waitress came to clear and wipe down the table.

"What would you like?" Salvatore asked me.

"Um, a cappuccino, please. Thanks."

"I'll have a double espresso and one of the éclairs if they're fresh."

"Baked just this morning," the waitress said, her tone unfriendly.

Salvatore excused her with a nod.

Voices picked up as conversation began again, and I wondered how many of them were talking about us.

Salvatore leaned back in his seat and looked at me. "You came here a lot growing up?"

I knew he wasn't oblivious to the stares or whispers, but he acted like he couldn't have cared less.

I nodded, trying to stop from glancing around. "Izzy and I would come every Sunday morning after church. The éclairs were my favorite."

"Why didn't you order one?"

"I don't feel very hungry."

"Take one." He raised his hand to get the waitress's attention.

"No," I reached out to make him take his arm down, to not draw any additional attention to us, but the waitress was already coming over.

"I don't think I can eat anything, Salvatore," I whispered.

He studied me, his eyes curious. Concerned? "Your niece will be there today, right?"

I nodded, glancing up at the waitress who stood quietly, clearly not happy about having to serve a Benedetti. Did they see me as a traitor? Did they know I'd been made to do this? To be with him? It was in that moment I realized they likely did not know about the contract. But even so, wasn't I myself confused?

"Let's get six of those éclairs boxed up to go too," he said to the waitress, then turned to me. "She has a sweet tooth from what I saw."

I smiled. "That's nice. She'll like that, and so will Izzy."

The waitress returned and delivered the coffee and Salvatore's pastry and set the additional box of eclairs up at the register. Salvatore took a big bite, and I chuckled.

"What?" he asked, looking for a napkin.

"You have some cream," I pointed, then reached over to wipe it off when he missed. "Right there." I pulled my hand away and without thinking, licked off the cream. He watched me, and as soon as I realized what I'd done, I pulled a napkin out of the dispenser and wiped off my finger.

"They're very good," Salvatore said, not commenting.

"You don't care that no one wants you here, do you?"

He raised his eyebrows and picked up his espresso. "No. Why should I? Besides, I'm not even sure it's true." He looked around the café. "What happened, happened five years ago."

That was when things had been at their worst. When fighting on the streets had turned this neighborhood from a quiet, safe place to a bloody one.

"And we've kept peace since."

"By killing off most of your enemies."

"Both sides lost people, Lucia. We just won the war *your* father started." He drank the last of his espresso and stood, looking pissed. "You finished?"

I rose to my feet. "I need to use the bathroom."

He nodded and took out his wallet as I made my way to the tiny bathroom. Once inside, I locked the door and gripped the sink, looking at my reflection. I had to find some way to be okay with all of this. This was my life now. I belonged to a man whose name I hated, but who made me question everything I believed. I needed to make sense of it all. To find some way to survive this. I splashed water onto my face and patted it dry, taking a deep breath before walking back out to find him waiting for me, his expression hard.

We drove to the house in silence. Turned out I didn't need to give Salvatore directions. He knew the way, and by the time he pulled up in front of the large, two-story brick home with the wraparound porch and swing hanging from a branch in the overgrown tree in the front yard, my heart was racing.

Salvatore switched off the engine and turned to me. He tucked a strand of hair behind my ear, his thumb resting against my cheek as his mouth moved into a small smile. A sort of truce, maybe.

"Relax," he said.

"It's that obvious?" I asked, holding onto the box of éclairs.

"Yeah." Salvatore's cell phone rang. He looked at the display but declined the call. "I'll walk you in, then I have to make a call."

I nodded, oddly grateful, and climbed out of the car.

"Aunt Lucia!"

I turned to find Effie running across the lawn toward us.

"Effie!" She crashed into my legs. Salvatore's hand at my back kept me upright. "I'm excited to see you too." I hugged her with one arm. "Look what Salvatore brought for you." She pulled back, and I opened the box of éclairs .

"Oh!" She squealed and looked with huge eyes from the box to him then back. "Thank you!"

The front door opened, and Izzy stepped outside followed by Luke.

"Huh?" I didn't realize Luke would be here.

Izzy came toward us, her mouth pasted into a smile. I glanced at Salvatore to find his eyes locked on Luke's.

"What the hell is he doing here?" he muttered. I wondered if he'd meant to say it out loud at all.

"Those look great," Izzy said, her eye on the box Effie held. She took my hand and pulled me to her side, her gaze on Salvatore. "Thanks for dropping her off."

"Oh, I can stay," he said, taking me by the arm and pulling me to stand beside him. "I'd love to see where Lucia grew up."

"Didn't you have to make a call?" I reminded him, unsure where my loyalties should lie.

His smile didn't reach his eyes. "It can wait."

"Luke came by to help. Luke, this is Salvatore Benedetti," Izzy said, introducing them.

The men eyed each other, neither offering a hand. "We know each other," Salvatore said.

I watched Luke, saw how he stood a little closer to my sister than he maybe should, remembered my conversation with Izzy yesterday.

"Mommy, can I have one already?" Effie asked.

My attention went to the little girl. I looked from her to Luke and back. But then Salvatore spoke, interrupting my thoughts.

"Want me to take the first bite, so you can be sure they're not poisoned?" he asked Izzy in Italian while placing a hand on top of Effie's head. I realized he'd spoken Italian so Effie wouldn't understand.

My sister's eyes hardened. "Go ahead, honey," she said to Effie, her gaze never leaving Salvatore.

"Thanks!" Effie, oblivious to the tension, chose the largest éclair and began eating.

"Okay, let's go inside and get started." I tugged my arm free from his hold, took Salvatore's arm, and dragged him with me into the house.

"Did you know Luke would be here?" he asked in a clipped tone.

"No. I'm just as surprised as you." I walked into the living room which, even on a sunny day, was dark because of the wide-covered porch, and today, with the heavy clouds overhead, Izzy had turned on several lamps even though it was early in the day. I stopped just inside the house, the faint but familiar scent of vanilla flooding my mind with memories. I'd forgotten that scent. Mom's favorite candles. Papa had always claimed to hate them, but he'd kept right on buying them even after she died. It was all too many years ago. An entire lifetime ago.

"Is there something going on between your sister and Luke?" Salvatore asked, his gaze on the pair outside, who stood having a heated discussion.

"They're cousins. They're just close, that's all." Was that all?

"I don't like it, Lucia. And I don't like you around him."

I faced him. "He's my cousin too. My parents are both dead now. I need all the family I can get."

"Sometimes family is bad for you."

I paused, trying to read what I saw in his eyes, but Salvatore had a talent for being unreadable. Feeling weak, I sat on the arm of the sofa and took a deep breath.

"Don't take them away from me too," I whispered without thinking, knowing he could do just that. What would happen then? Izzy would start a war. Hell, she and Luke were already planning it.

Salvatore came toward me. He took my hands and made me look at him. "I won't take them away."

"Promise it," I said after a long moment.

"I promise."

That was the second promise he'd made me.

Without another word, I led the way up to my bedroom, where Salvatore helped me pack up the things I wanted to keep, mostly books and old diaries I'd hidden. My bed stood where it had always been, just beneath one of the two windows. My father used to ask me how I could sleep there in the summer months—didn't the light wake me up too early?—but I loved it. I looked out onto the backyard, where he'd put up a second swing like the one in the front yard.

I sat down while Salvatore taped up the last box. It was when I picked up the pillow that I found it. A letter addressed to me, the envelope sealed, the handwriting familiar.

My father's.

I picked it up and stared at it. My father's suicide note had been brief. He'd said he was sorry. He'd said he'd failed everyone he loved.

I ran the pad of my finger over the blue ink before sliding my finger beneath the flap and tearing it. The sound stood out, almost as if it blocked out every other sound, every other person or thing. My heart pounded, and my hand trembled as I pulled out the folded sheet of paper.

Dear, dear Lucia,

I know this comes too little too late, and you won't ever know how sorry I am for the part I forced you to play in this terrible war. I want to say I had no choice. I want to blame anyone else. And for a time, I did. But that wasn't real.

One thing I've learned these last five years is to take responsibility for my actions, for their consequences. For your consequence. And this one, this final one, is the one I cannot reconcile. The single thing that has broken me.

I am so very sorry, Lucia. I am so ashamed of myself. I am a weak man, and I've burdened you with a weight too heavy. I can't live with this anymore. I will fail you again by being absent when the bastard comes to claim you. But you see, I cannot live with this for another moment longer. I cannot live, knowing they destroyed both of my daughters.

I hope you will forgive me. I do love you more than anything in this world.

Papa

A hand on my shoulder startled me, and I glanced up.

"You okay?"

It was Salvatore. I quickly crumpled the letter and threw it into the trash can, then wiped my face with the backs of my hands.

"I want to go." I said, looking around for something, what I had no idea. "I need... I can't."

"Shh."

He wrapped an arm around me and, without another word, pulled me into his chest and held me there, one hand rubbing my back, the other holding tight.

"Shh," he said again.

I choked on a sob and pressed my face into him,

for one moment letting his strength support me, lift the weight of all of this from me. But when in response to my surrender he hugged me back, I shook my head and wiped my face before breaking away from him. I couldn't look at him. I couldn't take comfort from him. He was the enemy. And I was betraying my family with every tender moment I shared with him.

I couldn't do this.

"Please…" I started.

With a nod, he ushered me out to the car. "Stay here."

Salvatore went back into the house and a few moments later returned, loaded the two boxes I'd packed into the trunk, and climbed behind the steering wheel. He glanced at me, the look in his eyes strange, cautious, measuring. Then, without a word, he turned the key and started the engine, taking us back to his house, back to my new home.

9
SALVATORE

I knew it wasn't right, but I did what any man would do in my situation. I fished out the letter Lucia had thrown into the trash and read it.

If I hadn't been sure before, I was now. The fucking bastard of a father was too weak to stay alive. Too weak to take responsibility even in this, his final letter to the daughter he betrayed. Did he even know what his letter would do to her? Did he know it would only add to the guilt she already felt with his loss?

Fucking bastard.

I paced my study, phone to my ear, when, finally, Roman picked up on the fifth ring. "I need you to do something for me, Uncle." I rarely called Roman that. Only when I needed to trust him absolutely. "Just for me."

"What is it?" he asked. He was too smart to agree to something without knowing the details.

"I know we have Luke DeMarco under surveillance, but I want more. I want to know where he spends his nights. I want to know exactly how much time he spends with Isabella DeMarco. And," was I really going to do this? "I want a paternity test run on the little girl, Effie. I want to know if he's her father."

"We share the same suspicions."

"And my father? What does he think?"

"He doesn't think she's a threat, so he hasn't looked into it."

"Isabella?"

"Yes." He paused. "Never underestimate your enemy, Salvatore. It will get you killed."

"No one knows that better than me, Uncle."

"I'll keep this between us for now."

"For now. I will go to my father once I have solid information."

"I'll work on it right away."

"Thank you."

I hung up the phone, that last part a lie. If my suspicions were correct, I couldn't go to my father with the details. My father did not need any more ammunition against Luke DeMarco, and something about what Lucia had said, asking me not to take them away, I felt it.

Luke was collecting supporters, that I knew, but

was Lucia's sister involved? If so, how deeply? Just how close were she and Luke? And what would I need to do if I what I believed was confirmed?

On top of everything else, I needed to gain Lucia's trust. I needed to be sure she'd do as I said and not act out during the birthday dinner. I needed to make sure my father knew I had control of her.

THE NEXT AFTERNOON, I pulled into Nordstrom's parking lot.

"I don't want to go to your father's party."

We climbed out of the car and went into the department store. She sounded defiant, but I heard the panic behind her words.

"I'm not going."

I touched her back to lead her inside. "Yes, you are. And you're going to behave while you're there."

"Why? Why can't you just go on your own?"

"Because he's expecting both of us." We stepped onto the escalator, Marco and another man following nearby. A piano played on the second floor. Before we reached it, I saw the salesgirl waiting for us.

"Why?" Lucia asked again.

Once off the escalator, I took her arms, rubbed them, and turned her toward me. There would be no discussion. She would go. Period. Even if it was the last place I wanted to take Lucia, we would both go. "Because I said so. Now be good." I leaned in, and to anyone who watched, it looked like I was planting a kiss on her temple, but instead, I whispered in her ear. "Or else I'll have to get creative again."

Her eyes searched mine when I pulled back, questioning, perhaps trying to gauge how far I'd go. Honestly, I didn't mind if she did push me.

"Mr. Benedetti," the salesgirl said, her high heels clicking toward us.

I turned to her. She couldn't be more than twenty.

"I'm Carla, and I'll help your..." She searched our ring fingers and modified, "I understand you're looking for an evening dress."

I chuckled and kept one hand at Lucia's back. "For Lucia. I'd look rather silly in an evening dress."

The girl laughed nervously and looked Lucia over. "Size four?"

Lucia nodded.

"Any preference as to length or cut?" We followed her as she led the way to the designer dresses.

My phone rang. When I saw Natalie's name displayed on the screen, I excused myself. Lucia raised her eyebrows but didn't question. Marco followed me, and the other guard kept close to Lucia.

"Hello?"

"Hi, Salvatore. It's Natalie. Is this a good time?"

"Yes, of course. Is everything all right?" She sounded tense.

"Dominic came by. He was here when I got home from work."

Natalie didn't trust Dominic. She had never liked him, and I'd seen Sergio have words with him. I never knew the details but suspected it had something to do with Natalie.

"What did he want?"

"He said he wanted to see his nephew. See how he's doing, since I won't take him to the house for visits."

Why in hell did Dominic care about a baby? He never had before.

"Salvatore?"

"I'm listening. How long was he there?"

"Just ten minutes. I wouldn't let him in. Talked to him on the front steps. What does he want, Salvatore?"

"I don't know, but I'll see him at my father's birthday dinner. I'll talk to him then. Do you feel safe? Do you want me to send someone over?"

"No, it's okay. I just...seeing him again...it brought back so much."

"I know." I heard her sniffle. "I'm sorry, Natalie." I heard Jacob fuss near the phone.

"It's okay, it'll be fine. He just surprised me. I'd better go get Jacob's dinner."

"I can come by myself if you want me to."

"You have your hands full. Really, I'll be fine. I feel better already, now that I've talked to you. It's fine."

"Let me at least send someone to keep an eye on the house."

"No. I don't want that for myself, and I don't want it for Jacob. We're out of this life. It's what Sergio would have wanted for us."

I nodded, even though she couldn't see. The salesgirl came around the corner, looking frazzled until she spotted me. I turned my back to wrap up my call.

"Okay, but if you feel unsafe or need anything, you call me, understand?"

"Yes. I will, Salvatore. Thank you."

We hung up, and I walked toward the girl, my mind going a thousand miles a minute, wondering what the hell Dominic was up to.

"She's ready with the first one." The girl sang out and pointed to the dressing room.

I followed her. It was a private room with a sofa and a long mirror with a curtain to separate the changing area. Once inside, the girl closed the door and disappeared behind the curtain.

"It's too low," Lucia complained.

"It looks amazing," the girl retorted.

A moment later, she pulled the curtain aside, and my eyes about popped out of my head. There stood Lucia, her expression annoyed, her long dark hair falling in waves over her shoulders, a cream-colored dress wrapped around her petite frame. The material fell heavy to her feet, which I could see were wrapped in silver-and-gold, high-heeled sandals. They added three inches to her height. The dress was cut low so that the V dipped all the way down to the high belt around her waist. Gemstones circled her waistline and edged the V between her breasts, clinging to her, displaying their small, round mounds beautifully.

"I think the hair should go up," the girl said, piling Lucia's hair on top of her head and forcing her farther out so that she stood before the mirror, her back to me. "To display this gorgeous back." The V of the neckline repeated on the back. "We'll need to alter it slightly here," she pointed out the pins at Lucia's shoulders. "But it'll be ready by tomorrow."

"You look beautiful," I said to Lucia.

Lucia's eyes found mine in the mirror. She looked at herself once more as if not quite believing it was her. I wondered if this was her first time in a dress like this.

"It's too..." she started, looking down at the V between her breasts.

"It's perfect." I stood and went to her, standing close behind her. Our eyes locked in the mirror. I took the clip out of her hair and let the mass tumble down her back. Lucia bit her lip and shuddered.

"Find us something more casual for tonight," I said to the girl without taking my eyes off Lucia. "Take your time."

"Yes, sir." The girl walked out, closing the door behind her.

I turned Lucia to face me. "I want you."

Her hands came up to my chest, and I brushed her hair off her shoulders. The light overhead flickered on and off, then settled for on. Without another word, I leaned in to kiss her. I loved kissing her. I'd seen her naked. I'd tasted her pussy, but this was our most intimate act yet, and I took my time, tasting her, her mouth soft, her tongue shy at first, submissive to mine, then bolder, curious in its exploration as the kiss deepened, drawing a moan from deep inside my chest.

A quick knock and the door opened. Lucia gasped, but the girl remained oblivious. She carried in an armful of dresses and spoke without giving us a glance as she hung them all up.

"And, what do you think?"

I looked Lucia over again, my gaze hovering on the exposed mounds of her breasts, my cock pressing against the crotch of my jeans.

"We'll take this one." My voice came out hoarse, and I cleared my throat. "You'll be able to deliver it altered tomorrow?"

"Yes, sir."

The girl beamed, and when I checked the price

tag, I understood why. She'd probably made more tonight on commission than a month on the floor.

"Let's get that one off and try another," she said, ushering Lucia behind the curtain.

"Out here. I want to see."

She stopped, confused, tilting her head to one side, but then glanced at Lucia who only stared back at me, her swollen lips slightly parted, her eyes a darker burnt caramel as opposed to their usual whiskey-brown.

"Here," I said, pointing to a spot before the mirror, where I could see her front and back.

"Yes, sir." The girl moved Lucia, who only watched me.

I leaned back in my seat as the salesgirl unhooked the belt and slowly slid the dress off Lucia, leaving her standing in panties, a pair of boyshorts like the ones she'd packed to Italy. That seemed so long ago now.

I abandoned looking at Lucia's eyes as I studied her nearly naked body, each time seeming like the first. Narrow shoulders; small, high, round breasts with nipples that tightened beneath my gaze; a flat belly; and long, slender, muscular legs. She was beautiful. Perfect. And my cock twitched in appreciation.

I had her, she was mine. But I wanted her to want it. To want me.

I swallowed as she raised her arms for the girl to

slide a short black dress over her head. This one hung loose to the low waist and had long sleeves with slits all the way through.

"Best part," the girl said, turning Lucia so she had her back to me. The back was cut out to the hips, accenting the silhouette of her figure seductively.

I nodded. "I want to see that one." I pointed to another, and the girl quietly obeyed, undressing Lucia and dressing her again. Turning her this way and that, all while my cock grew harder, Lucia's submission turning me on as much as having her naked did.

Once she'd gone through the rest of the dresses, the girl left us.

"What are we doing?" Lucia asked as she stood before me in just her panties and those sandals, her hands over her breasts, the spell broken.

"We're shopping. Don't cover your breasts."

For a moment, she resisted, her eyes questioning. But then, she obeyed and dropped her arms to her sides.

"Turn around."

She did, presenting me with her ass still clad in lace. I stood. She glanced over her shoulder but then faced the wall again.

"Hands up on the wall." I stood close enough to make sure she felt my breath on her shoulder, the heat of my body pulsing against hers. Leaning down,

I inhaled the clean scent of her hair, watched her nipples harden and goose bumps rise along the flesh of her arms. "I like looking at you, Lucia." I pressed my erection against her hip. "You don't know how badly I want you."

She swallowed as I ran the knuckles of one hand along her hip, then slid two fingers along the edge of her panties. "I like these." With both hands now, I traced the outline of lace on the soft swell of her ass. I then dragged them upward, exposing more of her cheeks as I set the material in the split between them, then tugged upward.

Lucia gasped.

"I like your ass." I wrapped one hand around to pinch her nipple. "I like your breasts." I slid it down over her belly and into her panties to cup the wet mound of her sex. "And I like your pussy." I rubbed her clit as she leaned against me, softening, a small moan escaping her lips. Wrapping my free hand around her neck, I drew her against me, still playing with the slick folds of her sex as I ground my cock against her back. "I want to bury my cock inside your pussy, Lucia. I want to bend you over here and fuck you so hard, everyone in this damn place knows it. Knows you're getting fucked. Knows you're mine."

She stiffened at my words, resisting, but her body jerked as she neared orgasm.

"Stop." Her voice was weak. A half-hearted plea.

"Give it to me."

"I..."

I pinched her clit, and she fisted her hands, leaning her forehead into the wall.

"Please. Don't. Not here."

"Come."

She shook her head but stayed as she was, not attempting to free herself, to drag my hand from her pussy.

"Come."

"No... Fuck."

Her knees buckled, but I kept her pressed against me, this time gripping a handful of hair and tugging her head backward. "Come, and I'll release you."

"I...said...no."

"Stubborn." I turned her to face me, kissed her, and worked her clit hard between thumb and forefinger. Her mouth opened to mine, and her arms wrapped around my neck, pushing and pulling, so close to orgasm yet resisting with all she had.

She broke away. "I...won't."

But I took her mouth again, and this time, I slid the hand that held her hair down into her panties, parting her ass cheeks, pressing my finger there, rubbing her tight little asshole until her knees gave way, and she cried out, gripping my neck, burying her face in my chest to stifle her moans as she came, her pussy soaking my fingers, my hand, her weight fully supported by me as her body gave out. She sighed, her breathing short, her eyes wet and dark when she turned them up to me. I wrapped my arms around her, smiling, victorious.

"I hate you," she murmured, closing her eyes when I claimed her mouth for the kiss I took, triumphant again.

"I'm not hungry."

"But you are stubborn," I said to Lucia, leaning in closer. "You're eating. Choose something, or I'll choose for you."

She glared but acquiesced. "Fine. I'll have the mushroom ravioli."

"Ravioli it is," the waiter said, giving me a look and taking our menus.

Once the clothes had been paid for, Lucia had dressed in the black backless dress, and we'd headed to a small Italian restaurant for dinner.

"I can't show my face at Nordstrom again. You know that, right?"

"No one saw your face," I said, winking, as I picked up a piece of bread and dipped it into a bowl of olive oil.

"You make me so mad!"

I chewed on the bread. "They have the best olive oil. You know, it's made from their own olives from their groves in Tuscany."

She took a piece of bread and violently dipped it before biting off a chunk, then sat back and gave me a look. "Did you wash your hands?"

I laughed so hard I nearly choked, and the patrons at the tables around us turned to stare. "I like the way you taste," I said, reaching under the table and sliding one hand up the inside of her thigh.

"You're terrible!" She caught my hand and shoved it away.

"That's not what you were saying in the dressing room."

The waiter brought over the bottle of wine I'd ordered. Lucia dropped her gaze to her lap, her cheeks flaming red.

He popped the cork and poured. "It's fine," I said after tasting it. He filled Lucia's glass first, then mine. "There's nothing to be embarrassed about," I said to her after the waiter left and we picked up our glasses.

"I just had a very loud orgasm in the fitting room at Nordstrom."

I smiled and shrugged a shoulder. I knew this resistance was in part due to her anxiety over my father's birthday party. "You're probably not the first," I teased, then gave her a wink and decided now was a good time to change the subject. "Your niece is cute."

She studied me, slowly sipping from her glass. "She is."

"You're close with your sister?"

"I was. Before…everything."

"What do you think of her moving into your father's house?"

"I'm glad she's moving in there. I don't know if I'm ready to sell it. And I'm glad she's staying nearby."

"Why didn't you see each other while you were at school? You could have. Nothing was forbidden."

She shrugged a shoulder. "You mean like when Marco was standing over us when she came to visit me at the house?"

I gave her my most patient smile. "You didn't want to."

"You don't know me or my family."

"I'm trying to get to know you. Just because you haven't been in touch with them doesn't mean you can't start again. They're your family."

"What about your brother? Are you close?"

"With Dominic?" She nodded. "No. Dominic is… not good."

"But you were close with Sergio?"

"Yes. Very."

Neither of us spoke until the waiter interrupted with our dishes. Once he left, Lucia looked at me.

"I'm sorry I didn't talk to my father before he died. I should have told him I forgave him."

"Do you? Forgive him, I mean?"

She shrugged a shoulder. "I think he was backed into a corner. And you're wrong, he wasn't just saving himself. He gave me up to save all of them. You...your father had murdered—"

"I'm getting bored of this conversation. It was a war. Both sides lost many lives. You and I both know that."

She sighed and pushed ravioli around her plate.

"But you're right. Your father was backed into a corner."

"Thanks for that."

I nodded as I stuffed a forkful of salmon into my mouth. We ate in silence for a few minutes. Every time I looked at her, she'd have her eyes on her plate.

"Your sister isn't married?" I knew she wasn't and suspected what the man I'd assigned to follow her would come back with.

"No."

"If I may ask, who is Effie's father?"

She picked up a ravioli and turned her gaze fully to mine. "You're welcome to ask. You'd just have to ask her." Her mouth spread into a victorious grin.

"Touché."

"Salvatore," she started a moment later. "This party," she put her fork down and wiped her mouth, shaking her head. "I don't know if I can. He hates me, and I feel the same toward him. I don't even know why you're nice to me."

I reached across the table to touch her hand. "I'm not him, Lucia."

She looked at my hand covering hers. It was so much bigger than hers. It swallowed her up. It was almost a physical manifestation of my power over her: I could make her disappear.

"Look." I turned her hand around and traced the lines of her palm with my thumb. "We don't have a choice. We will go to that party. There's no *if* about it, not even for me. You and me…it could be worse. He could have kept you himself or given you to my brother. You don't want that."

I knew she understood by the way her face changed a little, becoming more hesitant, but her expression told me she trusted me, at least more so than any member of my family. It was a start.

"I'm not saying you have to be grateful for any of it, but neither of us have a choice. We just need to go, to get through it. Just do as I say, don't make waves. We'll eat dinner; I'll be beside you the whole time. Keep under the radar, and don't give him any reason to have to prove anything. He will not miss another opportunity, Lucia."

"So do as you say. We're back to that again."

She rolled her eyes, but it was all an act underneath which, she was afraid. "Look at me."

She did, reluctantly.

"I can only keep you safe from him if you do as I say."

"I'll try."

"Are you finished?"

Lucia nodded. She'd eaten half her plate, which was good enough.

"Then let's go." I tossed some bills onto the table and stood. "I want to give you a closer look at those things you found in my bedroom."

10

LUCIA

He didn't try to hide his amusement at my expression when he said that. And if he did it to get my mind off the discussion of the party, it worked because the entire way back, all I could think about was that.

Once inside the house, Salvatore kept his hand at my back and told Rainey and Marco to go to bed. We then went into the living room to grab a bottle of vodka before he led me upstairs to his bedroom.

"Are you still curious?" he asked once we were inside and he'd closed the bedroom door. Uncapping the vodka, he took a swallow then handed me the bottle. Watching him, I did the same, then coughed and handed it back. He chuckled and drank once more before setting the bottle on the nightstand. He dimmed the lights and stripped the bed of its comforter before turning back to me. "Are you?"

"Salvatore—"

He wrapped one arm around my waist and put his forefinger to my lips. "I want you, Lucia. My cock is aching to be inside your warm little pussy." He kissed me, and I yielded, my body already reacting to his touch, wanting him. Remembering how he made me feel. How he made me come.

His fingers touched my shoulders, and I felt the dress dragged down over my arms and to my waist, leaving my bared breasts pressing against his chest. Salvatore stopped for a moment, pulling back, his dark eyes making my nipples tighten. With one hand, he tugged his shirt over his head. I watched, desire hot in my core as I took him in, his body big, muscular, powerful.

Large hands found my hips as he neared to kiss me again, our eyes open. He pushed the dress down and off. Salvatore stepped back, and I watched him strip off his jeans and briefs, wetting my lips at the sight of his thick cock ready for me.

He sat down on the edge of the bed, reached for the bottle, and drank again. When he held it out to me, I shook my head. He put the vodka back on the nightstand and gestured to my panties.

"Off."

My pussy clenched. I slid my fingers into the waistband and slid them down and stepped out of them. Salvatore's eyes went to my pussy, a hunger in his gaze he did not try to hide.

"Come here." He pointed between his wide-spread legs.

I went to him, and he took my hands, holding me. "Birth control?" he asked.

I was confused for a moment. "Yes. I...I'm on the pill." I'd had heavy periods for years and used the pill to manage the pain.

He nodded, his mouth closing around a breast, suckling first then biting the nipple. I gasped, not sure if the pain or the pleasure was the dominant sensation as he drew it out, all while watching me. He repeated the same on the other breast, leaving each one wet, cool in the air-conditioned room.

"Have you ever had cock in your mouth?" he asked, pushing me to my knees.

I shook my head. I was a virgin, he knew that. Placing my hands on his thighs, I eyed his thick cock and licked my lips, preparing.

Salvatore placed one hand at the back of my head. "Lick."

He drew me forward, and I dragged my tongue over the wet tip, tasting the salty drops collected there. I looked up to find his eyes on me, watching me take him. He guided me down over his length, the skin of his cock soft against the hardness. It made me want, being like this, being made to kneel before him, to pleasure him.

"Good girl, now open your mouth."

He guided his cock into my mouth all the while our gazes remained locked on each other.

"That's good."

He moaned and closed his eyes as he pumped his length slowly in and out of my mouth.

"That's very good."

He stood, kept a tight grip on my hair, and held himself inside me.

"I like looking at you like this, Lucia, on your knees, your mouth stuffed full with my cock. You don't know how badly I want to fuck your face, come down your throat."

As he said the last part, he pumped deeper, making me choke, holding himself there, his fingers tight in my hair when I tried to pull back.

I gasped for breath, pushing against his thighs.

He smiled then pulled out a little.

"Again," he said.

He thrust in deep, calling forth tears from the corners of my eyes as I struggled only to have his grip tighten, hurting me. And when he repeated once more, going a little deeper, all the while smiling, watching me, I had the strange idea he liked my tears, my struggles.

"But I won't come down your throat tonight," he said, dragging me off him by my hair. "Hands and knees," he said, tossing me onto the bed. "Ass to me."

I glanced at him, wondering if I should be turned

on by his rough treatment of me, knowing only that I was.

Once in the center of the bed on all fours, I looked over my shoulder, keeping my eyes on his. He looked me over and climbed on the bed behind me, his gaze on my ass, then my face. He reached for the leather cuff to my left and dragged it up onto the bed. Taking my wrist, he pulled my arm and bound it. He then moved to the other side and did the same so I lay with my face on the bed, my arms stretched out to either side, my ass in the air.

Salvatore moved behind me and knelt between my legs. He gripped my ass, spreading me wide.

"Look at me," he said.

I turned my cheek and watched, aroused, embarrassed, wanting. Something slid down my inner thigh. I knew it was my own arousal.

"You're dripping, Lucia."

He leaned his head down. His tongue must have caught the drop. He slid his tongue up all along my thigh until he reached my core.

I made some sound, momentarily burying my face in the mattress as he buried his in my pussy.

"I love to look at you like this, Lucia, all spread and open for me."

The rough scruff of his jaw scratched my tender flesh. He licked me, the tip of his tongue tickling my clit before dipping inside me. But before I could come, he straightened. I craned my neck to look at him again.

"And I love your sexy little asshole."

I tensed when his thumb pressed against it. "I'll fuck that hole too—"

When I protested, he grinned and pushed against the tight ring.

"When I want it, you'll give it to me. You'll get on your hands and knees just like you are right now, and you'll beg me to fuck your ass."

My mewling had his grin widening.

"But don't worry. That's not tonight. Tonight, I want to bury my cock inside your pussy. I'll go slowly at first, but what I want, Lucia, is to pound into your cunt until I feel your very center. Until you beg me to stop and beg me for more all at once. Until you scream my name."

I arched my back, biting my lip, wanting his hands on me, his mouth on me. Wanting him inside me.

"Make me come, Salvatore," I begged, my body shuddering at my request.

"You want it hard, don't you?"

"Mmm."

"Your first time, though?"

He knew that, though he still asked the question while rubbing his cock along my folds. His heat, his hardness, the softness of bare flesh on bare flesh. It all made my eyes roll to the back of my head.

"Yes."

"Are you scared?"

"No."

"Maybe I like you a little scared, Lucia."

The dark whisper made me shudder.

"Maybe I like to hold you down and fuck you hard while you scream. Maybe it turns me on." He lined himself up between my legs. "Keep your eyes on me. I want to watch you."

I nodded, swallowing as the head of his cock pressed against my entrance. "Maybe a little scared." My voice came out hoarse.

"Fear makes your cunt drip."

He pushed in then, more slowly than I expected, stretching me, the invasion feeling strange, my skin too tight, but as he moved in and out of me, I relaxed, closing my eyes, feeling. And it felt good.

"Eyes, Lucia."

I opened them, watching him, his face, as he rocked inside me, going a little deeper, taking more of me, pressing against a barrier that had my eyes go wide. I tried to rise, but he rubbed my back.

"Shh. Keep your eyes on me. It will only hurt for a minute. Then you'll be begging me to fuck you hard."

I fisted my hands, trying to pull my arms into myself. Salvatore leaned over my back, stretching his arms over mine, his cock lodged inside me.

"I want to feel all of you," he whispered, moving

slowly. "I want to feel your tight cunt squeeze my cock." He pulled out, then rolled his hips, going deeper. "I want to feel the warmth of your virgin blood."

He thrust then, making me cry out.

"I want to hear you cry out. I like it."

Another thrust, harder this time.

"I like feeling you come."

He slid one hand beneath me, trailing it over my breast, belly, finding my clit. "Oh, G—"

"Hard and soft. I want to fuck you raw."

He withdrew entirely, then pounded into me, kissing my shoulder, then biting it, his breath ragged.

"I'm going to come," I managed, his cock inside me hitting just the right spot, his fingers rubbing my clit hard; It was all too much: too much feeling, too much sensation, too much *him*. Hearing his labored breathing, feeling him swell even thicker inside me, it overwhelmed me. Moments later, I came, my cry sounding foreign, Salvatore's thrusts harder, faster. I felt raw, like he said, but all I wanted was him inside me, on top of me, having me, his fingers working, making me come.

"Fuck."

It was more of a grunt, and then he stilled, his cock twitching, releasing, filling me. I watched his face from the corner of my eye, his eyes so dark, they were black, and when he stilled, he collapsed on top of me, flattening me to the bed. His cock softened and slowly slid out. A rush of cum spilled over my thighs as he held me there, his face on my back. He undid the cuffs at my wrists before curling one hand possessively over the curve of my hip and kissing me gently at neck and shoulder until my eyes closed and I drifted off to sleep in his arms.

11

SALVATORE

Growing up, I'd loved coming to the house in the Adirondacks, but that felt like a hundred years ago. Now, as we neared the property, Lucia sat beside me in the car, everything about her tense. She looked beautiful in the cream-colored dress I'd chosen, her auburn hair piled high on her head, dark eye makeup accenting the almond shape of her whiskey-colored eyes.

I touched her knee as we pulled up to the security gate.

She startled.

"You'll be fine. I'll stay with you."

She nodded, but the tension kept rolling off her.

I hated this. Knew as I waved to the guard and pulled around back to the garage that she was here to be shown around, shown off, a token of my father's—of my family's—triumph. I also knew my father had not forgotten what she'd done at the funeral. He would punish her for it, and I had a feeling he'd do it tonight.

I just needed to keep her reined in nice and tight. After parking the car, I climbed out and met Lucia on her side.

"I feel sick."

I slid her hand inside mine and squeezed. "You'll be fine. Just breathe."

We were barely inside the front door when a woman's voice called out my name. It was Dalia, Roman's wife.

"Salvatore. There you are. I wasn't sure I'd see you tonight."

She leaned in, and I kissed her on both cheeks, as expected.

"Dalia," I said. I never called her Aunt Dalia. It didn't fit, not when she was only two years older than me. My uncle liked younger women.

She turned eager eyes to Lucia, who stood stiff beside me.

I introduced them. "Lucia, this is Dalia, my uncle Roman's wife. You've...met him." Shit. She'd met him five years ago on the day she'd signed the contract.

Luckily, she didn't register and only gave a faint shake of her head.

"Lucia *DeMarco*, isn't that right?"

Dalia could be a bitch but it only seemed to strengthen Lucia.

"Yes, that's right. Lucia DeMarco," she annunciated her last name slowly, standing up taller, her smile conquering, telling anyone who dared question that she would not be a victim.

I respected her for that, but it also made me worry. If my father saw her weak, if he thought she'd been broken, at least a little, he might lay off.

Dalia clearly wasn't expecting Lucia's response. "Well, lovely to meet you," she managed before excusing herself.

"Be careful," I whispered to Lucia. She gave me a cocky raising of the eyebrows.

"What do you mean? I was simply confirming that she was right."

"Don't make waves, Lucia. Once this night is over, you won't have to see these people again."

"Fuck these people."

I squeezed her hand hard.

"Ow!"

My father's guests turned to us as we moved through the room, not one even trying to hide their interest in Lucia. I let go of her hand to grab two glasses of champagne from a passing server.

"Drink," I said, handing it to her.

She took it and swallowed a big gulp.

"We need to see my father. He's waiting for us, I'm sure."

She downed the glass.

"Be good. Do not antagonize him. Remember what we talked about."

"Fine."

My father stood at the end of the room beside the fireplace. I knew he'd seen us, but he didn't let on and remained in a relaxed conversation with Roman and two other guests. But before we reached him, Dominic stepped into our path, his eyes hungrily sweeping over Lucia, making me wrap a hand around the back of her neck.

She was mine.

"Dominic," I said.

He dragged his eyes away from Lucia, the glimmer of fun disappearing the moment they met mine.

"Salvatore." He turned to Lucia again. "I don't think I've formally met the beautiful Lucia DeMarco."

Lucia shrunk into my hold. Dominic held out his hand to shake hers. It took her a moment, but she extended hers.

"Dominic," Lucia said.

I don't know why but I liked the fact that she didn't say it was nice to meet him.

"Dad's waiting for you. He's peeved you're late."

He took a sip of his beer, his eyes still on Lucia, who looked around the room, defiantly meeting the eye of every man and woman who glanced her way.

"Is he? Better not keep him waiting any longer, then. Excuse us." I made a point of knocking my shoulder against his and guided Lucia toward my father, who now watched our approach. His gaze, like Dominic's, traveled the length of her. It made my skin crawl.

I leaned down to whisper a reminder in Lucia's ear. "Behave."

She didn't reply but kept her eyes locked on my father's.

"Well, well," Franco Benedetti started, checking his watch. "Glad you could make time for us, Salvatore."

"Traffic," I lied, hating how whenever I was around him, I felt like a kid again, that eager-to-please child who never could. He didn't reply to my lie but turned to Lucia, appraising her dress.

"So nice to see so much more of you today than at the funeral," he said to her.

Her hands fisted at her sides, and I squeezed her neck in warning. Even though she tried to hide it, I knew she feared my father. It was just that her hatred of him overrode that fear.

"Another year of your life over," Lucia said, looking at the server who'd just appeared with a fresh tray of champagne. "I'll drink to that."

My father fumed. I stood uncomfortably by her side, wanting to shake her. To ask her what part of *behave* she didn't understand.

I heard Dominic's chuckle behind me. Roman placed a hand on my father's shoulder.

"Well, since my son has finally graced us with his presence, let's have dinner."

My fingers tight around the back of Lucia's neck, I held her while my father disappeared into the dining room. I took her into a corner of the hallway and turned her to face me, held her by the arms, and shook her once.

"If you don't want me to take my belt to your ass here and now, shut the fuck up, understand? Do *not* goad him. He is not a man for you to fuck with. He *will* retaliate."

"You're hurting me."

I looked at my hands wrapped so tight around her arms my knuckles had gone white. I released her, turned away, and ran a hand through my hair. I plastered on a fake smile when someone passed by.

"Why does he have power over you? Why do you care what he thinks?" she asked.

I spun around to face her, making her stumble backward. "Not here. Not now. Just keep your mouth shut. Am I clear?" I squeezed that last words out, desperate. We just needed to survive this dinner. She could go to our room, then, and we could leave early the following morning. But how many nights like this would we have to survive? And what would happen if she didn't do as I said, and she did goad him into action? What would he do?

Take her from me.

Take my place from me.

Give it all to Dominic.

She had no idea what she was doing.

"Let's go," I said.

Her gaze stabbed me, as if by forcing her in there, I was betraying her. In a way, I was. Because I was a coward, I was. But this was the only way.

Twenty-eight sets of eyes turned to us as we entered the dining room, my father's flat gaze locked on Lucia who, for once, didn't challenge him with her own. Instead, she kept her eyes on the intricate patterns of the fresco on the far wall, probably wishing she could disappear into it.

Alice in Wonderland. My mother had loved the story, and my father had surprised her with the fresco. Tenderness was not a trait I associated with my father, but he'd felt it. For her, at least. It was almost as though I never knew that version of Franco Benedetti, though, and in a way, it was sad.

My father pulled out the chair beside him. "Lucia."

Fuck. The only other empty seat stood at the foot of the table, as far from her as physically possible.

Lucia's footsteps dragged, and I had to nudge her forward. As the guests watched, I sat her down between my father and Dominic and, hands fisted, I walked to the empty chair and took it. Lucia's eyes met mine, and I burned my warnings in the look that passed between us, knowing she'd heed none of them.

Servers began to pour wine, and conversation flowed. I watched the lecherous eyes of both my brother and father consume her. She remained between them, eyes on her plate, her face tense as she pulled her arms tighter to herself. I'd come to know those little things she did, small physical movements she may not have been aware of herself, to protect herself. To hide away. Perhaps willing herself to disappear.

I felt powerless as course after course was served. I ate a few bites from each plate, forcing myself to join in the conversation or at least smile and pretend to be listening, but all I could do was watch her. She refused to eat a bite of food but drank glass after glass of wine and, after a glare in my direction, finally turned her attention to Dominic. He gave me a grin and brushed his fingertips over her shoulder.

I fumed, nearly breaking the stem of the wineglass I held. Clearing my throat, I stood and, with my knife clinking against the crystal of the glass, called everyone's attention.

"A toast."

Everyone picked up their glasses. Everyone except Lucia.

"To my father on his birthday."

We waited, the room silent as my father watched her, his fury visibly increasing. I willed her to pick up her glass, to take one last fucking sip, before I could excuse us and take her away, but she wouldn't do it. She was too stubborn to save her own damn neck.

"Happy birthday," I said, hoping to draw attention back to me. "And many more, father."

Everyone joined in, wishing him many more, and, after a moment, my father turned to me, acknowledged my toast with a raising of his glass, and drank, our gazes locked, his angry, dark, and foreboding.

He stood. The guests put knives and forks down and wiped their mouths, rising too. Lucia remained as she was. At least she knew to remain seated. As if the guests understood, they cleared the dining room quietly so only my father, brother, Lucia, and I remained. A server closed the doors.

"Punish her," he said, spitting the words. "Make it good, or I'll do it for you."

A grin played along Dominic's lips. I nodded once. Dominic and my father left the dining room. I looked at Lucia sitting there, her face insolent, her eyes the only part of her betraying her fear.

I took my jacket off and hung it over the back of a chair, then loosened my tie, unbuttoning the top buttons of my dress shirt before it choked me. All the while, my eyes remained locked on hers. I walked toward her, rolling my right shirt sleeve up as I went. I wondered if she knew what was coming, what had to happen now. Why the room adjacent to ours became suddenly so quiet, as if there wasn't an audience just beyond the doors to bear witness.

I reached for the buckle of my belt and undid it.

That was when she understood. She made to rise, but I was too close and caught her halfway up.

"Make this easy on yourself," I whispered, wondering if those in the other room heard the swoosh of my belt as I yanked it from its loops, pulled her up out of her chair, and pushed her to bend over the table that had yet to be wiped down.

"Salvatore," she began.

"Quiet." I shoved her dress up to her waist. She struggled, but I held her flat and pushed her panties down so they slipped from her hips and pooled around her ankles. "Count yourself lucky that he closed the doors."

"You can't mean to…"

I gripped a handful of her hair and leaned down close to her ear. "One fucking sip. You could have been drinking to his death for all I cared, but you couldn't do it. Now, you pay."

I straightened, keeping one hand on the flat of her back while I swung with the other, the sound of leather striking flesh coming instantaneously with the sharp intake of her breath.

"He'll require more than that," I said, lashing her again. "And forgive me, but so will I."

I whipped her hard, knowing I had to, wanting to

beat her for her stupidity, her inability to keep one fucking promise. Knowing if I didn't, he would. Or, worse, he'd let Dominic do it while I watched.

It took nearly thirty strokes, her screams becoming hoarse as she wept, lashing my heart as I lashed her flesh, hating myself, hating her for making me do this. Hating him, hating my father for his power over me. For the power I allowed him to have.

I only stopped when the quiet on the other side of the door grew into a soft murmur and the sound of silverware on dishes told me cake had been served. The vultures had been sated or perhaps had grown bored. I hated them all, but hated myself most of all.

When I lifted my hand from her back, she remained as she was, bent over the table, her dress hiked up to her waist, her ass bare. I adjusted the crotch of my pants before sliding the belt through the loops and buckling it. Red welts crisscrossed her ass and thighs, and when I placed the flat of a palm over her hip, heat throbbed against my hand.

I squeezed.

She mewled.

I picked up her panties and pocketed them before lifting her to stand. The skirt of her dress dropped to her ankles, covering her. I turned her to face me and held her tight to me as she wept into my chest, fists pounding against me. Hiccups interrupted her sobs, and I lifted her into my arms and, ignoring the stares of the waitstaff as I carried her up to our room from the server's stairs, I locked the bedroom door behind us. I sat on the bed, cradling her in my lap, refusing to let her go even as she fought me.

"I warned you."

She pounded her fists into my chest, trying to free herself, tears streaking her face black with mascara.

"You liked it!" she screamed as the evidence of my arousal stabbed her hip.

"I didn't like hurting you."

"You're hard, you prick! You liked it just fine!"

"I can't deny the fact I'm aroused." One corner of my mouth quirked upward. "But you deserved that one."

"I hate you!" She clawed her fingernails down the side of my face.

I flipped her onto the bed, gripped her wrists and spread them wide, straddling her hips. "I fucking warned you. You have only yourself to blame!"

"They all heard!"

"That was the point. Humiliation. You're lucky he didn't demand the doors stay open!" During her struggle, her dress had shifted, exposing one breast.

"Let me go! Don't look at me!"

She renewed her struggle, pissing me off when

she tried to line her knee up with my crotch. I transferred her wrists into one hand and held them over her head.

"I can look at you whenever I want." Gripping the V neck of the dress, I tore it down, the fabric giving way, the sound of it ripping somehow satisfying.

The harder Lucia fought against me, the harder my cock grew.

"I hate you!" she cried again.

I crushed my lips over hers, and for a moment, she stilled, maybe surprised.

I broke the kiss. "No, you don't." I kissed her again. I undid my pants, slid between her legs, and pinched her nipple with my free hand. "You make me crazy." My words came out angry. I pushed one of her legs open wider and then pulled back to look at her. She watched me, her hands clenched into fists. I lined my cock up at the entrance of her sex. "You drive me fucking insane."

I thrust in hard.

She grunted, her eyes locked on mine in defiance.

"Fuck you."

I thrust again, then again. "Fuck me." I wouldn't last long, but her wet cunt told me she wanted this too. "Your cunt is greedy."

"Harder," she gasped, hoarse from screaming.

"Fuck." I did what she said, fucking her harder,

watching her, not feeling like I had had nearly enough of her.

Easing my hand off her wrists, I brought both hands to her face. We were both panting. I pushed the hair that stuck to her forehead away and held her, lost in those eyes that now burned a fiery amber. Her mouth opened, and I kissed it, so close now.

"What are you doing to me?"

"What?" she asked, puzzled.

I must have said it aloud. Lucia's hands gripped my shoulders, her face getting that expression it did just before she came. I loved seeing her like this, watching her in those moments just before her release, her face as she let go. It was the single most arousing thing, that.

"I hate you," she whispered, her nails digging into my shoulders, my neck. She squeezed her eyes shut, coming. "I do."

"Lucia."

Her pussy throbbed around me, and as she came, so did I, stilling deep inside her, filling her, feeling like—for the first time since that goddamned contract—I'd claimed her. Like she was mine. She was well and truly mine.

12

LUCIA

I looked at the window. Sunlight filtered through the crack between the curtains. I blinked, confused for a moment, but the soreness between my legs and on my ass quickly reminded me of where I was.

The clock beside the bed read 7:04 a.m.

I dragged the silk sheet up over my naked body, sat up, flinched, and lay back down. Beside me, the empty pillow lay sideways. I touched it, leaned over and buried my nose in it, then reared back and shook my head.

What the *hell* was I doing?

He'd whipped me, humiliated me, then fucked me.

I'd come.

I'd begged him to fuck me harder.

I hated myself.

No, I hated him. I needed to remember that.

Why was it so hard to remember that?

I got out of bed and went into the bathroom. He must have showered recently. Steam still fogged up the corners of the mirror, and the scent of his aftershave hung in the air.

I found I liked it, felt somehow comforted by it.

The devil you know. That's all that was. I knew Salvatore. I knew his limits.

Fuck. I was fooling myself.

I used the bathroom, not surprised to find blood between my legs even though I wasn't having my period. He'd fucked me raw, like he said he would.

And you'd come.

I turned my back to the mirror, the dark, crisscrossed welts reminding me to hate him. To see him for what he was: a Benedetti. My enemy.

I touched the raised marks, pressed against them, forced myself to remember that he was my fucking enemy. I could not let myself trust him, let myself depend on him. He would hurt me. Wasn't this evidence of that?

This strange emotion—no, it was not emotion. Only confusion. I felt confused, but who wouldn't be if they were me? Isolated from family and under the *care*—more like under the thumb—of Salvatore Benedetti, I needed him for everything. Every fucking thing. And that was why I had any feeling for him whatsoever. Maybe it was a form of Stockholm Syndrome. I mean, this may not be a traditional kidnapping, but it wasn't like I was here by choice. Not my choice, anyway.

I turned on the shower and stepped under the hot stream. I wanted to scrub his touch from me. Wanted to scrub the memory of my reaction to him from my mind.

He'd fucking whipped me, and I'd begged him to fuck me.

I scrubbed my hair with shampoo and my body with soap, gritting my teeth when the hot water hit my ass. When I was finished, I climbed out and dried off. I wanted to be out of here. I'd only been told I had to stay the night. Not any longer. But what if his father made me stay? What if Salvatore had already gone? And left me behind.

Panicked, I hurried into the bedroom, found my cell phone in my purse, and dialed Isabella's number.

"Hello?"

"Izzy?" I was sure I'd woken her. "I'm calling too early. I'm sorry."

"No, no, it's okay. How are you?"

"I don't know. I'm in Franco Benedetti's house in the Adirondacks."

"What?"

Well, that woke her up. "I had to come. It was his birthday. We were required. I just..."

"Are you okay, Luce?"

I only heard concern in her voice now. I felt my eyes heat up, but I blinked hard. I didn't need tears. I hated weakness. Hated it! "I—"

The door opened then, and Salvatore walked inside carrying two mugs of coffee. I sighed in relief.

"Lucia, what's happened?" Isabella asked, likely having heard the sigh.

Salvatore looked at me quizzically and closed the door. He wore a pair of jeans and a T-shirt, his usual uniform, and he'd slicked back his dark hair. He mouthed the word, *Okay?*

I turned away.

"Never mind, I'm fine," I said to Izzy. "I thought he'd left me here," I whispered, hoping Salvatore wouldn't hear.

I heard a male voice asking what was going on in the background.

"Who is that?" I asked.

Isabella sighed. "No one. I'm getting up to come get you now."

"No, it's okay," I said, turning to find Salvatore sipping his coffee, watching me. "He's not going to leave me here," I said, the comment more a question to Salvatore.

He shook his head.

"I'll call you once we're home. Uh, I mean, back at his house." Fuck. What the hell was wrong with me? "I have to go."

"You're sure?"

"Yeah. Sorry to have called so early, sis."

"You're fine. You can call me anytime, day or night, understand?"

I nodded. "Thanks. Love you." I hadn't said that in more than five years.

There was a pause. "Love you."

I disconnected the call and slid the phone into my purse. "I thought you'd left me here."

"I wouldn't do that to you. Come here."

I went to him.

"You okay?"

I shrugged a shoulder, dropping my gaze to shield my eyes. Why did his asking make me feel so fucking needy? Why did him taking me into his arms make me want to sob? Because that's what it did. That's what having his arms around me right now, like he would keep me safe forever, even after last night, that's what they did. They made me want to weep.

The last time he'd held me like this, I'd pulled away. This time, I didn't. I let myself melt into him. Neither of us spoke. I squeezed my eyes shut against his chest, feeling confused and hurt and vulnerable and so fucking grateful he was here. None of it made sense.

"Can we go?" I asked when I could speak without crying.

He pulled back and looked at me, his thumb wiping away some of the moisture around my eyes.

"Not yet. I need to go down to breakfast, but I'll make an excuse for you. Get packed. We'll leave as soon as possible."

I nodded and went to sit on the bed but stood again as soon as my ass made contact.

"Lucia?"

I looked at him.

"Does it hurt?" His face told me he knew it was a stupid question.

"What do you think?"

He studied me, his forehead furrowing. He at least had the decency to look away for a moment.

"If it means anything, I didn't want to punish you on my father's order."

"But you did."

"I'm trying to tell you I'm sorry."

"Sometimes sorry isn't enough, Salvatore."

He stood there a moment, his eyes on mine. "Get packed. We'll leave as soon as we can."

He walked out the door and left me standing there in my towel.

His absence filled the space as soon as the door closed, and I hugged my arms around my belly, feeling more alone now than ever. But I forced myself to move. To get dressed. And as much as I hated it, to go down the stairs and face Franco Benedetti head-on.

I couldn't hide, I wouldn't. If I did, it showed that he'd won. That he'd shamed me, and I was hiding from him, afraid of him. Well, the latter was true, but I'd be damned if I'd let that fear get the better of me.

I dressed, packed my things, and pulled my wet hair into a bun before dabbing concealer under my eyes. I picked up my purse and walking out into the hallway. I paused, finding a staircase at either end. I looked over the banister, but all was quiet down below. I chose the stairs to my right and headed down, heard a door open and Salvatore's voice coming from it. I followed his voice, steeling my spine as my heart raced and my belly flipped.

I would not let Franco Benedetti win. I would not.

I reached the door and would have turned the knob but Franco's raised voice made me pull my hand away.

"You know what I expected of you!"

"I would not parade her through that room full of pariahs! She was humiliated enough! This is done. She's mine. I choose!"

Something pounded. I imagined a fist and a table. Was it Salvatore's? Was he defending me?

Then came Franco's laughter. Quiet at first, menacing, slowly growing louder, almost manic. Someone clapped his hands.

"My son, he finally grows some balls."

I fisted my hands, inhaling tightly.

"Fine, Salvatore. She's *your whore*. But remember, I gave her to you. I can as easily take her back. Take care of Luke DeMarco before there are any more supporters. One week, or Dominic will do it. I'm finished with him."

What? What did he mean, take care of Luke?

But then I heard footsteps, heavy and moving fast, and I charged toward the stairs. I bolted up then and ducked down behind the banister. Franco Benedetti stalked out of the room, his face tight with anger, his hands fisted at his sides.

I scurried back to the bedroom and closed the door, thinking, trying to make sense of it all. Should I call my sister and warn her about what I'd heard? Warn Luke? Or should I try to find out more first? See if Salvatore would tell me anything?

When a quick knock came, I jumped up, thinking it was Salvatore and that we could go. The door opened, but it was Dominic who stepped inside. He looked me over, his gaze odd, almost curious, but he remained at the entrance of the door.

"Hey," he said casually. A smile curved his lips upward, his voice sounded almost sweet. Too sweet. "I wanted to see if you were okay. My brother can be a brute and, to be honest, it sounded like he wasn't holding back last night."

I flushed. Was he talking about the whipping or the sex or both?

"I...I'm fine." I faltered.

He nodded and stepped inside. I didn't like him,

didn't like the way his eyes shifted around the room and over me.

"I'm glad." Again, his voice soft, his smile gentle. "If you ever need anything"—he grabbed a card out of his pocket—"this is my private number."

"I don't—"

"Just take it and hope you never have to use it. Like I said, my brother can be very physical. Brutal even. I've seen what he's done before, Lucia. I've cleaned it up."

What?

When I made no move, he closed the space between us, took my hand, turned it over, and pressed the card into my palm.

"What the fuck are you doing in here?"

I jumped at Salvatore's sudden appearance, but Dominic only gave him a smirk and picked something out from under his fingernail.

"Just checking in on Lucia. Since she wasn't feeling well and all. She looks good to me, though, considering."

"Get the fuck out of here, Dominic."

Dominic shrugged a shoulder and glanced back at me after taking a step toward the door.

"If you ever need anything, Lucia…"

"She won't be needing anything from you."

Salvatore stalked toward me, the look in his eyes chilling me as he squeezed my wrist and took the card from my hand. He didn't look at it. Didn't need to, I guessed.

Dominic walked out the door. Salvatore kicked it shut behind him, his hand still gripping my wrist.

"You're hurting me, Salvatore."

Anger, frustration, I don't know what it was, but whatever he was feeling, it rolled off him and slammed into me.

"It seems that's all I can do." He dropped my wrist. "We're leaving." He grabbed the suitcases and walked into the hallway.

I followed him out of the bedroom, wanting to be away from this house most of all, yet fearing Salvatore. Uncertain now if would save me or destroy me.

We didn't run into anyone as we left. Salvatore's car waited just outside the front doors. The man who must have brought it around handed him the keys. Salvatore loaded the bags into the trunk and opened my door, not waiting for me to get in before he moved around to his side. He was clearly as anxious as I to leave.

We didn't speak for the first twenty minutes of the ride back. Salvatore's tension literally rolled off him.

"Dominic will fuck with you. You're not to have anything to do with him, understand?" He didn't look at me but kept his eyes on the road.

"Is that an order?"

That made him turn his head toward me. "Yes."

"Or what, you'll whip me again? Doors open this time?"

His grip on the steering wheel tightened, his knuckles going white. "Don't push me, not now."

"What the hell happened back there?" His face tightened even more. "I heard, Salvatore. I heard you stand up for me. I heard your father lose his shit."

"Then you didn't learn your lesson about snooping."

"I wasn't snooping. I was coming down to have breakfast, show my face. Show him he hadn't won."

Salvatore snorted and shook his head, the smile that appeared on his face sad. "You don't get it, Lucia. He always wins."

"I told you before, everyone loses sometime."

"Not Franco Benedetti."

There was such a weight to him, to his words, that it made me sad. Just sad. But I needed to ask one more question. I needed to know one more thing.

"He said something about taking care of Luke."

Salvatore gave me a sideways glance. He didn't answer my question, but he sure knew how to distract me.

"I'm going to let you out of your contract. Once all is said and done, and I'm boss, you'll be free, Lucia."

13

SALVATORE

I couldn't win. No one could. What I said to her, I meant it. Franco Benedetti would win. And everyone else would lose.

Lucia went straight to her room when we got back to the house, and I shut myself up in my study. She hadn't talked to me the entire ride. Probably pissed at me, which I expected. I would deal with that later, though, because as soon as I booted up my laptop, I saw an e-mail from Roman regarding Luke's activities.

Luke had been busy indeed, meeting with various members of the Pagani family in the tristate area. We knew that, though. That wasn't new. It was the next part that intrigued me.

He was spending his nights in Isabella DeMarco's bed.

That's why it so surprised me to learn that I was wrong. That he wasn't Effie's father.

But that wasn't the strangest thing. In fact, what I saw made zero sense.

I picked up the phone and dialed Roman, but before he could answer, the door burst open. Lucia stood in the doorway, looking pissed off.

"So are you just going to lock yourself up in here and not talk to me at all?" She walked inside. "Because you're giving me fucking whiplash."

I put the lid of my laptop down just as Roman answered the phone. "Let me call you back." I got up and closed the door. "You ever hear of knocking?"

"What the hell is going on, Salvatore? What happened this morning? You were fine. We were fine. Then you had that breakfast meeting, and I don't know. It's like you keep pulling the fucking rug out from under me!"

"I told you, I'll give you your freedom as soon as I can. I thought you would want that."

"This isn't about that. You can't just throw that out there. And besides, how long until you're boss? And what if you change your mind?

I resumed my seat behind the desk but pushed away from it and crossed one ankle over my other knee. "I won't."

That silenced her for a second. She just stood there surprised.

"If you want a fight, I'm not in the mood," I said. "Not now."

She shifted her weight and folded her arms across her chest. "How about the truth, then? Are you in the mood for that? What is the Luke DeMarco problem you have to take care of?"

I let my gaze run over her. She'd changed into a pale yellow sundress, and I could see she wasn't wearing a bra underneath. My balls tightened, but I steeled myself. Lucia was fast becoming a weakness. My weakness. I needed to stop this. I meant what I said, that I'd release her from her contract. I needed to take care that when the time came, she wouldn't look back.

The best way to do that was to be a dick.

I leaned forward and placed my elbows on the desk. "How's your ass, Lucia?"

"My ass is none of your concern."

"Show me."

"Screw you."

"You want to know about Luke DeMarco?"

She eyed me warily but nodded.

"Fine. He's stirring up trouble. A lot of it."

"What did Franco mean when he told you to take care of it?" she asked.

"You aren't surprised by what I just told you?"

She shrugged a shoulder. "We'll always be enemies."

That took me a moment to digest. I decided to push further, see how much she knew.

"Why exactly did your father disown your sister?"

"Because she got pregnant."

"Doesn't that seem strange to you? I mean, this is modern day. Women have babies out of wedlock and alone all the time."

She studied me. What did she know? Did Isabella confide in her? How much?

"I don't know. I guess my father was old-fashioned."

"Has your sister ever questioned it? How he was willing to lose her and his grandchild?" I asked.

"My father didn't exactly make the best decisions regarding either of his daughters, did he?"

"No, I guess you're right."

"Why are you asking?"

"Just curious. Why don't you go for a swim. It's nice out."

"Why are you pushing me away? I thought—"

She sat gingerly on the edge of the couch, and the fact that I'd caused her that hurt messed with me. Was she innocent? Or did she know more than she let on? And if Luke wasn't Effie's father, then who was?

"What did you think?"

"You said some things last night."

She shook her head then brought her hands to her face, rubbing it before looking at me again.

"I am so confused. I don't know what I'm supposed to feel. I don't know where I stand, and as soon as I think I understand something, understand you, you strike out then pull back again."

Watching her, I rubbed the back of my neck and loudly inhaled, then exhaled, realizing I couldn't be a dick. Not to her. She deserved better. "It's best if we keep our distance, Lucia." *I don't want to hurt you, and it seems it's all I can do.*

She studied me, and the look inside those wide eyes screamed confusion. I understood it. I understood her comment about the whiplash.

My phone buzzed on the desk, and I glanced at it, seeing a text from Natalie.

"I need you!"

What the...

"Salvatore?" Lucia called me back to the present.

"Go for a swim," I said, standing and patting my pockets for my keys.

"So that's it? Go for a swim?" She snorted, rising too.

Finding them, I heard the phone buzz again.

"Hurry, please!"

"I have to go."

"No!"

She rushed me, gripping my arms before I made it to the door.

"You can't just walk away from this. From me! You can't just leave me here like this! I have a right to answers!"

I pulled her hands away and sat her down roughly on the couch. "I have to go. When I come back, we'll talk. I'm sorry, but I can't right now."

"It'll be too late then!"

My mind was too full with Natalie's frantic messages for Lucia's words to penetrate. I bolted out of the house and to the car that still sat parked in the driveway. I didn't look back, just drove as fast as I could to Natalie's house.

14

LUCIA

I couldn't believe this. He'd just left, walked out! I'd really thought last night, after what had happened in the bedroom, the things he'd said, I thought he felt something. And even as I'd told him I hated him, I didn't. I'd held fast, refusing to let go.

I felt something for him.

Then this morning, when he'd defended me, didn't that mean something? And what about when he'd been so possessive when he'd seen Dominic in our room?

God, I was stupid.

His cell phone buzzed again, and I got up. He'd forgotten it in his rush. The latest text was on the screen.

"Are you getting my messages? I need you!"

The name of the contact read Natalie.

Natalie *needed* him?

And he'd dropped everything for her. In a fucking heartbeat, he'd dropped everything and run out of the house, not even remembering to take his cell phone with him!

Fine. That was fine. She was probably the reason he'd release me from my contract. He didn't want me. I was a burden on him. He claimed not to have liked humiliating me last night, but he'd gotten hard doing it. He'd used me. He was getting off on it while he could. Probably cheating on Natalie while he was *forced* to keep me.

He made a fool out of me. I was a complete, fucking idiot.

He wanted Natalie? Fine. He could have her. He could fucking have her.

I walked into the bathroom that adjoined his study and dropped the cell phone into the toilet before I ran upstairs to my bedroom. I threw a few things into a duffel bag. I didn't care about anything anymore. I wasn't permitted to leave the grounds? I had to tell him where I was at all times?

He could go fuck himself. Or fuck her.

Fuck!

Flinging the duffel over my shoulder, I made my way to the garage. I knew they kept the keys to the cars there, and I'd seen the code Salvatore had punched into both the box that contained them and to open the gate yesterday. I was out of here. I was done.

Getting into a car was easy. Getting out of the garage easy. By the time I got to the gate, I saw Marco running down the driveway after me. I punched in the code to open the gate, but nothing happened.

"Shit."

I tried again, one eye on the rearview mirror as Marco's form neared. He ran fast.

I tried the code again, and again, nothing. I stopped, squeezing my eyes shut.

"Think. Think! You saw it yesterday!"

I tried again and exhaled in relief as the tall gates finally crept open, slow as fucking molasses. I inched the car forward, too aware of Marco just a few feet away as finally, finally, the gates opened wide enough that I hit the gas, the tires screaming against stones, kicking up dirt and rock and leaving him literally in the dust.

I grinned, seeing him pull his phone out and put it to his ear, no doubt trying to call Salvatore, tell him I'd broken one of his stupid rules. Too bad Salvatore's phone sat in the toilet.

That made me laugh.

I didn't calm down on the drive over to Isabella's house. The opposite, actually. What was the point of all of this? Why take me when he wanted someone else? Why?

Because daddy said he had to if he wanted to be boss.

This was so fucked up. Salvatore's father controlled him. He had to do what he did, or his father would take away what was his right. He'd give it all to Dominic. My life didn't matter. What I felt didn't matter.

Felt. No, I *felt* nothing. Nothing tender, at least.

But I was beginning to trust him.

The devil you know.

At least Salvatore's indifference to me kept me safe. Franco or Dominic, they would do worse things to me. Of that, I had no doubt.

So why did his indifference hurt me? What did I want?

Isabella's house looked empty when I got there. I pulled the car up in the driveway, far enough back that it wouldn't be visible from the street. I wondered if she kept the spare key where we used to in case we locked ourselves out. But as I walked down the long drive back to the house, I saw Isabella's face peer out of the kitchen window. I raised my hand in greeting, but she didn't wave. Her face grew worried. I saw her rush from the window and throw open the back door.

"Lucia?"

I fell into her arms, tears breaking loose, although I couldn't say exactly why. What would I tell her? How could I explain that I was jealous and hurt? That after all the things he'd done to me, all the things they'd done to me, I wanted him. Because I did. I wanted Salvatore.

"What's wrong? What's happened?"

We walked inside and went right into the kitchen.

"Sit down."

She pulled a chair out and set a box of tissues in front of me. She busied herself making some tea, casting glances my way as I blew my nose and mopped my face, forcing deep breaths in and out, trying to get myself under control. Isabella set a fresh cup of tea in front of me and then took the seat across from mine, taking a sip from her cup.

"What's happened?"

How much should I tell her? I wasn't worried about her judging me. I just didn't want her to think me weak. Or worse, a traitor.

"I'm so confused." I shook my head, picked up the mug of tea, and stared into the swirling dark liquid.

"Did he hurt you?"

Yes. Oh yes.

I swallowed a sip of tea then faced my sister. "I think he's having an affair."

She looked surprised. "Why do you think that?"

"Because we were in the middle of a conversation when he got a text from someone named Natalie and bolted. He was in such a hurry he left his phone behind. I read one of the messages."

"What did it say?"

"For him to hurry. That she *needed* him."

Isabella checked her watch. I went on.

"He just left me there and walked out in the middle of a conversation!"

"Wasn't Natalie the name of his brother's wife?"

"What? Dominic's married?"

"No, Dominic's not married. Sergio."

"Oh." Shit, how had I not remembered that? "He's having an affair with his dead-brother's wife?"

"Why are you jumping to that conclusion? It could be anything."

"Are you defending him?"

She sat back and folded her arms across her chest. "I guess I'm trying to figure out why you care."

I would almost say there was something accusing in the gaze she leveled me with. I rested my elbow on the table and dropped my forehead into my hand. "I don't fucking know."

Isabella's chair scraped away from the table. She got up and went over to her phone on the counter. She typed in what I assumed was a text message then turned back to me. She leaned against the counter and studied me with a strange expression on her face before she walked back over to me and rubbed my back.

"It's natural, I guess, if you're stuck living with someone who basically holds your whole life in his hands, to develop some feelings for that person. You're not in love with him, though."

I shoved her hand away. "In love? Who said anything about being in love?"

She sat back down. "I'm just saying don't beat yourself up over it. Good riddance, and hope he *is* fucking his dead-brother's wife!"

"Izzy!"

"I'm sorry, that came out cold. The most important thing is that you're out of there. And you're not going back."

"Where's Effie?" I suddenly realized the little girl wasn't here.

"She went swimming with her best friend, and they were going to have dinner together after. I should go get her soon."

"You should have seen Marco's face when I drove away."

"I bet that was something."

"Izzy, I overheard something this morning at Franco Benedetti's house. I wanted to talk to you about it."

"What?"

"Salvatore and his father were talking. I'm not sure if Dominic was there or not, but I heard his father say something about taking care of Luke."

She didn't seem surprised by what I said.

"They know you're trying to stir things up, Izzy. You have to be careful."

"That's Luke. Not me."

"Well, then you need to tell him to be careful. What's going on with you and him, anyway? I saw how he looked at you at the church, and he was here the other day. Are you two having an affair?"

"An affair. It sounds so illicit." She picked up her teacup and dumped its contents into the sink. "You're caught up on this affair thing today, aren't you?" she asked, her back to me.

"Is he Effie's father, Izzy? Is that why Papa—"

She snorted and looked off to the side. "Luke is not Effie's father."

"Who is?"

She turned and met my gaze, her expression cooler. "It's not important. What is important is figuring out what we're going to do to keep you away from Salvatore."

Isabella's cell phone rang, and she eyed the display. "I have to take this. I'll be right back."

She walked out of the kitchen and into the living room, surprising me with her sudden secrecy.

"This isn't a good time," I heard her whisper. Then I heard my name before she hung up and returned to the kitchen.

"Who was that?"

"The mom who took Effie swimming."

"Oh. You could have talked to her."

"It's fine. She was just checking in. Are you hungry? I can make you a sandwich."

"No, I'm good. I think I'll go lay down if you don't mind."

"Of course, go ahead."

I stood, feeling this space between us, something strange that hadn't been there before. But then she walked over to me and hugged me.

"You'll be okay, sis. I won't let him hurt you. I'll take care of everything."

An unease settled over me as I made my way up to my old bedroom. Something in her tone or posture was off...wrong. I couldn't quite put my finger on it, though. Maybe it was nothing. Maybe it was the five years between us. She'd changed too, just like all of us. She'd grown a little harder. But maybe that was what she'd needed to do to survive.

After a short rest and a microwave dinner later in the evening, I'd gotten ready and gone to sleep in my old bedroom, the sinking feeling never leaving my stomach. It wasn't too much later when I woke to rain beating against the window and voices arguing. I sat up and glanced at the time on my phone. It was a little after midnight. The display showed eight missed calls, all from—surprise, surprise—Salvatore.

I guess he'd gotten home from Natalie's. Asshole.

I ignored the messages, got out of bed, and

cracked the door open. The voices came from downstairs. It was Isabella and a man. Although I knew the voice, I couldn't place it. It didn't belong here.

"You promised me. I don't want him hurt!"

My sister sounded agitated.

"I'm placating. Relax."

"How the fuck can I relax? God, I wish this were over!"

I stepped out onto the landing and crept over to the stairs. Hearing the familiar creak on the third step, I froze, hoping they hadn't heard. They continued arguing.

"You need to go. You can't be here."

I suspected my sister didn't realize she was whispering that loud.

"I took care of what you wanted done. Don't I get a little reward?"

What you wanted done?

"I'm sure Salvatore will be here any minute. He's not stupid, he knows where she'd run to. Get out of here before he gets here."

Salvatore was coming?

"I parked a few blocks down. I'll duck into a room. No worries, babe."

Was that *Dominic*? Calling my sister *babe*?"

Tires screeched to a halt just outside the house. Headlights shone through the windows, and a car door slammed shut.

"Pussy whipped," the man said just as someone leaned on the doorbell.

I turned and ran into my room, pretending to just come out of it when I saw Izzy run to the door.

"Is that the doorbell?" I asked, not wanting her to know I'd overheard anything.

"Here we go," Izzy said.

I walked down the stairs. Izzy opened the front door.

A soaked and furious Salvatore stood just on the other side, his gaze fixed on me.

15

SALVATORE

"It's the middle of the night," Isabella said, standing in the doorway.

I looked over her shoulder and saw Lucia standing on the bottom step of the stairway. "I won't be long," I said, my eyes trained on Lucia. "I'm just here to collect what's mine." I then turned to Isabella. "Move."

"No."

"Move."

"I'll call the police."

"I own the police."

"It's okay, Izzy. Let him in."

Lucia stepped down from the stairs and folded her arms across her chest. She wore a short pink nightshirt that reached to just beneath her ass, and her hair looked like it did when she woke up: a beautiful mess.

"You don't have to listen to him," Isabella said, although she stepped aside.

Lucia's eyes were locked on mine.

"Get your things," I said to her.

"How's Natalie?"

"Natalie? That's why you left?" I'd gotten home to find my cell phone in the toilet. Had Natalie sent another text that Lucia had read? My phone was password protected, but the messages flashed and stayed on the screen for long enough that she wouldn't have needed the password.

Lucia stuck her chin out. She was jealous. She was fucking jealous.

I watched her, and the longer I did, the more nervous she became, shifting on her feet, biting her lip.

"Let's go home. We'll talk about it there."

"This is my home, Salvatore. I'm staying here."

I stepped toward her, dropping my gaze to her bare feet with their pretty pink toenails, before I took her arms and unfolded them. I attempted a smile. I'd been pissed when I'd gotten home to find out she'd run. Marco had tried to get hold of me, but all he'd been able to do was leave messages and assume I got them. But since my phone was in the toilet, I'd only found out about Lucia leaving when I got home around eleven at night.

But now, understanding why she'd run, I wasn't angry. I was surprised.

"You're coming with me," I said in a quiet whisper. I didn't care if her sister could hear or not. I also couldn't have cared any less what she thought of me. I'd talked to Roman about the DNA tests, and I was putting two and two together. "Your home is not here, not anymore. It's with me."

Lucia's eyes widened, and for a moment, I saw she wanted to believe, wanted to do as I said, but then Isabella cleared her throat.

"Luce, you don't have to do anything you don't want to do."

I glanced at her, feeling only disdain as things slowly fell into place, piece by piece. I turned my attention back to Lucia.

"I'll say it one more time. Get your things, and get in the car, or I will carry you out over my shoulder. But one way or another, you will be sleeping in my bed tonight."

I watched Lucia swallow and saw how her breasts tightened beneath the pink nightshirt.

She was turned on.

"What's it going to be?"

"Luce—"

I held a finger up to Isabella, not taking my eyes off Lucia. "This is between us."

Lucia stiffened, looking over my shoulder at her sister, then back at me, defiance in her gaze.

"You can't make me go."

I grinned. "I was hoping you'd say that."

She squealed, surprised I guessed, when I gripped her hips and heaved her over my shoulder, slapping her ass hard when she kicked her legs and pounded my back with her fists.

"I'm calling the police!" Isabella ran into the kitchen.

I ignored her and moved us out the door, sheets of rain soaking us both.

"Let me down!"

"I gave you a choice," I said, opening the passenger-side door and dropping her into the seat. She immediately tried to spring out, but I pressed her back with the flat of my hand against her chest. "You chose wrong." I clicked her seat belt and shut her door, locking it until I got into the driver's seat. I hit the gas, propelling us forward.

"You can't just…take me like that!"

"Put your seat belt back on." She'd unbuckled it. What did she think she'd do, jump out of a car going sixty miles per hour?

I made sure the door was locked just in case.

"I swear, Lucia, if I have to pull over to discipline you—"

"Slow down!" she screamed as I took a turn.

"Fasten your fucking seat belt."

"I hate you."

She fastened it as I merged onto the highway. "You say that a lot. Mostly when you're turned on."

"I'm not turned on!"

I glanced from her face to her nipples and back. "No, obviously not," I said, returning my attention to the road.

She covered herself with her arms. "You have no right, Salvatore."

"I have every right. You signed a contract."

"I was sixteen, and I had no choice!"

"And what's your choice now? Huh? Break it? Risk your family's safety?"

"You wouldn't hurt them."

I glanced at her again, some part of me glad she knew that. But I wasn't the only danger. "I may not, but others would."

"Are you going to threaten me with that for the rest of my life?"

I just shook my head and concentrated on the road. I had more important things on my mind at the moment. Like figuring out what the hell had happened that afternoon.

By the time we pulled inside the gates and up the drive, the silence between us hung like thick, impenetrable fog. Rain still poured down. Since the garage structure was separate from the main house, I parked as close to the front door as possible and climbed out. Lucia had already opened her door and sat measuring the distance between the car and the house.

"Your feet are bare. I'll carry you." I leaned in to lift her, getting soaked for the third time that night.

"I'm fine. Don't touch me."

"Stop fighting me. The stones will cut your feet." With one arm beneath her knees and the other at her back, I lifted her out.

"I said don't touch me!"

Just as I leaned to close the car door, she hoisted herself out of my arms and fell to her hands and knees with a grunt.

"Lucia!"

"Stay away from me!" She scrambled to her feet and made for the front lawn.

"Godamnit!" I chased her, although there wasn't anywhere for her to go. If it wasn't pouring down rain, I'd have left her to it. Although knowing her, she'd tear herself up, trying to climb over the gates.

She ran fast, but the slippery ground beneath her bare feet hindered her progress. She fell twice more before I finally caught up to her. When I wrapped an arm around her waist to haul her up, she kicked out, knocking my legs out from under me so that I fell on top of her.

"Leave me alone! Why can't you just *leave me alone*?"

She fought like a feral cat, scratching and kicking until I lay my full weight on her, caught both of her wrists, and trapped her beneath me.

"Stop! Stop fighting me!"

"I hate you. I hate you, and I will never stop."

I looked down at her, tears and rain soaking her face.

"You will stop."

"Why did you come for me? What do you want from me?"

"What do I want?" I looked at her face flushed with exertion, her mouth open to suck in gulps of air, her dark hair fanned out around her head, stuck to her face, soaked and dirty. "What do I want?" She jerked her body. I touched my forehead to hers, her eyes burning amber now. "This," I said, and kissed her.

She tried to say something, but whatever it was, I swallowed it up. Her soft wet lips yielded beneath mine. Even as she attempted to fight, her body gave itself over, her mouth surrendering. She made a small sound as I deepened the kiss, tasting her, pressing her harder into the earth, my cock like steel against her soft belly.

"I want this," I said, claiming her mouth again while I reached with one hand to take my cock out of my pants. Her nightie had already ridden up to midbelly. "This." I kissed her again, this time softer, on her lips, then her chin, her cheek. I wanted to see her face, her eyes. Slipping my fingers beneath her panties, I drew them aside. She bit her lips, watching me. "I want you." I thrust into her, and she arched her back, closing her eyes momentarily. "You." I drove in again, her tight pussy wet like a glove around my cock. "I want you, Lucia," I said finally, taking her wrists in my hands and pinning them out to her sides, watching her face as I fucked her, just a few more short, hard thrusts before she clenched around me, coming, making that sound she made, crushing my cock until I stilled, squeezing her wrists harder, coming, heart racing, not breathing until I'd emptied.

The rain slowed, finally, as if it matched our moods. I kissed her and slowly slid out, kneeling to zip my jeans before lifting her up. She let me this time. Let me carry her into the house and up to the second floor and through my bedroom to the master bath, where I ran the shower and placed her inside. I followed, still fully clothed, stripping first her and then myself beneath the warm flow of water.

"I want *you*, Lucia," I said yet again, pressing her back against the wall, kissing her. "As wrong as it is, I want you."

Lucia lay in my bed, the cuts on her knees and palms bandaged, warm beneath the covers. Safe in my arms.

"Natalie is my sister-in-law. Sergio's wife." She had her back to me, so I couldn't see her face. "She has a son who was at daycare while she worked her usual hours. When she got there to pick him up, he was gone. The daycare provider had fucked up, releasing Jacob to someone who claimed to be his uncle."

She turned her head to look at me, then shifted to lie on her back. I kept my arm over her belly, my hand closed possessively around her hip.

"She was frantic, as you can imagine."

"Did they find him?"

I nodded. "It was Dominic, I'm certain. He'd dropped him off at her parent's house but only after a couple of hours."

"Is Jacob okay?"

"He's fine now. He's only a year and a half, so he couldn't tell us much. Dropped off with an armful of toys and an ice-cream cone that had melted all over him. He apparently ran into his grandmother's arms and sobbed, calling for his mom."

"Why would Dominic do that?"

"To show he could." That's what pissed me off the most. This was the one thing that could terrorize Natalie.

"I can't imagine what Natalie must have felt."

I nodded. I'd never seen her like I did today, not even when she'd learned Sergio had been killed.

"I'm the only person she trusts, Lucia. I couldn't abandon her or my nephew."

"You should have told me."

"I know."

"I assumed... I thought she was your... That you

were having an affair." She lowered her lashes, her face growing pink with embarrassment.

"I told you I wouldn't do that. The contract—"

"It doesn't say anything about that."

"I'm not interested in anyone or anything else at the moment, Lucia." The words *at the moment* made me pause. I wondered if she noticed them. "Don't worry. I will still release you from the contract when the time comes."

She grew quieter. "I'm tired."

I pulled her tight against my chest and rested my chin on top of her head. "Go to sleep."

Lucia still slept deeply when I woke early the next morning. Kissing her softly on her forehead, I climbed out of bed and tucked her back in, then left a note, and drove to Dominic's house. He lived about forty-five minutes away. When I got there, I saw my father's sedan in the circular driveway. I wondered what he was doing here. If he was meeting with Dominic about the Luke DeMarco situation.

Stop being so fucking paranoid.

If it wasn't for Lucia, would I give a fuck if Dominic became the next boss? Would I care? Or would I take the opportunity and walk away? Although walking away wasn't really an option. Nothing in this life came that easy.

I shook it off. I needed to focus. Parking my car behind my father's, I walked to the front door, my anger from yesterday coming back white-hot as I approached. Lucia had tempered it. She'd cooled the anger, turned it into something else. She'd awakened a different side of me, one I'd tried to keep buried for a very long time. I'd always thought that part of me weak, but it was actually the opposite.

I rang the doorbell. A woman I'd only seen here twice before answered. As soon as she recognized me, I saw the momentary note of panic on her face.

"Mr. Benedetti, was Dominic expecting you?"

"No, it's a surprise visit." She seemed nervous and stood blocking the doorway.

"He's in a meeting, sir, and he said no interruptions."

"Did he?" I glanced behind her. A woman vacuumed the living room, but apart from that, the house stood still. "Well, I need to see him, so please step aside."

"I'm afraid I can't do that, sir."

"What's your name?"

"Patricia, sir."

"Patricia, I need to see my brother. I need you to step aside."

"Sir," she glanced behind her, clearly uncertain what to do. "I'm not supposed to…"

I smiled as wide as I could, feeling the gesture

crinkle the corners of my eyes. "I'll take full responsibility, Patricia. Don't worry."

She hesitated, and I took advantage, nudging her out of my way as I entered the house. I went straight for Dominic's study located around back. A man stood at the door, but my presence clearly surprised him. I just grinned and walked right past him. I'd put my hand on the doorknob before I felt his hand fall on my shoulder.

I gave it a sideways glance, eyebrows raised, before meeting his gaze.

His eyes went wide, and the weight of his hand lessened.

He knew who I was. Good.

"Sir—" he started.

"Step back."

It took him a moment, and I didn't wait for him to decide. Instead, I turned the handle and pushed the door open to find Dominic, Roman, and my father sitting around the circular table inside.

They all turned at the interruption, my father and Roman surprised, Dominic furious.

"Isn't this cozy," I said, narrowing my eyes on Roman, the man I trusted most out of the three.

"I told you *nobody*!" Dominic roared to the man who'd stood guard and rose to his feet.

"Sir—"

The guard mumbled something, but I didn't care about that. Instead, when Dominic rounded the table, I pounced on him, grabbing his collar and dragging him backward until I had him pinned against the wall.

"What the—" my dad's voice came.

"Salvatore!"

Roman's shout registered, but all I could see were Dominic's eyes, the look in them both evil and proud, like the cocky prick he was.

He knew exactly why I was here.

"What did you want, taking Jacob?"

His grin widened. "Get your fucking hands off me."

"You scared the shit out of Natalie!"

"What's going on?" my father asked behind me.

"Nothing—" Dominic started.

"It's called fucking kidnapping, asshole!" I said before slamming him hard against the wall.

"Salvatore, get off him," Roman said, his voice the calmest of all. "Let him go."

"Yeah, Salvatore, get off me," Dominic mimicked Roman.

His face, his tone, they infuriated me. He didn't give a shit about anything or anyone. Not Jacob. Not Natalie, not anyone. "You fucking prick." I released him, and Dominic straightened, attempting to fix his collar, but as he did, I drew my fist back and struck his jaw so hard, his head slammed back into the wall, and he stumbled. "You don't even give a shit, do you?" I straightened him, and this time, drove my fist into his gut. "You don't give a shit about scaring that little boy. About scaring the crap out of your brother's wife."

It took three men and Roman to drag me off him, but before they did, I'd landed one more punch on Dominic's jaw. He struggled to stand, his grin angry as he wiped blood from his lip.

"What the *hell* are you talking about, Salvatore?" my father demanded.

I noticed then how he stood back, watching, a weariness in his eyes.

"Why don't you tell him?" I said, fighting against the men who held me, watching Dominic, his expression pissed, bruises already coloring his face. "Tell him what you did."

"He's my nephew too."

"Fuck you, you've never cared about that."

"Enough!" My father's voice bellowed through the room. "Sit him down."

The men holding me shoved me into a seat and held me there. I watched my father stalk toward Dominic. I'd never seen him do that with him before.

"Did you hurt Jacob?" he asked, his tone low, threatening.

"I didn't hurt him. I took him toy shopping and bought him a fucking ice-cream cone!"

"You scared him. He's just a child. Your brother's son!" I said.

"Dominic?" my father asked, some of the color drained from his face.

I freed myself of the men who held me and stood. "I have just one message for you." My voice came low and deep. "Stay away from Natalie and Jacob, or God help me—"

"Dominic!" my father snapped.

I walked out, shaking out of the hold of one of Dominic's men. "I'm leaving. Keep your hands off me."

"Did you lay a finger on Sergio's boy?" I heard my father ask.

I didn't look back. I walked out the door and back to my car, satisfied with having beaten Dominic, but not quite trusting that my threat would keep Jacob and Natalie safe.

As I started the engine and turned the wheel, movement at the front door caught my attention. It was Patricia. She glanced behind her several times as she made her way toward me. I rolled down my window.

"Mr. Benedetti." She was out of breath.

"Yes?"

"Your uncle asked me to give this to you." She slipped a note to me and quickly backed away from the car.

"Thank you, Patricia," I said absently as I unfolded it and read the brief, hurriedly written note: *Dominic visited Isabella DeMarco late last night, just before your arrival there.*

Dominic was there? I'd gone inside—well, I'd gotten as far as the foyer. Did Lucia know Dominic was there and keep it from me? And did this confirm my growing suspicion?

16

LUCIA

I woke suddenly, sucking in a breath, my throat incredibly dry.

Looking around, I remembered where I was, remembered the night before. I lay in Salvatore's bed, his scent still on his pillow, the indentation where his head had been now containing a small piece of paper.

Unfolding it, I read:

I need to take care of some business. I will be back this afternoon. I have Marco's phone, and I've programmed the number into yours in case you need anything.

   Salvatore

I set it down and closed my eyes, feeling

sheepish at what I'd done, dropping his phone into the toilet.

But now, I had to face the thing that had woken me, as unbelievable as it was. I wished I'd kept my father's note rather than throwing it away. At the time, I'd been so upset.

My father had committed suicide because he couldn't live with the decisions he'd made. Because he hadn't been able to come to terms with the fact that when I turned twenty-one, Salvatore would claim me as his. Did he have any idea how that letter would make me feel? Did he know he laid more guilt on my shoulders with that letter than he had in signing the contract that bound me to the Benedetti family?

But there was something else. He'd said something I'd just remembered moments before waking. He'd blamed the Benedettis for destroying *both* his daughters.

I'd thought—when I'd heard the man's voice last night, I'd thought I'd recognized it, but it wasn't a familiar voice. I'd thought it was Dominic Benedetti. But what would he be doing at my sister's house? Isabella hated them more than I did.

But what my father had said...

"No."

I sat up and pushed the blankets off. I was naked and saw that Salvatore had carefully bandaged my knees and the heels of my palms from where I'd torn myself up, running from him last night. When he'd caught up with me, he'd been fierce but also tender. Caring.

I shook my head and got out of bed. Back in my own bedroom, I dressed in running clothes. Running always helped clear my head, and I needed my head cleared really bad right now. Once dressed, I headed out. I heard Rainey in the kitchen and someone vacuuming in another part of the house.

I started at a slow jog, trying to choose some music, but then I stopped, wrapped the earbuds around the phone, and tucked it into my pocket. I didn't want music today. I'd listen to the sounds of the forest.

Last night, when I'd asked him what he wanted, Salvatore had said he wanted me.

"At this moment."

The swell inside my chest deflated instantly at the memory. He had to have me. It's not like I was his choice.

I shook that thought aside. I needed to figure out what was going on. I needed to talk to Izzy, but how? How could I tell her I'd heard a man's voice without giving myself away? How offended would she be if I asked if Dominic Benedetti were at her house?

But what if it *was* him? What if she'd known him for far longer than I realized?

And what if she knew about what he'd done to that little boy, kidnapping Natalie's son like that?

"I took care of what you wanted done."

No. No way. Izzy would never have arranged for something as terrible as the kidnapping of a child. And I should be ashamed of myself for thinking it.

I pushed myself to run faster, even though I hadn't properly warmed up yet, and broke a sweat within a few minutes. I ran harder than I usually ran, but I needed more, needed to burn and exhaust my muscles, purge myself.

When did things get so complicated? Isabella and I were DeMarcos. We hated the Benedetti family. That was simple. It was black-and-white. But this? This attraction, this pull toward Salvatore? My yielding to him? It didn't make sense. And my questions about Izzy. About what my father potentially referred to in his letter. About having heard Dominic's voice in her house late at night.

I was running too fast on unfamiliar terrain and not paying attention, so when I tripped over the exposed root of a large tree and went flying, I shouldn't have been surprised. But when I tried to stand, I had to haul myself up with my arms. My left ankle was already starting to swell and hum with pain.

"Shit."

I looked back toward the house, but I'd run too deep into the woods to see any more than the decorative chimney tops. I forced myself to stand, leaning all my weight on my right leg. Holding on to nearby trees, I hobbled toward the house. It wasn't more than five minutes, though, before I realized I'd never get back there on my own, not with my ankle quickly doubling in size.

Fishing my phone out of my pocket, I unwrapped the earbuds and stuck one in my ear. I then scrolled down to where Salvatore had entered Marco's number and dialed.

He answered quickly, sounding like my call surprised him. "Lucia?"

"You know how you said to try and not get lost when I'm running?

He chuckled, audibly relaxing. "Are you lost?"

"No, that's not it. I'm not lost, and I didn't even have any music blaring, but—"

"What?" he cut me off, his tone anxious. "What is it?"

"I caught my foot on a tree root and fell. I'm trying to get back to the house on my own, but my ankle's swelling and hurts pretty badly."

"Get your weight off it, and elevate it if you can. I'm coming. Just pulling into the gates now. Do you know which trail you took?"

"I headed east, same as the morning you ran into me, but I've already passed the spot where we stopped last time."

"Okay, I'm on my way. Just keep talking to me, so I can hear you."

I heard the sound of stones beneath the car's tires. He really had just gotten back.

"Where did you go?" I asked, since he said to keep talking.

"To see my brother."

Could I tell him my suspicions? But he continued talking as he walked—the front door opening, him saying something to Marco, sliding the glass doors open before the sounds of his footsteps crunching on the forest floor reached my ears as he hurried to me.

"My father, Roman, and he were in a meeting. Some days, I question my trust in Roman."

"You do? Trust him, I mean?"

"Out of the three, yes. Sergio did too. But I know if push came to shove, he'd take care of himself first."

"Was it Dominic who took Jacob? Did he admit it?"

"Yeah."

"I can hear you! I mean, not just on the phone."

"Hot-pink running shorts?" he asked.

I glanced down and smiled. "I guess it's a good thing."

"It'd be hard to miss you in those," he said, hanging up as he came into view. He wore his usual uniform: dark T-shirt and jeans. And he made my mouth water.

Salvatore scanned me from head to toe and knelt

down by my hurt foot, making me flinch as he lightly touched my swollen ankle.

"Ouch. Hey, your hands!" His knuckles were raw and bruised.

He looked at them as if seeing them for the first time and smiled proudly. "You should see Dominic's face."

"You beat him up?"

He nodded, his attention back on my ankle. "I'm going to lift you up and carry you back. Just let me make a call."

He dialed, and I realized he'd called Rainey as soon as he said her name.

"Can you get Dr. Mooney out here for me? Lucia's hurt her ankle. I don't think it's broken, but I'd like him to have a look anyway."

"I don't need a doctor, I just need some ice," I said, but he pretty much ignored me.

"Thanks, Rainey." He hung up and turned to me. "Let's not take any chances."

He lifted me up in his arms, and I blinked back tears with the movement.

"Sorry."

"It's okay."

"This is getting to be a habit."

"You carrying me into the house?"

He nodded, navigating his way carefully through the forest so as not to hit branches with my hurt ankle.

"Can I ask you a question, Lucia?"

"Sure."

"How did I not see Dominic when I came to get you last night?"

How did he know?

"It was dark, but I'm pretty sure I would have seen him," he continued.

"I wasn't sure it was him. I overheard them from upstairs, but I never saw who it was."

"So I'm right, he was there."

"You mean you didn't know?" I looked at him, confused.

"Not one hundred percent."

"Why did you ask it that way, then?" He'd tricked me.

"Wouldn't you have tried to protect your sister rather than tell me the truth?"

We neared the house, and I saw Rainey waiting by the doors, a large bag of ice in hand.

"Answer my question, Lucia."

I looked into his deep-blue eyes, seeing not darkness, not rage or hate. I saw instead goodness, as much as one could be good in our world. "Probably," I answered honestly.

He nodded. "Thank you."

"Doctor will be here in twenty minutes. He said to keep it iced and elevated," Rainey said as we entered the house.

Salvatore laid me on the couch and rested my hurt ankle in his lap as he sat beside me.

Rainey smiled and handed me a cup of her homemade lemonade and two Advil.

"Thought you might need these."

I returned her smile as I popped the pills in my mouth. "Thank you. You're a lifesaver." Rainey went to wait for the doctor, and I took a sip of the lemonade, yelping when Salvatore tugged my shoe off. "That hurt."

"I'm sorry."

He gently peeled my sock off, inspected the swelling limb, then placed the ice bag on my ankle.

"How did you know about Dominic?"

"I've had men watching the house since the day I saw Luke there. Luke's involved in some dangerous things. I truly hope, for her sake, that Isabella isn't a part of those things, Lucia."

I didn't miss the warning, but Salvatore wouldn't hurt her. He'd promised.

Salvatore continued. "I guess I was surprised to hear it was Dominic who made a visit in the middle of the night rather than Luke. Is she sleeping with both of them?"

"Salvatore! You don't know that! *I* don't know that! She's not some kind of—" I couldn't say the word.

"I don't care if she sleeps with a hundred men in

one night, Lucia. But I do care if she's fucking my brother."

"She wouldn't! She hates him. She hates all of you!" I tried to take my ankle off his lap, but he placed the palm of his hand firmly on my thigh.

"Who is Effie's father, Lucia?"

I looked at him, my breath coming in loud and heavy, my eyes watering with the accusation. It was like he was picking information from my brain. Things I hadn't yet come to understand, things I couldn't have be true.

"Why do you do this? Every time I feel like we're finally getting somewhere, feel like I maybe understand you, why do you have to fuck it all up?"

Two sets of footsteps came from the foyer. "This way, Doctor," Rainey said, ushering him in.

Salvatore and I had devolved into some kind of staring contest. I finally had to forfeit when a tear rolled down my cheek. I turned away.

"Dr. Mooney," Salvatore said. "You'll excuse me for not standing, but I think I'd only cause her pain to move her leg."

He did. He only caused me pain. Every. Single. Time.

17

SALVATORE

I stepped out of the room when I saw Roman's call come in and left Dr. Mooney to wrap Lucia's leg. I was right; just a sprain, but painful nonetheless.

"Roman," I said as I entered my study and shut the door.

"Well, you know how to make an entrance."

"He kidnapped Jacob from the daycare. This is after he'd gone to Natalie's house a few days ago, and she'd refused to let him in. He was sending a message, Roman. I wanted to be sure he received mine loud and clear."

"Well, your father was pissed. You were gone for most of that, though."

"Really? Franco Benedetti pissed at the son that's not me for a change?"

"Franco can be pigheaded sometimes, Salvatore.

We both know that. He's tougher on you because he knows you'll be the one replacing him, but he can't ignore Dominic. Franco is more aware than you think of the potential threat Dominic presents, and this stunt with Jacob banished any doubts he may have still clung to."

"Finally," I said sarcastically.

"Either way, unless Dominic is stupid, he won't go near Natalie or Jacob again. Franco's gone out there himself to make sure she knows she and his grandson will have his protection."

"Neither Dominic nor I hold a candle to Sergio, even in death." I hated that I felt this pang of jealousy toward Sergio, as tiny as it was. I'd known this all my life, but it had never come between us. And I wouldn't let it now. "Never have and never will."

"The fact that Sergio is gone still hurts your father. He doesn't love you any less. He's just missing one child. He is human, after all."

I didn't comment.

"I want to talk to you about the DNA test, Salvatore."

"Go on." I hadn't yet had a chance to read through the rest of the report to get a clearer understanding of the results.

"When the results came back, disqualifying Luke as the father, I used a sample from myself. Family shares DNA, in some cases more than in others, but there is always something."

Roman had studied genealogy for a while and was in the process of compiling his family tree.

"What made you do that?" Was I ready to hear what he would tell me?

"A hunch. Effie DeMarco shares at least some of our DNA, Salvatore."

I sat down. Hearing it was different than thinking it.

"I'm obviously not the little girl's father, but I'm running more tests today. I took a sample from Dominic's home."

"What, did you swab him?" I chuckled, but there wasn't any humor behind it.

"Took the hair off his brush."

"When will you know for sure?"

"I'm hoping within twenty-four hours."

"Does my father know anything about this?"

"No. Nothing. He won't find out unless I'm one hundred percent certain."

I leaned back, exhaling. "So Dominic's been having an affair with Isabella DeMarco for five years?"

"That I don't know."

"Where do his loyalties lie, I wonder? And how does Luke DeMarco play into this? This just got a hell of a lot more complicated."

"Talk to Lucia. See if you can glean any information at all. She may not be aware herself, Salvatore."

"I think she's innocent." No, I knew it. And this knowledge would only hurt her.

"I'll get back to you as soon as I know more."

"Thank you, Roman."

I made one more call to check on Natalie, who had called in sick to work and was spending the day with Jacob at home. She knew my father was on his way, and although not pleased about it, she seemed reasonably calm and promised to call me once he'd left.

When I returned to the living room, Dr. Mooney was just packing up his things.

"Just keep it iced and wrapped. You'll be fine in no time. I've already ordered crutches. They'll be here hopefully within the next hour or two."

"How long will I need those?" Lucia asked.

"Only as long as you feel pain when putting any weight on your leg. I don't think long, a week or two."

"Thank you, Dr. Mooney." I extended my hand and shook his.

"You're welcome, Salvatore." He turned back to Lucia and shook her hand as well. "It was nice to meet you, my dear. Call if you need anything at all."

"I will. Thanks again."

Rainey walked Dr. Mooney out, and I took a seat beside Lucia.

"I don't want to talk to you right now."

"I didn't mean to upset you with my question, Lucia."

"But you did, Salvatore. That's the point. Ever hear the saying 'the road to hell is paved with good intentions?'"

"Let's go sit by the pool before it gets too hot."

"I said I don't—"

Ignoring her, I lifted her into my arms and carried her out. Lucia simply sighed.

"Can you bring my lemonade at least?"

"Sure. Would you like something to eat?"

She gave me a cautious look. "I think I smelled cake."

I had too. Rainey had been baking. "I'll be right back."

In the kitchen, I sliced two chunks of the still-warm cinnamon cake I found cooling on the counter and set them on a tray along with two fresh glasses of lemonade. Back outside, I handed one of the plates to Lucia and placed her lemonade on the table beside her lounge chair before taking the seat by hers.

"This is Rainey's signature cake." Not bothering with the fork, I picked up the fat chunk I'd sliced for myself and bit into it. "God, it's delicious."

"I'm going to get fat," Lucia said through her mouthful.

"I'll make sure you get enough exercise."

She glanced at me from the corner of her eye,

then returned her attention to the cake on her plate in her lap.

"We need to talk about last night."

"I thought we had."

"About what you overheard."

Her wary gaze met mine. "She's my sister, Salvatore."

"Jacob was very afraid, Lucia. If Isabella had anything to do with that, I think it's important I know."

She rubbed her face with both hands then pushed her fingers into her hair and pulled at the roots. "I don't know, Salvatore. What happened to that little boy, what Dominic did, was cruel. I hope to God my sister wasn't involved in anything like that. The Izzy I knew wouldn't be. She'd never hurt a child. And I know he wasn't physically hurt, but taking him without his mom knowing? Freaking her out like that, and scaring the little boy? I just—"

She looked away and shook her head. When she turned back to me, her eyes glistened with tears.

"Thing is, I don't know her anymore. I've shut everyone out for so long that I don't even know who *I* am anymore. I thought this was black-and-white. I hated the Benedetti family. Period. But my sister involved in or even possibly orchestrating something like the kidnapping of a child?"

She shook her head again, her face lined with worry.

"She's a mother herself. How...what's happened to us?"

"Too much hate. Too much power," I said. "Too much of a lust for blood and vengeance. War never makes friends out of enemies. The opposite. It solidifies that hate. The war between Benedetti and DeMarco may have been fought in our fathers' time, but we inherit the hate, the bad blood. It doesn't just go away. It carries down generation to generation."

"I don't hate you."

"You have every right to."

"I don't. You're not like them, Salvatore."

But I was. I had killed. I had taken. I had lived off blood money. I'd shed that very blood with my own two hands. Standing up to my father after whipping Lucia, though, and then today—walking away, not giving a shit about what he thought—was I changing? Was I finally growing out of my father's shadow and casting my own?

And would mine be as dark as his?

"I asked Roman to run a paternity test on Effie, Lucia."

"I don't want to know."

She started to stand but then realized she couldn't without my help. Which was precisely why I'd laid her on one of the lounge chairs rather than sitting her on a chair.

I touched her arm. "You have to know."

She closed her eyes and reopened them after a minute but remained silent, waiting.

"Luke isn't her father."

From the look on her face, I had the feeling she knew that.

"She carries DNA from my family." Christ, was I saying this out loud?

A tear rolled down each of Lucia's cheeks, and I knew she knew.

"They're testing Dominic's DNA now. We'll know for sure soon whether Dominic Benedetti fathered Effie DeMarco."

It was a long moment before she spoke. I didn't know how Lucia would take what I told her. On the one hand, she'd seen enough evidence to suspect the truth. She'd seen it herself before I told it. On the other hand, Isabella was still her sister, and I was still the enemy's son. I was her keeper. The man who'd signed a contract, claiming ownership of her.

"What do you want out of this, Salvatore? When all is said and done, what do you want?"

I'd been straddling the seat and now... I lay back and looked out across the pool toward the forest. It was so quiet here. So still. So peaceful.

I turned back to her. "I want to live a quiet life. I don't want to look over my shoulder at every turn. I don't want to see an enemy in every set of eyes I meet, every hand I shake. I want the people I love to be safe. I want them be happy." Strange. Six months ago, I would have added 'I want my brother to be alive' into that list, but something had shifted. Somehow, I'd come to accept that he was gone. Not the cruelty or the unfairness of the act, but the knowledge that he was gone. And that my life lay here.

She cleared her throat and blinked her pretty, innocent eyes, casting them somewhere in the space between us. I didn't take my eyes off her.

Lucia was all the innocence in my life.

She was my redemption.

And I wanted her. Her presence here, us together, as tumultuous as it was, as wrong as I was for keeping her, it saved me. *She* saved me.

And that was why I would keep my promise and release her once I could. Once I knew she would be safe and out of harm's way.

"What do *you* want, Lucia?"

She met my gaze, shrugged her shoulders, and gave me a tiny but sad smile. "Same things, I guess."

"You'll have them. I promise."

Another promise to her. Another one I didn't know I could keep. But I would try. I would try every day up until my last breath to give her what she wanted. A life. Simple, peaceful, beautiful.

Like her.

It was in that moment I realized I loved her. Somewhere, somehow, I'd fallen in love with her.

But my debt to her was greater than anything I felt, any hurt or loss I'd experience. And because of that debt, I would never say those words aloud, not to her, not to anyone. She'd been locked away most of her life. All of her brief adult life. I was the only man she'd known—a cruel trick of fate. If I said the words, I knew what would happen. Lucia would mistake survival for love. Because right now, she needed me to survive. To survive my family. To survive the war that I'd mistakenly thought over. I would stay alive for her. I would fight for her. I would do everything in my power to save her. Nothing else mattered, not even my own life. Everything from this point forward would be for her.

"I want to make love to you, Lucia."

She looked at me, confused, although her body began to prepare. I could see it in the slight dilation of her pupils, the stiffening of her nipples, the parting of her lips.

"I want you to want it. I want you to give me the word. Up until now, I've taken it from you."

"Salvatore—"

I held up my hand. "I've taken it."

She touched my arm. "Salvatore—"

I moved to stop her from speaking. She combed her fingers into the hair at my forehead and tugged.

"You're so damn stubborn."

She leaned in to kiss me, her mouth soft, her tongue sweet as it probed my lips. She pulled back and looked at me, swallowing.

"I want it. I want you. Make love to me,

Salvatore."

I wrapped her in my arms and kissed her, lifting her up as I stood, cradling her to me, carrying her to the door of my study. Our lips still locked, we entered. I took her to the couch, sat her on it, and kneeled before her between her spread knees. Her eyes on mine, she pulled first her top, then her sports bra off, her round breasts settling into place, the nipples already tight. I worked her other shoe off her foot and then slipped my fingers into the waistband of her shorts and panties. She lifted up a little, allowing me to drag them down and off so she sat before me naked.

"Spread your legs wider and lean back," I said, tugging my shirt off.

She did as I said, opening herself wide, leaning back, offering me her pussy. With my thumbs on either side of her lips, I opened her farther and brought my mouth to her, licking her length once before taking her clit into my mouth, still watching her as she leaned her head back and closed her eyes.

"Fuck, Salvatore, I love that."

I sucked, pulling her toward me so her ass hung off the couch. I pushed one finger inside her, and when she tightened her muscles around it, I stopped sucking, licking her clit instead, teasing it. She opened her eyes.

"You like when I eat your pussy?"

She nodded and tried to drag my head back.

I smiled. "Greedy girl." I stood, rid myself of my clothes, and stroked myself, loving how she watched me, her hungry eyes never leaving me.

"I want to suck your cock, Salvatore."

Placing my knees on either side of her on the couch, I straddled her and brought myself to her mouth. She took my cock in her hands, sliding one beneath to cup me, and opened her mouth, licking the tip before taking me into her hot, wet mouth.

"Fuck, Lucia, I love you sucking my cock." I rocked my hips against her, moving slowly, relishing the wet heat of her on my swelling dick until I needed to fuck her faster. I pulled out then and lay her on her back on the couch before taking the leg she hadn't hurt and pushing it back so I could see all of her. "I love looking at you too, at your dripping pussy." I rocked myself into her, sucking in a breath as I did. "Knowing it belongs to me."

"Hard, please."

I shook my head. "Not yet." I moved slowly, taking my time, penetrating her deeply before sliding out, feeling every inch of her until she nearly screamed for me to make her come.

"Please, Salvatore!"

"I want something else today," I said, pulling out fully and going to my desk.

She lifted her head, her expression confused, annoyed. I opened one of the drawers and found what I wanted, a bottle of lotion.

She looked at it, then at me. "What?"

I took the lid off and squeezed some of the scentless cream onto my hand, coating my cock in it while she watched. It took all the restraint I had not to shoot my load right then and there while fucking my palm.

"What do I want?" I asked, smearing more of the lotion on myself.

She nodded. I pulled her good leg out, bent it at the knee, and pushed it toward her chest. I then squeezed half the bottle of lotion onto the flat of her belly.

"I want to fuck your ass."

Her eyes went wide, and she opened her mouth, but I stopped her, dipping one finger into the lotion and taking the tip of it to her asshole.

"I think you'll like it," I said, circling the tight, virgin ring, smearing lotion all over it. "But first, I'm going to fill your sexy little hole with this." I dipped my finger in the lotion again, and she watched, a slight flush to her cheeks, caution in her eyes alongside the curiosity.

After several times circling, I pressed against the hole, and she gasped as my lubricated fingertip penetrated. I waited, watching her face as she took it, relaxing enough a few moments later so that I could press deeper.

She sucked in a breath and gripped the side of the couch. I moved slowly until she was taking the length of one finger easily in and out of her tight little ass. I then pulled out to dip my finger into more of the lotion and repeated.

"You like my finger fucking your ass, Lucia?"

She made some sound and averted her gaze before giving me the smallest nod.

"No, look at me. I want to watch you take me." I slid a second finger in, causing her to tighten all her muscles again, her eyes wide on mine. "Take it." I thrust a little harder, then circled inside her, smearing lotion along her walls. "When I fuck your asshole properly, I'm going to watch you take me then too. I'm going to watch you when you stretch and come and I'm going to watch you when I fill you with my seed."

"Salvatore, I..."

"Wait, Lucia. Wait until my cock is inside you before you come." I pulled both fingers out and smeared the last of the lube onto them, dipping them back into her more easily now. "That's it, it feels good, right?"

She nodded.

"When your ankle is healed, I'm going to have you bend over my desk and bare your ass. You're going to like this so much that when I tell you to beg me to fuck your ass, you're going to do it. You're going to spread yourself wide and arch your back and beg me to fill your ass with my cock."

"I can't...I'm coming."

She closed her eyes, and the walls of her ass clenched around my fingers. I watched her come, watched her slide one hand to her clit and rub herself as she moaned, her pussy leaking, my fingers thrusting in and out of her ass.

"Bad girl," I said once she'd come down. I pulled my fingers out of her and lifted both her legs up, pressing them against her sides to make taking my cock easier. "I'm thicker than my fingers, but we'll go slow until you're ready."

She nodded.

"Touch your clit, Lucia. Make yourself come again, this time with my cock inside your ass."

She did as I said, rubbing herself slowly as I lined up the head of my cock against her asshole and slowly began to push into her, taking my time, stopping when her muscles tightened, watching her face, feeling her body to know when she was ready for more.

"Salvatore, it's too big. It hurts."

"Shh. Relax. Open for me." I moved in and out of her, one inch at a time, slowly rocking my hips, wanting to drive into her but holding back until she came again. I was about two-thirds of the way in.

"Fuck, Salvatore!"

This orgasm took her more violently, her walls clenching, relaxing, opening for me to fill her fully.

"God, you're so fucking tight." I held myself deep inside her for a moment, knowing I wouldn't last long. When I began to move, she cried out, her fingers still working her clit, another orgasm on the heels of the last until she called out my name. The sound of my name on her lips, the feel of her around me, took me over the edge until my cock throbbed and I emptied inside her, filling her, owning her, owning every part of her.

I SAT in the tub with Lucia between my legs, her bandaged ankle resting on the edge. We'd barely settled in when Marco barged into my bedroom, calling out my name, probably only stopping when he realized from the pile of clothes I'd dumped just inside the doorway that I wasn't alone.

"Shit. Sorry."

"Give me twenty minutes," I called out.

"It's urgent."

I glanced at Lucia. Marco wasn't one to cry wolf.

"I'll be right back," I said to her as I climbed out I settled her against the back of the tub.

"What's urgent?" she asked.

I dried off and wrapped a towel around my hips. "No idea." I went into the bedroom. One look at Marco told me this was bad. "What is it?"

He glanced toward the bathroom. I followed his gaze, then walked over closer to him.

"What's happened, Marco?" I asked more quietly, so Lucia wouldn't hear.

"There's been a shooting."

My entire body tightened. "Who?"

"Luke DeMarco. He's being airlifted to Bellevue Hospital right now."

"Fuck."

"What's happened, Salvatore?" I turned to find Lucia wrapped in a towel, hopping on one leg, leaning her weight against the wall.

"It's Luke." I went to her, put her arm over my shoulder, and propped her up by her waist. "He's been shot."

"Oh my God! Is he okay?"

"Not sure yet."

"I have to call Izzy. She wasn't there, was she?"

"I don't know."

"Shit, my phone is downstairs."

"Here," Marco said, handing her his.

She looked at him as if she were surprised, but took it and dialed.

A knock came at the door. Rainey peeked her head inside and held up the crutches Dr. Mooney had ordered.

"Already here," she said, her smile fading when she saw the looks on our faces.

"Thank you, Rainey," I said, taking them from her. "Maybe you can make us all a pot of coffee."

Lucia looked up at me. "I'm on my way, Izzy," she

said into her phone. "I'll be there as soon as I can." She hung up.

"Salvatore, I have to go to them."

I nodded. "We'll get dressed and go."

Lucia blushed, and Marco and Rainey awkwardly left the room. I went into her bedroom and chose some clothes: a dress and a sweater in case it was cool at the hospital. I helped her get her clothes on before getting dressed myself. I handed her the crutches that had just been delivered.

"Thanks."

Since she had never used crutches before—and there was no time to practice—I ended up carrying Lucia down the stairs—it was just faster that way—and asked Marco to follow us.

"Did your sister know anything?" I asked Lucia once we were in the car and on our way.

"No. Only that he was in critical condition. He took two bullets, one to the stomach, the other in his shoulder. She's a mess."

I checked my watch. "It's about an hour's drive from here without traffic."

"Crap."

My mind raced with thoughts of who'd done it, and I couldn't shake the feeling the assailant was closer to home than I'd like once I'd learned the truth. But we'd deal with that if and when we had to. Right now, I had to get Lucia to the hospital and find out what the hell was going on.

18

LUCIA

Salvatore made call after call as he drove us to the hospital, first to his uncle, then to Marco who tailed us, then to Dominic. Dominic didn't pick up his call. He also arranged for security to be added to the hospital, for which I was grateful.

I tried Isabella twice but never got hold of her. With traffic, by the time we got to the hospital, it was well over an hour later. Salvatore's phone rang once more just as he parked the car. He checked the display, and I glimpsed the name. It was his father.

"I have to take this."

I nodded, opening my door and setting my crutches outside. What a time to sprain my ankle!

"Marco," Salvatore called out once Marco had parked his car. "Take Lucia upstairs, and stay with her until I get there."

Marco nodded and took my arm, helping me out of the car.

"I got it," I snapped, hating feeling helpless. I glanced at Salvatore, who walked away with the phone to his ear. Marco followed me into the hospital. At reception, I found out where they'd taken Luke. I went as quickly as I could to the trauma unit and found Isabella holding Effie's hand, her face one of frustration and worry, her eyes weary and red.

"Izzy."

She turned, a look of relief quickly replaced by surprise at my state.

"It's nothing, just a sprain. I fell while running."

She got up, and we hugged.

"Aunt Lucia, are you hurt too?" Effie asked.

"I'll be okay. It's just a sprain, kiddo." I gave her a hug then turned to Izzy, who was watching Marco talk to two other men I just noticed.

"Salvatore?" she asked, gesturing toward them.

I nodded. "He wanted security for Luke and for us.

She snorted. "He's probably the one who put Luke in here!"

"Wait. No, he was with me."

She rolled her eyes. "Don't be so naive, Lucia. All he has to do is give the word!"

"Mama?"

Izzy wiped away a tear and looked down at her daughter.

"Let's calm down." I touched my sister's shoulder, and she sighed.

"Sorry, honey. It's fine," she told Effie. "Everything's going to be fine."

"Uncle Luke is hurt," she said to me.

"I know. Hey, I saw a vending machine just around the corner." I dug into my purse and found my wallet, took out some dollar bills, and handed them to her. "Go get us some chocolate bars, okay?"

She looked at her mom, who nodded.

"Marco, will you keep an eye on her?" I asked.

"Of course."

Wow, this was a different Marco than the inflexible man I'd met thus far.

"Here, some sodas too." I handed Effie more money to keep her busy. She went with Marco. "Let's sit down. Tell me what happened," I said to Isabella once Effie was out of earshot.

"He was at the stupid bowling alley," she started, taking a crumpled-up tissue out of her purse and wiping her dripping eyes. "He always goes there in the mornings, so the bastards knew where to find him. He'd just gone to get a cup of coffee, and two guys came in and opened fire."

"Jesus."

"The owner who was working the bar took a bullet in his arm. He'll be okay."

"Anyone else hurt?"

She shook her head. "No."

"Any idea who?"

She shook her head. "They wore ski masks."

"I guess they would. Why do you think it was Salvatore's men?" I asked.

She shook her head with a flat look in her eyes. "Who else but someone from the Benedetti family." She turned her attention to digging for something in her purse.

"Dominic is part of that family," I said, watching her.

She glanced up, her lips narrow, her face tight.

"He was at your house the other night."

She stood. "This isn't the time, Lucia."

"What was he doing there?" I asked, following her, the crutches an irritating nuisance.

She kept her back to me, shaking her head, watching Effie push buttons on the vending machine.

"Izzy, what's going on?"

She faced me finally. "A big fucking mess, that's what."

"Are you having an affair with Dominic Benedetti?"

Izzy threw her arms up into the air. "There you go again, another affair. First it was Luke, now it's Dominic? Excuse me, sis, but I'm not going to justify that with an answer."

"Ms. DeMarco?" a doctor called out, rounding the corner.

"Yes?" Isabella went to him, and I followed, hobbling behind her.

"Your cousin's injuries are very serious. We're operating now, but it will be several hours. I can't speak to the outcome just yet."

"He can't die," she started, her eyes watering, her voice desperate. "You can't let him die."

The doctor looked to be immune to her emotion. Probably so used to doling out bad news, it just didn't faze him anymore.

"Mommy, I got you a Snickers bar," Effie started, coming back toward us with the candy bars, Marco behind her carrying cans of soda, looking as much out of place following her as possible. It would have been comical if we weren't standing in a hospital waiting room with Luke in critical condition a few doors down.

"What did you get for me?" I asked, lifting her up and turning her away while Izzy wiped her tears.

"A Twix. Same as me."

"I love Twix. Good choice."

"I thought you might."

"I'll check in with you as soon as I have some information, but it will be several hours before he'll be out of surgery," the doctor said.

I watched them. Izzy nodded her head. When I set Effie down, she went to her.

"Here, mommy." She held out the candy.

Isabella took it then hugged the little girl. "I love you, honey."

"It's just a Snickers," Effie said, confused, and tried to squirm out of the tight squeeze.

Salvatore walked in just then, and I felt an immediate sense of relief. His expression, however, showed how preoccupied he was. Isabella glared at him, but he watched her with concern.

"What are you doing here? Not enough that you had to attend my father's funeral? You had to come see this too?"

"I'm here for Lucia."

She snorted.

"How is he?" Salvatore asked me.

"Critical. They'll be in surgery for a few hours."

"Mommy, is Uncle Luke going to be okay? I got him his favorite candy bar too."

"That was sweet of you," Izzy said, then looked up at me. "It may be best if Effie goes home. There's nothing for her to do here."

"I'll take her. You stay. Just call me as soon as you hear anything, okay?"

"I will."

"I want to stay with you, mommy."

Isabella hugged her daughter again. "I'll be home as soon as I can, but there's nothing for you to do here. Go home, and bake some of those cookies Uncle Luke likes. Then you can bring them with you when he wakes up, okay?"

"What kind of cookies?" I asked to distract Effie.

Effie studied her mom then gave her a tight squeeze, whispering something in her ear before turning away. A tear rolled down Isabella's cheek.

"It'll be okay," I said, hugging her while holding Effie's hand. "He'll pull through. He's almost as stubborn as you, after all."

She gave me a smile, then turned to Salvatore. "Are you staying with them at the house?" Her tone changed utterly when she addressed him.

"I'll take them there, and I've already got men stationed outside. I have to attend a meeting but will be back as soon as possible."

"Of course, another meeting. You see what comes of those meetings," she said, gesturing to the door the doctor had disappeared behind.

"Izzy," I leaned in close so Effie wouldn't hear. "Salvatore didn't do this. I promise you that."

"Take care of my daughter, and take care of yourself." She hugged me. "I have a gun in my bedroom," she added in a whisper. "Nightstand drawer."

I pulled back. She had a gun? By her bed?

"Here are my keys." She pulled her car keys off and handed me the ring. I took it, still not quite believing what she'd just told me.

"Let's go, Lucia," Salvatore said after giving Marco some orders.

"Call me if you hear anything. Come on, Effie."

Effie and I followed Salvatore to the elevator and

out to his car. Once we settled Effie and my crutches in the backseat, we climbed in. I spoke with Effie as we drove to her house, which was about half an hour from the hospital. Although she tried to hide her unease, it was evident she was anxious and unsure. Salvatore said only a few words, preoccupied. Maybe grateful for Effie's presence, since that meant I couldn't question him.

Once we got to the house, I saw two cars parked along the curb with two men inside each one. Salvatore pulled up in the driveway, and we all climbed out, me last, since I had to figure out how to use the damned crutches, and putting weight on my foot made me wince every time. Effie held my crutches while I climbed out and watched me while Salvatore walked over to the men sitting in the cars by the curb and, I assumed, gave them instructions before returning to us.

"Ready?" he asked, closing the door behind me.

Effie nodded and walked ahead to the front door.

"What meeting are you going to?" I asked, not sure if I liked him going to any meeting after Luke had just been shot.

"Luke's shooting is just one of the incidents. Two of our businesses have been attacked as well."

"What businesses?" I knew they had several shops, and I didn't want to know what those shops fronted for.

"Doesn't matter," he said. "What matters is that

what I feared would happen in time, what *Luke* was working on, is here now."

"Luke? But—"

"He's in the hospital, I know."

"Is it Dominic?"

His face changed, and he looked just beyond me. "I'm not sure, Lucia."

"What aren't you telling me?"

"That the time for war, it's dawning."

Salvatore's phone rang, and he reached into his pocket to get it. "I'll call you right back," he said and disconnected the call. "Let's get you inside and settled. I'd rather have you at home, but this will have to do for now."

We headed for the door. Salvatore slid the key into the lock and opened it. Effie went directly into the kitchen, leaving us alone for the time being.

"You'll be safe here. I'm leaving four men outside. They won't let anyone in."

"Or out, I'm guessing." He turned to me and took my face in his hands.

"Correct."

He looked at me for a long moment.

"This is one I really, really need to trust you on, Lucia. I don't have time to go looking for you, and I can't keep you safe if you disappear."

"I'm not going anywhere."

"Good, because if you do, I'll take my belt to your

ass again, and this time, it'll be a month before you can sit down."

"I said I'm not," I snapped, not wanting that memory.

He nodded then kissed my mouth, his hands still on either cheek.

After walking him out, I glanced once more at the cars parked out front. One man sat inside each one. I wasn't sure where the others had gone. Probably around the house. I didn't care as long as they didn't come inside. I closed the door and went to the kitchen to find Effie had taken out flour and a big bag of M&M's, but even she wasn't snacking on them.

"I can't reach the other stuff," she said, her tone somber. "M&M cookies are Uncle Luke's favorites. Mommy has the recipe on her iPad."

I smiled and squatted down to her level, rubbing her arms. "The doctors are going to do everything they can to make sure he's okay, understand?"

She nodded, but her face remained serious. "He and mommy had a fight last night. I heard them."

"Their fight doesn't have anything to do with what happened. You know that, right?"

"I'm scared, Aunt Lucia. What if he's not okay? What if he doesn't wake up anymore?"

How could I answer that question, when I didn't know myself the outcome? I stood and looked around, finding an apron, my mom's, in the drawer she kept it in, neatly folded as if she'd just had it on yesterday. My dad hadn't gotten rid of anything of hers. In fact, I was sure the closet in his bedroom would still be full of her clothes unless Isabella had packed everything up. I hoped she hadn't.

I slid the apron over my head and tied the strings at my back. "This used to be your grandmother's apron," I said to Effie.

"She's in heaven," Effie said as she opened the same drawer and took out a second, smaller apron. "This one is mine. I got it for my birthday."

"Oh, that's a pretty one. Shall I help you tie it?"

She nodded.

"Okay, let's get started. Where does mommy keep her iPad?"

"Here."

I followed her into the living room, where she opened a drawer in the coffee table and pulled out the tablet, punching in the code before handing it to me.

"It's 0-0-0-0." Effie shook her head. "I cracked that one in no time."

I ruffled Effie's hair and led her back to the kitchen, looked up the recipe saved in the Favorites tab, and we got to work. It took much more time than I expected because Effie insisted on using only the colors of M&M's that Luke liked best, and she patterned them into individual smiley faces. We spent the rest of the day playing in her room or watching TV, and I reheated lasagna I found in the fridge for dinner. At eight o'clock, I took her to her room and read her a story before putting her to bed, anxious that I hadn't heard from Isabella yet. When I'd tried her phone a few times, it had gone right to voice mail.

I dialed Salvatore, who answered on the third ring.

"Hey, it's me."

"Everything okay?"

He sounded rushed. "Yes, it's fine. I'm just wondering when your meeting will be finished."

He sighed. "I'm not sure, but I'll be there as soon as I can. Just lock the doors and go to bed if you're tired. Have you heard from your sister?"

"No, and she won't pick up the phone." Someone called his name, a man I thought might be Roman.

"I have to get back, Lucia."

"Okay. Call me when you're done. I don't care about the time."

"Make sure the doors are locked."

"I will."

"Be safe."

"You too." We hung up. I walked around the house for the fifth time and made sure all the doors were locked. The cars were still parked outside, and I spied one man in the backyard at the far end. Still, I didn't feel safe. I had no idea what was going on, and being here I felt exposed, like I was a sitting duck.

Shoving those thoughts aside, I made a pot of tea then closed the curtains on all the windows. From the bookshelf in the study, I found some old photo albums. Taking two of them, I settled on the couch to wait for my sister to call or come home.

That was when I heard the creaking of a door and footsteps coming from the back bedroom, the one my parents had converted on the main floor.

I turned my head. "Effie?" But it couldn't be her. I'd waited until she'd fallen asleep upstairs.

The hair on the back of my neck stood on end, and I watched the dark hallway as the steps grew closer. Terrified and unable to drag my gaze away from the shadowy space, I fumbled for my cell phone on the coffee table.

I knew who it was. Who it had to be. But still, when Dominic stepped into the light in the living room, I gasped, shocked, suddenly shaking when my gaze fell on the pistol he held at his side.

"Toss the phone, Lucia."

19

SALVATORE

I walked back into the meeting room at my father's house. About a dozen men were gathered around the table, all family, cousins and uncles. My father raised his eyebrows but didn't comment on my having left the room to take the call.

I hated leaving Lucia alone. She didn't know to what extent things had progressed in the last twelve hours. Hell, I was shocked to hear it all myself.

After I'd left Dominic's house, my father had apparently gone ballistic on my brother. Roman filled me in on the details. Franco had been furious with Dominic. So much so that he'd apologized to Natalie himself. I knew he was going to her house to make sure she knew he would protect her, but to apologize? That wasn't Franco Benedetti's style.

He'd also stationed men at her house when she'd refused to come to the city with him and stay at his house until things settled. She'd had no choice in the matter. He would do whatever he needed to do to protect his grandson.

And he had sent Dominic to the house in Florida to cool off. To *"get his head out of his ass"* were apparently his exact words.

The shooting of Luke DeMarco had surprised my father. It wasn't done on his order and obviously not on mine. The video footage only showed two masked men walking into the bowling alley and opening fire. It was a wonder more people weren't hurt.

Two of our businesses, one a restaurant and another, a bicycle shop, both of which fronted for money-laundering operations, had been attacked, but no one had been killed. Nothing of the businesses connected directly to us, so investigators would not find anything linking the crimes, but this was only the beginning. Money was taken from both businesses, but the amount of cash wouldn't have warranted the burglaries.

No, a message was being sent.

This was the prelude to a war.

But Luke DeMarco's shooting threw us off. He was working with the Pagani family. Why would he have been attacked?

That was the piece that gave us all pause.

"I feel real uneasy about this," I said. "They wouldn't have attacked DeMarco. Hell, if things had progressed to this point, DeMarco wouldn't have been at a fucking bowling alley. Something isn't right. It's someone else."

"Isabella?" my father asked.

Roman glanced at me.

"I saw her at the hospital. She's beside herself."

"You were at the hospital?" he asked.

I'd told Roman where I was, but not my father. "They're Lucia's family."

His lips tightened. "You miss the point of everything."

"By point of everything, you mean my treatment of Lucia." I knew. It wasn't a question. "If it's the fact I'm not a monster to her, then you're right, I miss your point. Maybe you should have given her to Dominic after all." The thought sickened me, but my saying it out loud to him, and in front of other members of the family, it only reaffirmed the fact that I would never allow that to happen.

My father made no reply, which surprised me. But it also strengthened me.

Every man in the room seemed to be holding their breath.

"Leave Lucia out of this. She's my concern and mine alone. Period. Let's talk about the damage done, who's behind it, and what we're doing about it."

He exhaled but turned his attention back to the task at hand. I assumed he'd deal with me later, but when that time came, he'd learn there would be no more dealing with me. My strings had been cut. I was no longer his puppet.

Maybe it took that contract to teach me that, to break me from my weakness, my cowardice when it came to Franco Benedetti. If any good could come out of something as terrible as stealing a life, this had to be it.

"Back to who is behind this," Roman began. "I believe the Pagani family is carrying out the attacks. I don't believe Isabella DeMarco would have her cousin assassinated. Assuming that was the intent."

"What else would it be? They put two bullets in him," I said.

Roman agreed. "Maybe Isabella is a bigger threat than we gave her credit for. Maybe Luke was an underling, a cover for her."

"Maybe the Pagani family is acting alone?" I added.

"No." My father shook his head. "I've spoken with the senior Paul Pagani."

Paul Pagani Sr., an eighty-six-year-old man who still refused to hand over the reins of the family business to his son. Although knowing the son, I understood why.

"He has not authorized any shootings, and he is aware of talks between DeMarco and his son. When he learned of it, he forbade any action."

"But his son could have gone behind his back," Roman added.

"And attempted to kill Luke DeMarco?" Stefano, one of my cousins, asked.

"There's something we're missing," I said, shaking my head.

I caught Roman's concerned look.

"Pagani has stated if it is his men who carried out the shootings without his permission, they'll be dealt with, but I'm not satisfied," my father said. His phone rang, and he looked at the display. "Excuse me."

He stood, and although he didn't leave the room, he turned his back to the table and walked a few steps away.

The men at the table continued to talk, but Roman and I remained silent, listening to the call.

"What do you mean?" my father asked, checking his watch. "That was hours ago." Silence on the line. "You've tried him? His driver?" Silence. "Fine. Reschedule it. And find him."

When he turned to us again, he immediately met my gaze and gestured to the door. Roman also stood, and the three of us stepped into the hall and closed the conference room door behind us.

"Dominic didn't make his flight."

"What do you mean?" I asked, alarm bells sounding.

"I mean that was the fucking captain, calling to

say he was about to lose his time slot," my father snapped.

I watched him try to call Dominic, but the call went directly to voice mail.

"His driver is missing as well."

"Missing?" Roman asked.

My father placed another call and spoke into the phone. "Get Natalie and Jacob packed up and to my house. I don't care what you have to do to make that happen, but get them here now."

"I have to go," I said, pulling my phone from my pocket.

"Godamnit, I need you here, Salvatore!"

I stopped, took a deep breath in, and turned to face him.

"Dominic has always wanted what you have," my father stated. "What you will inherit from me once I am ready to retire. That's no secret, not for any of us."

I listened in silence.

"I don't like all of the things he does," he continued, the words obviously difficult to say. "I sometimes don't like who he is." He breathed in deeply. "But he is still your brother."

I shifted on my feet. My father didn't usually resort to making me feel guilty to do something I didn't want to do, and I wasn't sure that's what he was doing now, but what he said triggered something akin to guilt inside me.

"I was harsh with him when I learned what he did to Natalie," he said.

"No, not harsh," I disagreed. "It needed to be done. Dominic was the only person in the wrong on that one. Question is, does he realize it? Does *he* think so?"

My father ran his hand through his thinning hair and sat on the chair just beneath the window. Seeing him weary—it was strange, felt wrong. I'd only ever seen my father as strong. All powerful. And ultimately, always in control.

I always thought I'd celebrate his fall, his weakening.

I went to him and placed a hand on his shoulder. "I'll look for him."

He sighed, nodded his head, then met my eyes and took my hand. "I'm too fucking old for this."

"Go upstairs, Franco. I'll handle the meeting," Roman offered.

My father looked at him, shook his head, and steeled his spine before standing. "I'll handle it."

Roman nodded. We both knew he couldn't not handle this one. It would be seen as ultimate weakness.

"Dominic is unsatisfied. Always has been," he said to me. "I've always pushed him to want more. It corrupted him in a way."

I wanted to tell him it wasn't his fault, but wasn't it? At least partially?

He put his hand on my shoulder and came to within inches of me. He tapped his forefinger against his head. "He's not right, not now. He can't accept his place. But remember, he is your brother. Find him, and bring him home. Do that, and I'll take care of him."

20

LUCIA

"What the hell are you doing here?" I asked, standing and leaning my weight on my crutches. I didn't feel half as confident as I somehow managed to sound. "How did you get in?"

He stood in the light just on the other side of the coffee table looking disheveled, his shirt untucked, his hair messy, his face bruised. He gave me a lopsided grin, and I really looked at him for the first time, the dimple on his right cheek disarming me momentarily. His eyes were a light blue-gray, the lashes thick and darker than his blond hair. He was tall, well over six feet, but he had a leaner build than Salvatore, although still muscular. Powerful.

I returned my gaze to his face, saw his grin widen. The darkness in his eyes reminded me who he was.

He tucked the gun into the back of his jeans before reaching into his pocket and taking something out.

I cocked my head to the side when he held it out to show me, not understanding right away.

"I have a key."

It dawned on me that he held a key to my old house. To the house where my sister and niece lived.

"Isabella gave it to me."

"I don't understand." But I did. I just hadn't come to terms with it yet. I studied him, taking in his features, comparing them to Effie's. Although she hadn't inherited his blond hair, she had similar eyes, although hers were warm, innocent. The rest was Isabella, but there was one thing she shared with Dominic: that dimple in her right cheek. That was from her father.

No.

I had to stop this. What was I thinking? I was talking about my sister here. And Effie's father could be anyone. It wouldn't be him.

What about the tests?

Nothing was definitive, not yet.

And the key. Why did Isabella give him a key?

"You're lying. My sister wouldn't have given you a key."

"Why not?"

"She hates you."

He snorted then went to the liquor cabinet and poured himself a drink. "Want one?"

"No."

He leaned against the cabinet and watched me as he brought the tumbler to his lips and swallowed the deep amber liquid. I hoped it burned on the way down.

"What do you see in my brother?" he asked.

"What do you want, Dominic? What are you doing here?"

"He's a puppet to our father. A weak little windup toy who does as he's told. Who humiliated you. What in hell do you see in him?"

"I see his heart. I see what's real behind the mask he puts on for you, for your father."

At that he chuckled and poured himself another drink. "That's fresh. Now Sergio," he began, drinking deeply. "He was a man's man. A man to be respected, like me. Even Franco Benedetti respected him."

"And you think kidnapping his son makes you respectable? It makes you a monster. A weak, hateful monster."

He laughed and stalked toward me. I forced myself to stand my ground, even when he stood only inches away, breathing whiskey on my face as his gaze roamed over my body. He looked me in the eye.

"Well then, you may need to actually open your eyes and see the other monsters much closer to home."

A car pulled up outside, and I exhaled in relief. He stepped away just as a key turned in the lock, and Isabella walked into the house. She stopped in the doorway as soon as she saw him. They exchanged a look before she turned her gaze on me.

I watched her, then him, then her again.

And I was certain.

"What are you doing here?" she asked Dominic, her tone much too casual as she closed the door behind her.

"What, do you two compare notes or something?" he asked, finishing his drink and setting his glass down. "I'm hungry." He went into the kitchen, leaving us alone.

"Izzy? What the hell is going on?"

She plopped her bag down on the coffee table and rubbed her eyes with her hands. She looked defeated in that moment, and I saw through the tough facade she put on more and more.

"Luke's out of surgery," she said, heading to where Dominic had left his glass, filling it with the same whiskey and drinking it down. "He's going to make it."

She stood quietly a moment before her body slumped, and she broke into sobs. I went to her and embraced her, the crutches tucked awkwardly under my arms. I held her so tight that she finally surrendered herself, letting herself go, weeping, hugging me back.

"I thought…I thought…God, if he died?" She sucked in a loud breath and wiped her eyes, leaning back. "I prayed, Lucia. I haven't prayed in five years." She shook her head. "I love him. I love him, and all I've done is hurt him."

"Luke?" I was so confused.

She nodded, and we walked over to the sofa and sat down.

"He was adopted," she started, as if that was what I was concerned about. "We're not blood relatives."

"I know, Izzy. God, I know. It's okay. I don't care. It's fine."

"I owe you an explanation. Multiple, probably."

I nodded.

"Five years ago, more than that, actually, I met Dominic. It was accidental, nothing planned. I was seventeen. It was a party in the woods, and I didn't know who he was. Same for him. He didn't know me, and we didn't exchange last names. It was just Dominic and Isabella. That's all. We hit it off, and things got heated over the next few weeks. Months."

"You still didn't know who he was?" I didn't believe that.

"By then we knew. Hell, by our third date, we knew. But there was something there. I don't know what it was, maybe even the whole Romeo and Juliette with warring families and the romance of it all, the sneaking around, meeting in the woods, sitting under the stars. Just us. Together."

"You fell in love with Dominic Benedetti?"

She nodded her head. "He wasn't like this, not then. We were each other's firsts. First love, first..."

"Then you got pregnant."

"Yes. It was right around when things were coming to a head between the families. Dominic was going to tell his father. I told Papa."

"That's why he was so mad."

She nodded sadly. "I was pregnant with the enemy's child. Never mind that I was barely an adult and unmarried."

"He disowned you because it was Dominic's?"

"Yes. He couldn't accept it. It shamed him. Infuriated him. Looking at me pissed him off. I think I was the ultimate reminder of his disgrace."

"How long did he know before you left?"

"A month. He gave me an ultimatum. Abort the baby or lose everything."

"Abortion? Papa?" He was a devout Catholic. As old school as they came.

She nodded, her eyes glistening again. "I couldn't do that." She glanced up the stairs. "I'm so glad I didn't."

"Does Franco Benedetti know?"

"No. Dominic never told him. In fact, we stopped seeing each other as soon as I found out I was pregnant. Well, it trickled to a stop. But things were different then. He sent money, though, after I left."

"Well, isn't he a prince?"

"We were both kids, Lucia, and I've forgiven him. You don't have to, but this is between him and me."

"Does Effie know?"

She shook her head. "No one does."

"Well, I think Salvatore may." She opened her mouth, but I continued. "He and Roman suspected it was Luke, and Roman had DNA tests done."

"Fuck."

"When it came back that Luke couldn't be the father, Roman, who apparently had his suspicions, used his own DNA to test against it. Traces matched, and he's running Dominic's now."

"My fucking uncle is always sticking his big fucking nose where it doesn't belong." Dominic leaned against the entrance to the kitchen eating a sandwich, not bothering to hide the fact he was eavesdropping. "Not that it fucking matters. Not anymore."

Isabella stood, suddenly fuming, and went to him. "Was it you? Did you order the hit on Luke?"

He walked around her, biting off another piece, chewing like he didn't have a care in the world. "I didn't realize you *loved* him," he sneered.

She grabbed his arm, making him turn to face her. "We had an agreement! Goddamn you, we had a fucking agreement!"

"You're the one who wanted him involved."

"I couldn't meet with them, you know that!"

"Meet with who?" I asked.

They both looked at me as if they were surprised I still stood there.

"The Pagani family. Paul Jr., the old man's son and wannabe successor," Dominic filled in, stuffing the last of his sandwich into his mouth. "Fucking asshole."

"Old school. They won't deal with a woman," Isabella said.

"Deal with a woman over what?"

"What I told you when I first came to Salvatore's house."

"What, starting another war? Reclaiming our place as what, the biggest and baddest? The family who sheds the most blood? Izzy, what are you doing? I don't want this. You can't want it."

"I did, at first." She dropped into a chair. "But now, after what happened? After I saw him like that, Luke hooked up to too many machines to count, barely alive? Jesus, how could we..."

She stopped and turned toward Dominic, then stood and went to him. She poked a finger into his chest.

"Did you order the fucking shooting? Did you order them to kill Luke?"

"You're starting to bore me. What happened to my vengeful little bitch?"

"Fuck you, Dominic."

"Fuck you, Isabella." He took her glass and finished it before slamming it down on the coffee table. "You may be over it, but I'm not. No way I'm standing by and letting my father hand everything over to my half-wit brother. No. Fucking. Way."

The door flew open right then, and Salvatore burst in, his face a mask of fury as he slammed Dominic against the closest wall, his forearm crushing his neck. "How the fuck did you get in here?"

Dominic shoved him back and chuckled. "Check inside the house before you plant guards outside it, dumbass."

"Mommy?"

Effie's voice had all of us turning toward the stairs. The fighting had woken her up. She stood there, clutching her teddy bear and watching us.

"Honey!" Isabella ran up to her and took her in her arms. "Uncle Luke is going to be okay, baby!"

"He is?"

"He is."

"I'm so glad. Can we go see him?"

"He's still sleeping, but soon. I'll take you to him, and you can give him all those cookies you made."

"They're delicious, Effie," Dominic yelled up.

Salvatore's stood at Dominic's side, hands fisted.

"Thanks, Dominic."

Effie's relaxed familiarity with Dominic

surprised me and, when I glanced at Salvatore, I saw that it surprised him as well.

"It's late," Isabella said over her shoulder. "Go home." She turned and walked up the stairs with Effie.

"Why was everyone yelling?" I heard Effie asking her mom as their voices disappeared down the hall. I didn't hear my sister's answer.

"Well, she always was good at dismissing anyone she had no use for," Dominic bit out.

"Fuck you. Dad's looking for you. Go home."

"You go home. And take your pretty little plaything with you before I decide to have a taste myself. Her sister was pretty good."

Salvatore reared up to punch him, but I grabbed his arm. "He's not worth it, Salvatore."

"Get out." Salvatore didn't look at me, but stood nose to nose with his brother.

"I wasn't planning on staying."

It was a moment before he walked out the front door.

Salvatore turned to me and took me into his arms.

"Are you okay? Did he hurt you?"

"I'm fine. He didn't do anything to me."

"He was right. I should have checked the house."

Salvatore stepped back and looked me over as if he wanted to see with his own eyes that Dominic hadn't hurt me.

"Stop. Nothing happened. And everything is out in the open now."

His eyes searched mine, and I touched his face with my hand.

"Take me home, Salvatore."

21

SALVATORE

Lucia sat silently beside me.

"What is it?" I asked after a few minutes.

"Effie is Dominic's daughter. Isabella confirmed it."

"I'm not surprised."

"They fell in love, Salvatore. They were young and just fell in love. You were right in what you thought. That's why Papa sent her away, disowning her. He gave her an ultimatum: abort or leave. She left."

I remained silent, understanding a little more of Isabella. I'd pegged her to be a hateful, power-hungry bitch. She might well be, but she was also stronger than I gave her credit for.

"Dominic was supposed to tell your father, but he never did."

I glanced at Lucia. "I can't say I'm surprised."

"He let her go all alone." Lucia looked off into the distance. "He sent her money, though." She rolled her eyes.

"Lucia." I don't know why I felt the need to defend Dominic. I wasn't, really; I just needed to explain how things were at our house. How my father was. "My father is a very domineering man. When we were kids, Sergio was the only one brave enough to stand up to him." She opened her mouth to speak, her expression unbelieving. "Wait. I'm not defending Dominic or what he did. I'm just telling you there is more to his story, another layer, like there is with your sister."

I'm not sure if she accepted that or not.

"Luke and Isabella, they're in love," she said, changing the subject.

"I heard he's out of surgery, and that he's going to make it."

"I'm so relieved."

"There are still too many questions, Lucia. This isn't over."

"Who shot Luke?"

I shook my head. "Unclear. Luke was working with the younger Pagani, Paul Jr. His father forbade any interaction once he found out what his son was up to."

"I think Dominic is more involved than you know, Salvatore."

"What do you mean?"

"He and Isabella, I think they have been working together. She said they had an agreement."

Fuck.

"I think she's wondering if Dominic ordered Luke's shooting."

"So my little brother is working with Isabella DeMarco and Paul Pagani to bring down his own family?"

Our gazes locked, but neither of us said more.

As we pulled up to the tall gates of the house, I fished my phone out of my pocket and dialed Roman.

"What are you doing?" Lucia asked.

Roman answered.

"Where are you?" I asked.

"At your father's. The last of the family is just leaving."

"Are Natalie and Jacob there?"

"Just got here. She's pissed."

"Well, don't unpack her."

"What do you mean?"

"I'm calling a family meeting. It's an emergency. I want you to bring Natalie and Jacob to my house. And I want my father and Dominic here."

"What?" Lucia asked.

"What meeting?" Roman asked. "What's going on?"

"Tomorrow morning, I want a second meeting

with you, my father, Dominic, both Paul Pagani Sr. and Jr., and Isabella DeMarco. I want you to arrange it."

"Izzy?" Lucia asked, her eyes wide as I pulled the car to a stop at the front door.

"I'll give you an hour to get the family over here. Call the others for tomorrow morning. Seven o'clock. That should give them enough time to get here. This is going to end."

"Let's meet with the family first and discuss this, Salvatore. I think it would be wise for us to—"

"This is fucking ending, Uncle. Period."

I disconnected the call and turned to Lucia.

"Salvatore, you can't involve my sister."

"She's already involved, Lucia. She involved herself."

"No, I won't allow it!"

"You won't *allow* it?" I asked, getting out of the car and going around to her side. She'd already swung the door open and had her crutches on the ground, trying to climb out. I took the crutches in one hand and lifted her out with the other.

"Put me down. I can do this."

"I don't have time for this, Lucia."

"I said put me down!"

"Christ. You are the most pigheaded..." I set her down, and she leaned on me until she could get the crutches under her. "Let's go inside."

"You want my sister in with that room full of killers?"

"It will be a peaceful meeting." We entered the house, and I closed the front door behind us. "This is my house. I make the rules." I dialed another number on my phone. Once it started to ring, I covered the mouthpiece and turned back to Lucia. "Go upstairs to your room. You'll wait for me there."

"I am not a goddamned child!"

"Then stop acting like one."

Marco answered the call. He was still at the hospital. "Yes?"

"I need you back at the house. Arrange for two men to stay at the hospital. I'm calling a meeting for tomorrow morning. I need more men here. We'll have the Pagani father and son along with Isabella DeMarco. The Paganis will bring their own guard. I'm calling for no weapons, but I want the manpower here."

"I'm on it."

"Thank you." I could trust Marco to take care of things every time.

"You already sound like you're the boss of the family," Lucia taunted, still standing there, not having moved an inch.

I checked the time and tucked my phone into my pocket before turning to her. I looked her over, her dress rumpled, her eyes looking a little tired, but she was still too damn pretty.

"You need some time?" I asked, closing the space between us. "With me?" Sliding a hand to her waist, I tugged her close.

"Salvatore, this isn't—"

"Shh." I kissed her mouth and took one of the crutches away while the other one slipped out from under her arm as she wrapped it around my neck. "Let's go upstairs."

She gasped when I lifted her, cradling her in my arms. I carried her up to my bedroom. I sat her on the bed and tugged her dress over her head before pushing her to lie on her back. After stripping off my shirt, jeans, and briefs—all while Lucia watched with rapidly darkening eyes—I slid her panties over her hips and off her legs. I brought them to my nose and inhaled deeply.

"Salvatore!" She tried to tug them away, but I held them just out of reach.

"I like your smell," I said, leaning over her to kiss her, swallowing her moan in my mouth. She tasted so sweet, so innocent. I dragged my mouth from hers and trailed kisses down over her jaw and to her throat, across her collarbone and down to one breast, then the other, drawing out the nipples, making her cry out when I bit just a little harder than she liked.

I ran my tongue down the center of her chest and tickled her belly button before sliding it lower. I settling myself between her legs to take her clit into my mouth.

Lucia sighed heavily.

"You taste fucking amazing."

She curled her fingers into my hair and tugged. "Wait."

"Why?" I asked, looking up at her, her scent intoxicating.

"I want to taste you." She pushed herself up on her elbows. "Please."

I nodded and lifted her slightly, lying on my back and setting her on my hips so she straddled me. "Does it hurt?" I asked.

"Huh?" She seemed confused.

"Your ankle?"

She shook her head.

With my hands on her hips, I guided her folds over my cock.

"I want to taste you," she said.

"Patience." I smiled, liking her greedy, a little dirty. I'd corrupt her, and I'd make sure she loved every minute of it. "Turn around, and put your knees on either side of my face."

She hesitated only for a moment before turning, presenting me with her beautiful ass, then, her gorgeous, dripping cunt just over my face. She lowered herself to her elbows, and I pulled her to me, pausing to bite my lip when she flicked her little wet tongue over the tip of my cock before sealing her lips around it.

"Fuck, baby." I brought her to my face, tickling her with the little bit of stubble I needed to shave off. I dipped my thumb into her wet cunt before sliding it up to her asshole and pressing there, not penetrating, not yet, only holding it there as I tickled her clit with my tongue while she went to work on my cock.

I'd only ever been with experienced women. Having Lucia's innocent mouth on my cock made me heady. What she lacked in experience, she made up for with lustful enthusiasm: sucking my cock, licking it, taking me to the point she gagged, all while I teased then sucked her clit and slid another finger into her cunt while my thumb kept its pressure on her ass. She arched her back, moaning, as she worked me with her hand, like she'd watched me do, and sucked. My cock swelled even thicker. When my release was moments away, I closed my mouth around her clit and sucked hard, penetrating her ass with my finger as I did. She cried out, the sound muffled by my thick, throbbing cock, and she stilled when I came, emptying into her mouth while she throbbed around my finger, pressing herself into my face, squeezing every ounce of pleasure from my tongue.

A moment later, Lucia lay beside me spent, her hair splayed out on the pillow, some of it falling on my face. She turned to me and slid one leg between mine.

"I liked that," she said, kissing me.

"I'm glad, because I'll want your little mouth around me often." I checked my watch. They'd be here in twenty minutes. All I wanted to do was hold her, stay here with her, but I had to take care of business. "Go to sleep, Lucia." I climbed out of bed and covered her with the blanket.

She shook her head and rose up on an elbow.

"My sister, Salvatore."

"She'll be fine. But if she orchestrated Jacob's kidnapping, she'll need to answer for that."

"You're not going to let anyone hurt her."

It wasn't a question, but I answered it anyway. "No. I'll keep her safe. My intention is to keep everyone safe and end this."

"I want to be there with her."

"I want you to stay out of family business."

"My sister is my family."

I shook my head, my tone harder when I spoke. "Your sister is in over her head, and I want her out of it too. Can I trust you to stay here, or do I have to bind you?" I needed her to know this conversation was over.

She glanced at the restraints, perhaps remembering how easily I could do just what I said.

"You make me really mad," she said.

"Mad I can handle. I just need you safe."

She nodded.

"I need to have a shower. Stay."

"Can I at least call Izzy?"

"That's okay by me." I tossed her my phone and walked into the bathroom to have a quick shower before everyone got there. It was going to be a long night.

I WASN'T surprised when Dominic didn't show up.

I also wasn't surprised to find Lucia making her way down the stairs, dressed, clumsily working her crutches.

My father and Roman stood in the foyer watching her, my father looking at her with tired eyes rather that the contempt he normally showed. I walked up to her with a look that said I'd deal with her later, but when I tried to take her crutches and carry her down, she refused.

"I'm not an invalid. I just need to get used to these. Besides, my ankle can take a little weight." She flinched as she demonstrated putting a bit of weight on it.

"Pigheaded."

I walked the steps with her to make sure she didn't fall. By the time we got down, Natalie walked into the house with a sleeping Jacob in her arms.

"Father, Roman, why don't you go ahead into the dining room."

They both nodded and left. Everyone was tired.

Rainey went to Natalie and took the bag off her shoulder. I'd woken her to prepare a room.

"Natalie, I'm sorry to keep you and Jacob up so late, but I thought you'd be more comfortable here," I said.

"I'd be most comfortable in my own house," she said, glaring at my father's receding back.

Lucia giggled, then had the presence of mind to cover it up with a cough.

"This is Lucia," I said. "Lucia, Natalie. And my nephew Jacob."

Jacob stirred, opening his eyes then closing them again. I watched how Lucia looked at Natalie and saw Natalie with renewed eyes. I'd known her for so long, and she'd been so much like a sister to me from day one that I sometimes forgot how attractive she was, even with her long dark hair wound into a bun, wearing no makeup, and dressed in an old pair of pajamas.

"Nice to meet you," Lucia said. She then peeked at Jacob. "You probably want to get him to bed."

"And me too. It's nice to meet you. Salvatore's told me about you."

They both glanced at me.

"Should I be worried?" Lucia asked.

Natalie smiled and shook her head. "Not given the way he looks at you," Natalie said with a wink.

"Why don't you go up with Natalie and help her get herself and Jacob settled," I said to Lucia. I then pulled her in close. "And this time, stay up there," I whispered, squeezing her ass so she knew she'd pay if she came down again.

"Fine. I don't want to be around your father anyway."

I didn't offer to help her upstairs this time. She'd refuse anyway. Instead, I went into the dining room and closed the doors.

"Where's Dominic?" I asked.

"Don't know," my father answered.

"I thought he'd come home," I said.

"Why would you think that?" my father asked.

"Because I talked with him. He was at Isabella DeMarco's house."

My father's lips tightened. "What the fuck was he doing there?"

It wasn't my place to tell him about Effie. I'd let Dominic do that when he was ready. Strange. I realized just then how difficult these last five years must have been for my brother. He'd abandoned his child and a woman he'd at one point cared about all out of fear of my father's disapproval, his wrath. He'd wanted his acceptance, his approval, as much as I had. Maybe he still did. He was as much a puppet to my domineering father as I was.

Roman cleared his throat.

"Why do I get the feeling you two know more than you're letting on?" my father asked.

"Let me make a call. I think I may know where he is," Roman said, standing.

"It's important he's here," I said. "Critical, actually."

He nodded and made the call. My father and I waited in awkward silence until Roman returned. Rainey knocked and entered with a tray holding a bottle of whiskey and several glasses. I poured for everyone and sent her to bed. She'd need to be up early to greet the remainder of our guests. It was only a few hours before they got here.

"I know who was behind things."

My father drank his glass of whiskey then pulled the bottle over to pour a second.

"Isabella DeMarco and Dominic have been working together with Pagani's son, Paul Jr. Luke was just the front man, acting on her behalf."

"I knew that fucking bitch would be trouble. Only good DeMarco is a dead DeMarco," my father said.

"That's enough," I said more calmly than I expected I could. "I called this meeting to put an end to this stupidity. This feud that's torn your own family apart. When will it be enough for you?"

"When I'm dead."

"Don't push me."

"Gentlemen, we're on the same side," Roman said, standing between us with a hand on both our shoulders. "I'm having someone pick Dominic up and bring him here."

"Where is he?" I asked.

"He has a bar he likes to go to."

Roman didn't expound on that, and I left it alone.

"He's got some explaining to do, that fucking bastard," Franco said. "Cancel the meeting. I'll deal with my son myself. You deal with the DeMarco cunt, and Pagani will deal with his son." He rose to his feet. "I'm fucking tired. You called me here for this bullshit?"

"Sit down," I spoke quietly, not rising but remaining where I sat, feeling more in control than I ever had in my life. I knew what I wanted, what I needed to do. It would all truly end tonight.

"Be careful, son," he said, but he lowered himself back down into his chair.

"We're dealing with this publicly. We're forgiving what's happened thus far and calling a truce."

"You're not boss yet, Salvatore. I decide, not you."

"I already decided, old man. Let it be."

"Franco," Roman started.

My father kept his eyes on me, but listened.

"Let's do this Salvatore's way and end this. It's grown too far out of proportion," Roman said.

"And how do you propose to get Dominic to agree?" Franco asked.

That was where we were all at a loss. He couldn't be given a property to manage, not as volatile as he was. He'd bring war wherever he went. He needed to be controlled, but I didn't know how. I was truly at a loss when it came to Dominic.

"I will talk to him," I said. I'd give him one more chance, talk to him like maybe I should have been talking to him all along. Maybe he'd have come to me five years ago when he was in trouble if I'd been a better brother to him.

By the time Dominic arrived, it was almost five o'clock in the morning. He stank of liquor and stumbled in making a lot of noise, propped up by two men who worked for my father.

"You called, brother?"

The lids of his eyes were drooping, and the bruises I'd given him earlier had colored a dark purple.

"Summoning me to your grand estate?" he said, slurring his words as he gestured around the house.

"Get him in the fucking shower."

"I'll make coffee," Roman said.

Marco had also arrived in the meantime, and men were being arranged throughout the property. We had about two hours before everyone would get here. According to Roman, Pagani Sr., wasn't surprised by the call, which meant he'd already talked to his son. Good. The less surprises, the better.

Isabella was a different story. Roman had spoken with her and told her the reason for the meeting. Maybe it was vanity, a feeling of being acknowledged as head of the DeMarco family, because for all intents and purposes, she was. We just underestimated the DeMarco family's level of activity. It was stupid on our part. Isabella would be here bright and early, as anxious as me to put this behind her, now that she realized what she could have lost.

I had Dominic taken to a bedroom downstairs, knowing he'd raise hell wherever he was just because he was Dominic and he was piss drunk. Roman remained with my father while I went to check on Dominic's progress.

"You're not boss yet," was the greeting he threw at me when I walked into the bedroom.

"You at least smell a little better," I said, tossing one of my dress shirts at him. "Put this on." I'd changed too, wearing a suit minus the jacket.

"You want me looking respectable for those assholes?" he asked, but he took it.

"I know about Effie," I said, sitting down.

He met my eyes but remained silent.

"You haven't told anyone all these years?"

"What, that I knocked up a DeMarco? All while father hands you one on a silver fucking platter." He shook his head in disgust. "You're the golden boy, aren't you? First it was Sergio, then you. Fuck Dominic."

I wanted to punch him but had to remind myself why he was being defensive. "I'm sorry I didn't make it easier for you to talk to me."

"Don't get sentimental on me now." He said, then returned his attention to buttoning his shirt before continuing. "Does father know?"

"No. Only Roman and I. That's how it'll stay unless you decide to tell him."

He nodded, and I knew it was as close to an actual thank-you that I would get.

"Tell me about Luke DeMarco's shooting."

Nothing.

"Isabella and you were working together with Pagani, Jr."

He snorted. "He is a colossal fuckup. Fucking dimwit."

"That we can agree on. They'll be here soon, Dominic. We're all going to be in a room together. I would rather know the truth now, from you."

A knock came on the door.

"Sir."

It was Marco. "Come in."

He opened the door and glanced at Dominic but spoke to me. "Isabella DeMarco is here."

I checked my watch. "She's early." It was barely six a.m. "Does Lucia know?"

Marco gave me a short nod.

"Of course she does. Where are they?"

"Your study."

"All right. I'll be right there. Make sure they stay in there until I get there."

"I will."

He closed the door. I turned back to Dominic, who'd finished dressing and was now combing his hair, studying me.

"Last chance to tell me everything."

"Go get everyone under control, brother. I'll see you when it's time for the meeting."

"Suit yourself." I walked out of the room and directly to my study.

Lucia and Isabella sat on the couch talking in whispers when I walked in. Lucia at least had the grace to give me a meek smile.

"You shouldn't be here," I said to her.

"She's my sister, Salvatore."

"Why do I feel like I'm hitting a wall at every turn?" I asked.

"For once, I'm taking his side, Lucia. This is my business, and I don't want you involved," Isabella said, standing.

"I'm not letting you face those men alone."

"She's not alone. I will be there with her," I said.

"Luce, I did this. I brought this on us. I had Dominic kidnap Jacob. I ultimately was responsible for Luke being shot." She turned to me. "I'm so sorry about Jacob. I just, I wanted to scare Franco. I didn't even think about Natalie. It was all about sending a message to Franco. Everything. And every time I look at Effie's face and hold her in my arms, I keep thinking about Natalie. How she must have felt. How scared Jacob must have felt. I'm sorry. I was wrong."

Lucia squeezed her hand.

I nodded. "Is it over?"

"Yes. For me. But I'm not sure how much control I have or ever had. The burglaries—we'd talked about it but hadn't decided on anything. And Luke... I hope Dominic didn't order that."

"I don't know myself, but we'll soon find out."

Before I could say more, loud voices—two men yelling—interrupted us. Dominic and my father.

"Stay here," I said, rushing to the door and out. They were in the dining room, Roman, my father, and Dominic.

"You betray your own family!" Franco yelled, his face hot with fury.

"What was in it for me? What was ever in it for me? Why in hell did you even have me?" Dominic countered, all drunkenness having left his system, the heat of his anger perhaps having burnt it out. "After Sergio died, it all went to Salvatore. What about me?"

"You're the youngest. I can't fucking help that."

"The backup to the backup."

"You're stupid if that's what you think!"

"So worried about your grandson. Everything is about Sergio. His boy. Taking care of Jacob."

"Like I would take care of yours!"

"Really?"

"Everyone calm the fuck down." I walked into the room, but neither my father nor Dominic noticed my arrival.

Isabella walked in behind me, her gaze locked on Dominic. When my father stalked up to her, she stood taller, and I stood beside her.

"You stupid little bitch," he started.

"Stop! All of you! What is this, fucking preschool? We're all going to sit down, and we're all going to talk."

"Salvatore."

Roman said my name and walked into the room. I just then realized he'd been absent.

"I just got off the phone with Paul Pagani, Sr. Neither he nor his son will be here after all. He's already addressed his son's responsibility and taken care of it. Jr. won't be a problem, he assures us. The moneys that were taken have been returned, and he's given his word his allegiance is to the head of the Benedetti family."

I nodded. "Then this will truly be a family meeting."

"Apart from this whore," Franco muttered.

The tension in the room was palpable. No one

moved to sit, and it looked like either Dominic or my father would explode at any minute.

I sighed, shaking my head, but before I could speak, Dominic drew a pistol and held it at his side.

"She's the mother of your other grandchild, old man, but you're too fucking stupid to see it, aren't you?"

"Dominic, give me the gun," I said, shadowing him as he moved around the table to where my father stood, but it was like he couldn't hear me. Couldn't see me. Couldn't see anyone but our father.

"I was too much of a coward to tell you she was pregnant with my baby. *Mine*, you stupid fuck."

"Dominic," I started, cautious.

Franco watched him, glancing at Isabella for a moment as he finally understood. But Dominic wasn't finished.

"You never cared about me. All your love went to Sergio."

"That's not true," our father said. "He was just firstborn."

"Fuck firstborn! This isn't the fucking Dark Ages. It doesn't fucking matter."

"You betrayed your family. I accepted you as my own, and you betrayed me."

All heads snapped to my father then.

Roman approached Franco and whispered something into his ear. I turned to Dominic to see his face as he slowly understood what was being said.

"No, I'll tell this bastard who he is." My father shoved Roman away. "Son of a fucking foot soldier who thinks he should be head of *my* family."

"You're lying," Dominic said, raising the pistol.

"Dominic, give me the gun," I said, mirroring every move he made.

I heard a gasp at the door, and Isabella moved, shielding Lucia, who'd just walked in.

"Dominic, please, give me the gun."

"You all thought your mother was a saint. Died a martyr." Franco snorted. "You didn't know her very well. None of you did."

"You're a fucking liar, old man," Dominic spewed.

"She whored herself out."

"He's not worth it," I said to my brother. "He's lying, and he's not worth it." But it was like he couldn't hear me at all.

"Don't you dare talk about her like that." Dominic wiped his face with the back of the hand that held the pistol.

"Like your bitch," Franco said, gesturing to Isabella.

That was it, it was finished. Dominic aimed, my father's face changed to one of surprise, of shock. I don't know if any of us thought he'd do it. Thought he'd actually pull the trigger.

I grabbed Dominic's arm, but he cocked the gun. My father's mouth opened, another taunt leaving it, pushing Dominic to the breaking point.

Gunshots never sound the way you think they should. They're louder, deadlier, and a hell of a lot faster than in the movies.

Lucia's scream was all I heard. Everything else was background noise. She drowned it all out with her scream.

I lunged between them, intending to push my father out of the way, to save him. To save Dominic from doing something he'd regret for the rest of his life.

But it never worked that way in real life either. Never like the movies. The heroes didn't walk away, arms raised, triumphant.

More often, they got hurt.

They got killed.

I did knock my father out of the way. Landing on him was softer than the damned marble floors I always hated. A second later, and I'd have been too late.

Or maybe I already was.

Lucia screamed again, dropping to her knees, her hands bloodied, her face splattered with it. Her crutches clanked to the floor near my head as she grabbed my face, looking over her shoulder, shoving someone away. Her tears kept dropping on my face, and she kept wiping them away again and again, talking, I think. Her mouth moved, but no sound came. No sound. Only pain. Only fire in my side.

When I put my hand to the place, it felt warm and wet, and when I reached to touch her pretty, pretty face, I covered it in red, smearing it down over her jaw, her neck, down until she faded from view. The last thing I felt was her hair tickling my face, her body pressing against mine, the movements desperate.

22

LUCIA

"Salvatore, no!"

I held his face with one hand and pressed my other hand to the place on his side that wouldn't stop bleeding. I kissed him. Kissed him and kissed him. When I tried to push the hair back from his forehead, I left blood in its place. His blood. God, there was so much of it. Too much.

"Don't die."

He hadn't promised me that. He'd made me three promises, but he'd never promised me he wouldn't die.

I'd never asked him to promise that. I'd never...

"Don't die," I whispered just to him.

He was too still, and when my sister touched my shoulder, and I looked up at her through the blur the haze of my tears caused, I sucked in a trembling breath. Her face, the look in her eyes, telling me it was bad.

"There's a helicopter on its way to take him to the hospital," she whispered, kneeling down beside me, holding me when I turned my attention back to him.

They would take him away. They would take him away, and I would never see him again. Why did they do that? Why did they take them away? How could you hold an empty space? How could you say good-bye?

My lip trembled. I bent down to his face, his beautiful face so pale, so still. My hair made a curtain between us and the room, and I listened for his breath, tried to feel it on my skin, feel its soft warmth. I wanted him to call me pigheaded again.

I wanted to hear him telling me he would keep everyone safe.

He had. He'd kept that promise.

Why hadn't I made him promise to keep himself safe?

"I'm sorry," I whispered.

"Lucia."

My sister said my name, but I ignored her.

"I should have made you promise," I said, tears rolling from my face onto his. I smeared the blood with them, trying to clean him, remembering then that he had made one promise to me he hadn't yet kept. "You have to wake up, Salvatore," I stated, gaining some strength. He kept his promises. He wouldn't not. "You promised me you'd give me what I wanted. The life I wanted. You promised. You have to wake up now."

"Lucia," Isabella said again.

"Go away," I told her, still cleaning his face with my tears.

"Ma'am."

Other hands were on me, another voice was talking to me.

"Lucia, they're here. They're going to take him to the hospital. You have to let them see Salvatore."

I kept one hand on Salvatore's chest, trying not to think about the fact it was still. I looked up at the men, at the room around me, and I leaned away, letting them look at Salvatore. Letting them start their work.

Two other men lifted Franco Benedetti onto a stretcher. Roman looked at all of us, his face one of shock, blood splatters marring it and ruining his perfect suit.

"Ma'am, we need to take them now."

"Which hospital?" Isabella asked.

"Bellevue."

"Come on," Isabella said, dragging me to my feet.

"He's not dead?" I asked, confused.

The paramedic gave me a cautious look. "We'll do what we can for him."

"Let's go," Isabella said again. "We need to get to the hospital. They'll be much faster with the chopper."

"What's happened?" Natalie asked from the doorway, her face crumpling when she saw Salvatore unconscious on the stretcher.

I looked around the room, searching for him, for Dominic. "Where is he?" I asked my sister. "Where is he?" Anger gave me strength, but my sister held fast to me.

"Salvatore got in the way between Dominic and his father," Isabella said to Natalie.

"Where the hell is Dominic?" I screamed to anyone who would answer.

"Let's go," Isabella said. "Salvatore needs you now."

That got my attention. I turned to her and nodded. I followed her to the front door, cursing the crutches and my damn ankle.

"He's so fucking stupid," I said to her as she drove too fast off the grounds.

"He wanted to save everyone," she modified.

"Why did they take Franco?"

"Heart attack."

A fresh onslaught of tears came, and I sucked in a loud breath. "He did it for nothing. He tried to save that horrible man for nothing."

Isabella took my hand and squeezed it, forcing me to look at her. "He's not dead yet. He needs you to believe in him, understand? You can't be weak now, not now, Lucia. He needs you."

I looked at her face. She looked much older than her twenty-two years all of a sudden, and her eyes— they held lifetimes of sadness inside them.

"How's Luke?" I asked, remembering.

She focused her attention back on the road. "No change."

"Where's Dominic?"

"He slipped out." She shook her head. "I saw his face. He just kept looking at Salvatore, lying at his feet. For so long, it was what he wanted, but then, when it happened…"

"Where is he?"

"His face, Lucia. I'd never seen him look like that before. Not ever."

But I didn't care about Dominic or what he felt or what his face looked like. I would kill him with my bare hands when I saw him.

My sister was right, though. Salvatore needed me now, and I would focus all my energy on him. He was a survivor. He would survive. He had to.

When we arrived at the hospital, he was in surgery. They'd brought him to the same unit where Luke had been.

Déjà vu.

Only this time, the doctor wouldn't talk to us. We weren't family.

"Fuck! I just want to know if he's alive!"

"Ma'am, you need to calm down," the doctor said.

"Lucia."

I heard a man's voice behind me. I turned to find Roman walking into the waiting room, his face cleaned of blood, although his shirt still had splatters of it.

"They're operating. There's nothing for them to tell." He turned to the doctor. "Add Lucia DeMarco to the list," he said. "Keep her updated on Salvatore Benedetti's condition."

The doctor nodded and made a note of what I assumed was my name and walked away.

"Thank you," I said to Roman.

He nodded and sat down. Defeat was the one word I would use to describe him in that moment.

"What about Franco?" Isabella asked.

"Stable"

"Of course. Of course he's stable while his son is in there possibly dying." I sank down into a chair, and Isabella wrapped her arms around me.

"Shh. Remember, you have to be strong. He needs you now more than ever."

I nodded, wiping away tears and snot.

We sat in the waiting room for a long time. Isabella excused herself to make some calls, to make sure the sitter could stay with Effie longer, to check on Luke. Roman and I remained silent, lost in our own misery. All the while, my ankle throbbed.

"He should never have goaded Dominic like that. He'd sworn never to do it."

I turned to Roman. "What are you talking about?" I hadn't been in the room, not until it was almost the very end.

Roman glanced at me. "Franco isn't Dominic's father, but he loved my sister. Loved her enough to keep it hushed. To act like Dominic was his son all along. He had no right to tell him like this."

"You're worried about Dominic? He deserves to be the one in there, not Salvatore."

He met my gaze. "No one should be in there. Period."

"I may be a horrible person, but I don't agree."

He sighed. "You're nowhere near a horrible person."

He got up and left the room. I remained where I was. Isabella stayed with me until, almost four hours later, a doctor finally came out, looking for next of kin.

"That's me," I said, although it wasn't quite me. "Lucia DeMarco."

He checked his sheet of paper. Satisfied, he looked back at me. The space of that second stretched to an hour, and I dreamed the worst, thought I should prepare myself to hear it, but how did one prepare to hear something that terrible?

"Mr. Benedetti is an incredibly lucky man. And his will to live is tremendous."

I smiled, feeling a thousand pounds lift from me. "He's going to make it?"

"He shouldn't have, not given the route the bullet took, but he is. He's asking for you."

"I can see him?"

"Only for a few minutes. He needs to rest. We'll sedate him, but he's insisting on seeing you first."

"He's pigheaded," I said, wiping away fresh tears. I followed the doctor, a joy filling me that I'd never in my life felt before. Never knew possible.

I walked into the private room, where machines beeped and doctors and nurses worked around the bed where Salvatore lay, eyes closing, then opening, turning his head away from the nurse who tried to attach yet another tube.

"Salvatore!" I hobbled over to him and took the seat someone pushed behind me.

He opened his eyes and gave me a weak smile. He kept opening and closing his hand, and I placed mine inside it. He stilled then, lay back, and shut his eyes. I sat there and watched, not sure if he held my hand or I held his, not sure it mattered anymore. I watched him sleep, counted the needles in his arms, watched them inject something into the tube of one of the IVs.

"He will be out for a while. You can go home and get some rest. We'll call you when he's awake."

"No," I said, not taking my eyes off him. "I'm staying here."

"Ma'am…"

I felt Salvatore's tiny attempt at squeezing my hand and turned to the doctor. "I'm just as pigheaded, just so you know. I'm not leaving."

23

SALVATORE

I probably dreamed Lucia calling herself pigheaded, but it made me smile all the same. And every time I opened my eyes, there she was, sitting by my side. At first, she still had blood on her. My blood. Then she looked like she'd showered and changed. I saw Roman too, but she was my constant.

She'd remembered what I'd said. What I'd promised her. I vaguely recalled her voice, telling me I hadn't yet kept the promise to give her the life she wanted.

I had changed rooms. I knew it from the way the light came in the window. I wasn't sure how long I'd been in the hospital until finally, I opened my eyes, feeling a little less groggy, and the things around me didn't seem so like a mirage.

Was it a mirage? Was Lucia a mirage?

"Hey."

I looked up at her beautiful, smiling face. She still sat in the same place, holding my hand, watching me.

"Hey." It felt strange to speak.

"How do you feel?"

"Like I've been run over by a truck."

"Do you remember what happened?"

My mind traveled back to that morning. My father, Roman, Isabella, and I in my dining room. Dominic. Dominic with a gun. My father telling him he wasn't his son. Calling our mother a whore.

Something beeped, and the door opened. A nurse rushed inside.

I took a deep breath, and the beeping leveled, but the nurse gave me a warning look.

"It's good to see you're awake, Mr. Benedetti, but you need to stay calm, or we'll have to sedate you again."

I opened my mouth to tell her to fuck off, but Lucia squeezed my hand and spoke to her.

"It's okay. I'll make sure he stays calm."

"Thank you."

The nurse left, and I looked back at Lucia.

"They called you pigheaded," she said. "Well, I did actually, but they agreed."

I smiled, but it hurt to speak or move. And as

much as I wanted to keep looking at her, my eyelids began to droop.

"Go to sleep. I'll be here when you wake up."

I did, unable not to, and when I woke next, I was in a different room yet again, this one less sterile-looking. Lucia again sat by my bed, talking to her sister, who sat on another chair, and Effie, who was watching TV with the sound muted.

"He's awake," Isabella said.

Lucia turned to me. "Finally. I didn't mean sleep for three more days."

This was surreal. "I want to sit up."

"Bossy already," she teased and handed me a remote control. "Here, push this button. Stop if it's painful."

I pushed, and the bed moved. Effie came over to watch, entranced by the operation.

"Wow! Can I get one of those, Mommy?"

"No," came Isabella's voice.

I smiled and came to a stop when the slight throb at my side became painful. "How long has it been?"

"Almost two weeks."

"I baked you some M&M cookies" Effie said, coming over with a tin. "They helped Luke, and he's out of the hospital now. If you eat these, you'll be out soon too."

"That so?" I asked.

Lucia took the cookie Effie had fished out for me. "I'll give it to him after his dinner, okay? We don't want to spoil his first proper hospital meal, after all."

I made a face, and so did Effie. She then turned to me. "Grilled cheese is the only safe thing," she whispered. "And no matter what you do, do not eat the pea soup."

I laughed but had to quit; it hurt too much.

"All right," Isabella said, taking Effie's hand. "Time for us to go." She looked at me. "I'm glad you didn't die."

"Thank you?" I guessed.

Lucia walked them out then returned to me. "Effie's a hoot," she said.

"Yes. And I'm staying away from that pea soup. I trust that kid." It grew quiet as our smiles faded.

"I thought you were dead. I couldn't feel you breathe, and you were so still. And the blood..."

Her eyes filled with tears.

I reached up to touch her face, although my arm felt sore even with that small movement. "I'm not that easy to kill off."

"I kept the clothes I was wearing."

"Huh?"

She shrugged a shoulder. "With the blood."

I must have made a face when I got what she was saying.

"I know, it's creepy."

"You can throw those away now. I'm not going anywhere. I have a promise to keep."

She smiled.

"Where's Dominic?"

She shook her head. "No one knows. He disappeared after that night. Good riddance."

"He's not my father's son."

"I know."

"He wasn't trying to kill me. You know that, right?"

"I don't care, Salvatore. He almost did."

I decided to drop it for now. "My father?"

"He had a heart attack, but he's fine. He's home already. Roman's been running the show apparently. Probably waiting for you to get well enough to take over." She snorted, her face changing, darkening.

"He had a heart attack?"

"I guess seeing one son shoot another was too much even for his cold heart."

A knock came on the door. We both turned to see Roman peek his head in.

"I heard he was awake."

"Come in," Lucia said and stepped aside.

"Where are your crutches?" Salvatore asked me.

"You've been out a while. Long enough, my ankle's mostly fine."

"You should use them—"

"Bossy."

"I need to talk to you," Roman said to me, glancing at Lucia.

"I'll wait outside," Lucia said, picking up her bag.

"You can stay," I told her.

She shook her head. "It's fine. I'll get some coffee."

"Thank you," Roman said.

Once she was gone, he sat in the seat she'd occupied and took a folder out of his briefcase.

"How are you feeling?"

"I've been better. What's going on? Fill me in."

"You know about your father's heart attack?"

I nodded.

"Well, Franco is home and recovering. He's not doing well, though, Salvatore."

I didn't reply.

"He wanted to come and see you, but the doctor advised him against it."

"Okay." Was he telling me that so my feelings wouldn't be hurt?

"He knows you saved his life."

"I didn't do it for him. I did it because I knew my brother would regret it for the rest of his."

"You have every right to feel the way you feel."

"I don't need you to tell me that."

He inhaled a deep breath.

"Where's Dominic?"

"I don't know. He disappeared after the shooting.

No one knows. He didn't go home, didn't pack, didn't take anything with him. Just left."

"Is it true?"

Roman nodded.

"And you knew?"

"I'm the only one apart from your mother and father who knew. He regrets having told him."

"He should."

I cursed my father for having told Dominic like that. What purpose did it serve? It would only wound Dominic. Perhaps irreparably.

"Franco is no longer able to manage the family, the businesses, anything, Salvatore. I've been doing it until you're recovered."

We studied each other for a long time. I just couldn't tell what my uncle was looking for.

"I have papers here, things I want to go over."

A small knock came on the door. Lucia opened it.

"Not now," I said to him. "Just take care of everything for now."

"I can come back," Lucia said.

"No, you stay. Roman, thanks for your visit."

Roman took his dismissal with grace and left. Lucia sat back down in the same chair.

"Coffee is so crappy here," she said, setting the untouched paper cup on the table nearby.

Before we had a chance to talk, though, the doctor walked in to look things over and told me I'd be home in three days' time. Lucia vacated her chair and stood back and watched, giving the doctor room. Every time I looked at her when she didn't know I was, I saw the worry on her face. My mind traveled back to what I'd told her. What I'd promised her. Freedom, as soon as I was boss. Freedom, once I knew she was safe. A quiet life. Happiness. I wanted it for everyone I loved. I wanted it especially for her.

24

LUCIA

Salvatore moved into a bedroom downstairs while he recovered. I slept beside him, taking care not to touch the still tender spot the bullet had ripped into. I knew he felt pain, but he insisted on less and less medication, saying he could manage it. Within a day of being home, he could walk on his own to the bathroom, although it wore him out.

"I hate this," he grumbled a week later after one of his visits to the bathroom. "I hate being weak."

I tucked the blanket up to his waist. "You're getting stronger every day."

"Not fast enough."

"You hate having someone else take care of you. You're so used to taking care of everyone and everything and being in charge of it all but can't stand to be in a position where you need others yourself."

He studied me, then looked beyond me to the waning light outside the window.

"Let's sit outside."

"I'll get your wheelchair." I'd already stood to unfold it. He hadn't used it except for the time they'd rolled him in here in it.

"No."

I looked back to find him rising on his own.

"Jesus, Salvatore, it'll only take longer if you don't take care—"

"I said no,"

He leveled his gaze on mine, giving me a glimpse of the man I knew him to be—rough and tough and sexy as hell.

He must have seen the change in me too, because his expression softened, and his gaze rolled over my body.

I swallowed, my nipples tightening, my belly fluttering. Just one look from him, and I shuddered.

"Okay," I said, clearing my throat. Then, without asking his permission, I opened the bedroom door and called out to Marco. "He's too stubborn to use the wheelchair, and I can't support his weight, so maybe you can walk with him."

Marco gave Salvatore a look then glanced back at me. What he saw in my face must have trumped what he saw in Salvatore's, because he put Salvatore's arm over his shoulder and held on to his waist.

"Come on, boss."

Salvatore shook his head. "You'll answer for that later," he told me.

"Is that another promise?" I gave him a dirty grin and walked ahead, taking my time, knowing he was watching my ass as I led the way out back.

Once Salvatore was settled, Marco left us. We sat quietly, watching the light dance along the surface of the swimming pool. Salvatore held my hand.

"I've been thinking," he said, then stopped.

I glanced at him, but he looked straight ahead.

"I'm going to hand it all over to Roman."

"What?" I didn't expect that.

Salvatore looked at me. "I only have one thing to do as boss, then I'm walking away."

One thing. I knew what that was. It was what I had wanted.

"You're free, Lucia. I'll talk to Roman tomorrow, destroy the contract, and draw up a new one, so they can't touch you or your family ever again. You'll be free of me, of all of us."

Free of him?

I watched his eyes. Soft again. Like they'd looked the day we'd been forced to sign that terrible piece of paper. Gentle. I'd been wrong when I'd thought he was like them. A monster. This was the real Salvatore. It had always been there, lying beneath the fear.

Only thing was, I didn't know if I wanted to be free of him at all anymore.

I cleared my throat. "I can't leave you alone while you're not yet recovered."

"I'll be fine," he said, then looked away from me again.

"Salvatore—"

We started to speak at once, but he won. "I'll make sure you have enough money to set yourself up, buy a house, take some time—"

I pulled my hand free of his. "I told you before. I don't need your money." I turned the back of my head to him in case he saw me wipe away a stupid tear.

We were back to this.

He picked up my hand and squeezed, making me look at him. If he saw my eyes were wet, he didn't mention it.

"I'm going to take care of you, whether you like it or not, so just accept it as a part of life."

"Do you know what you're going to do?" I asked, swallowing a lump in my throat, not sure what else to talk about, needing there not to be any silence between us because in that silence, I would fall apart.

"Sell this house. Move. Look for Dominic. I don't know."

"You're worried about him."

"Yeah. He needs someone now, after everything. Not sure he wants it to be me, but I'm going to try."

"Can you walk away from it, though? Can you just up and leave?"

"I'm going to." There was a long pause. "What about you? Where do *you* want to go?"

"My sister is putting the house up for sale. I think it's a good idea to start fresh. She, Luke, and Effie are looking at Florida." For a moment, I thought I would go too, but then the thought of being without him made me stop. Didn't I want this? Didn't I want my freedom?

Strange, how priorities shifted. I thought I'd always want revenge for what they had done to my family, but that had all slipped away. All the anger, the hate, it just wore me down to think about it, and now, it was gone.

"Salvatore," I started, but again, we spoke at once, our voices and gazes colliding.

"If you don't know…it will take some time to sell the house. Maybe you can stay…" He trailed off.

I nodded. "That would be good. Izzy and Luke need their space, and I can help you get the house ready and make sure you're—"

He took my face in his hand and drew it to himself to kiss me, swallowing up the empty words.

"I want to make love to you."

"The doctor said—"

"I need you, Lucia. I've needed you for so long."

25

SALVATORE

I kept my promise to Lucia. Roman came to the house the following morning and handed me the initial contract she and I had signed. I set it aside and had him draw up another one. This one forgave any and all debt any DeMarco owed any Benedetti, real or perceived, and the two families were no longer bound in any way. And it could not be overturned at any time in the future.

I signed it and had a copy sent to Isabella. I would deliver a copy to my father personally. This insane vendetta was finished. I ended it as one of the two things I did during my hours-long rule over the Benedetti family before I gave everything—the reign, the rule, the power—over to Roman.

It was another week before I could move back upstairs to my own bedroom and another month before I was fully healed. All that time, Lucia stayed with me, caring for me like I didn't remember ever being cared for by anyone apart from my mother.

I also saw Natalie and Jacob. She came to give me the news she too was moving away, along with her parents. She didn't trust anyone but me, and with Roman now taking over and Dominic somewhere out there, she didn't feel safe. She promised to keep in touch with me, though, and I let her go, let her take my nephew with her. I would miss them. It was another piece of Sergio that was gone, but I knew part of him would always be with me, no matter what.

As far as the house, it turned out I didn't have to put it on the market. An anonymous buyer bought it outright, furnished, within hours of my talking to a real-estate agent. We needed to be out within two weeks. I let Rainey go with a hefty bonus to tide her over until she found work. I didn't need to worry about Marco. He would go to work for my uncle. Lucia and I simply had to pack up our personal things, and we were free to truly walk away.

Those last two weeks in the house were strangely more bitter than sweet. Lucia would go to Florida, where her sister had already gone with Effie, while Luke took care of the selling of their house. I hadn't yet decided what I would do. I couldn't think about it for some reason. And I still had one more person to see before I could close this long chapter of my life.

"Can we take the Bugatti?" Lucia asked, a glint in her eye when we got to the garage.

"No." That was my baby, and she was insisting on driving 'considering my injuries.' "We can take the BMW."

She pouted but picked up the keys.

"It's not that I don't trust you driving it," I started, "although I don't. But the less bumpy the ride, the better."

"My driving is just fine."

"We'll see."

"You nervous?" she asked.

"About your driving?" I joked, but I knew what she meant.

She only glanced at me as she pulled out of the garage.

"Not nervous, just want it over. I know he's my father, and maybe it's wrong, but I don't feel anything close to love for him."

"Have you forgiven him?"

I thought about it. "For being a complete and utter failure where it counted?"

She shrugged a shoulder, but her gaze was serious. "Regret sucks, Salvatore."

I knew she still had some of that.

"I actually have, I think. The way he's chosen to live his life—well, look at him. He's alone. He'll die alone. Roman will be there for him, but not us. I don't feel any anger toward him anymore. It's like it's sated or something. Not because I'm happy he's alone. I'm not. But he made his bed, and I'm making my peace. It's all I can do."

"You're good, Salvatore."

Once we reached my father's house, I climbed out of the car. I held the envelope containing the new contract. It was symbolic, nothing else, but it was necessary for closure.

"Ready?"

Lucia wound her arm through mine. We'd gotten used to each other's company, but when she did things like this, touching me like this, it still felt strange, special. It made my heartbeat quicken.

"You don't have to go in there." I watched her; she watched the house.

"I want to be there with you, Salvatore," she said, turning to me.

"Are you sure?"

"Yes."

We both took a deep breath and walked up the stairs and to the large, foreboding double doors. I rang the bell, and Roman opened the door, expecting us.

"Morning," he said, quickly hiding his surprise at seeing Lucia.

"Morning."

"Come in. He's waiting for you in the study." I nodded and took a step. Roman put his hand on my shoulder.

"Should I keep Lucia company—"

"No, thank you," I said, tucking her arm tighter to me.

He stepped back. "I'm glad you came."

I nodded, and we moved forward, neither of us speaking. Knocking once on the study door, I pushed it open, not expecting to find what I found. I heard Lucia's gasp, but I had schooled my face for so many years that masking my surprise came more easily than I thought it would.

"Salvatore," my father said after glancing at Lucia on my arm.

"Father." They'd moved a hospital bed into his study. It stood in place of his desk, which was pushed to the side. I remembered that desk, how I'd trembled on the opposite side of it when I'd been called in for this reprimand or that growing up. There had always been something he was displeased with.

"Don't just stand there, come inside. It's not contagious."

His bitterness held an edge of regret. I heard it clearly.

We both entered. He adjusted his positon, so he sat up taller. He looked so much smaller than the last time I'd seen him. So much older. Dark circles ringed his eyes, and his cheeks looked sunken. He must have lost about twenty pounds too.

"I came to say good-bye," I said, not wanting to delay this any further.

He once again glanced at Lucia before returning his gaze to mine.

"I assume you've seen the contract?"

"Roman showed it to me."

"Well, here's your own copy." I set it on the foot of the bed. "You were wrong to tell Dominic. He never needed to know."

He took in a deep breath, and his hand trembled, but his eyes remained fixed and hard.

"It was a mistake," he said. "One I will pay for until the end." No one spoke for a long moment. "Will I see you again?"

"No."

He lowered his gaze to the envelope then back to me.

"I forgive you," Lucia said, surprising me. "I forgive you for everything you did, all the hurt you caused."

He only stared at her, but I couldn't read his eyes.

"We never could please you, huh? None of us, not my brothers, not our mother, not really."

"I've never been an easy man, son. Don't think I don't know that. And don't think I don't know I've made mistakes. I only did what was best for my family."

"I believe you believe that."

I released Lucia's hand then and went to him.

Leaning down, I kissed the top of his head. "Goodbye, father."

His eyes glistened when they met mine, and he nodded but didn't speak. I walked away and took Lucia's hand. Without a backward glance, we left the house, got into the car, and drove away.

It was silent for a very long time, and I wasn't even sure where I was driving to.

"I want to scrub my skin," I said finally, inhaling a loud breath. "I want to burn my clothes and wash with scalding hot water."

"Pull over, Salvatore."

"I want—"

"Pull over."

I did. Lucia reached over and wrapped her arms around me. I buried my face in her shoulder and wept like no man should weep. "I've never wanted to leave a place so badly. I've never wanted to leave a person—"

"Shh."

"So many lives wasted."

She held me, and I clung to her. A lifetime's worth of pain and sadness welled out of me. So much was lost for so many of us, all of it so pointless, so unnecessary. So much death, so much anger and jealousy and hate. So much I needed to purge until there was nothing left, nothing at all but this broken, exhausted body.

When I pulled back, I found Lucia's face stained

with tears. She wiped mine away, just kept brushing my face with her thumbs, looking at me, looking at me, not letting me go.

"Don't leave," I said finally. "I don't want to lose you, Lucia. Not you too. You deserve so much better than this, than me..." She hugged me to her again, fresh tears pouring from her eyes. "I have no right..."

"Come with me," she said, pulling back. "Come with me now, and we'll start again. A new beginning."

I shook my head. "I shouldn't have asked...I'm—my world, Lucia, it's dark. It's so damn dark inside. You deserve light. You deserve carefree and happy and light. So much light."

"And you don't think you do? You stubborn fool."

She kissed me, a salty kiss.

"My brother—"

"Come with me," she said again, this time more firmly. "Right now. We'll drive. Come with me, please, Salvatore."

"I love you, do you know that?" How could a grown man weep like this?

"It's you who doesn't know I love you."

When she kissed me that time, something inside me shifted. I felt it like a physical thing in my chest, my gut. I squeezed my eyes shut and felt her, her body in my arms, her lips on mine, her tears wet on my face. I kissed her back, inhaling deeply, my tongue inside her mouth, my hands pulling her closer and closer because I couldn't be away again. I couldn't have her away again. And so, when we pulled back, I smiled and turned the car around, and I drove south, leaving everything behind and just driving away with the girl I loved beside me.

LUCIA'S EPILOGUE
SIX MONTHS LATER

We did it. We drove to Florida. We drove as far as we could from New Jersey and ended up on the very tip of Key West. We bought a modest old house with a strip of private beach and started again.

The renovations on the house would probably take us over a year to complete, but I liked it. It was built in the 70s, and the seller was the son of the sole owners of the place who had done zero updates since its build. It needed a lot of work, but work was a good thing. It kept us occupied, kept our minds busy, especially Salvatore's.

It was strange at first, as though he didn't know how to be without the Benedetti mafia behind him. Around him. Taking up all of his energy. Defining him. There was no one to take care of here besides us. Natalie and Jacob had settled in California.

Roman took care of the family business with few questions for Salvatore. He'd been so involved when Franco had been boss that he was a natural fit. I didn't think Salvatore regretted handing everything over, but this life was very different than the one he'd had.

My sister and Luke lived south of Miami, which was just shy of a four-hour drive to Key West. At first, the tension between Luke and Salvatore had been high, but both men had something in common. They'd both nearly died. They both realized what was important, and that was family. I wished they lived closer. I wanted to be around my sister and Effie after having missed out on so many years, but this worked, and it was better than what I'd had for five years.

As happy as Salvatore and I were with the simplicity of things here, there was one thing that bothered him. Dominic's absence.

He'd hired several investigators but came up short at every turn. Dominic had vanished, and Salvatore struggled to come to terms with that.

I stood outside of our little house at the barbecue looking out at the beach, startling when I heard him.

"You smell like a steak," Salvatore said, suddenly behind me, his mouth on the back of my neck.

"Christ! How do you always sneak up on me?"

He'd walked around back where I was grilling

two steaks. He'd been gone most of the day, picking up supplies.

He laughed and held out a bouquet of sunflowers. "You're too involved in your head, that's how."

I was too involved for a reason.

"I missed you." His mouth found mine.

"Me too." I kissed him back and took them. "These are pretty. Thanks."

"I'm glad you like them." He looked at the grill. "Early for dinner, isn't it?"

"I'm just hungry."

"Well, I'm not hungry for food just yet," he said sliding his hands down and into the back of my shorts. He squeezed my ass, kissing me deeply, his big body bigger, even more muscular since we'd started working on the house. His skin had darkened in the Florida sunshine. He seemed to smile more, and his face looked more relaxed. I didn't think it would be possible for him to be even sexier than before, but he was.

"I've been thinking about this all day."

He picked me up. I wrapped my legs around his hips and my arms around his neck.

"I haven't fucked you on the picnic table yet," he said, pushing my shirt aside and taking a nipple into his mouth.

"You are a dirty, dirty man, Salvatore."

"I think you like it, Lucia."

He set me on the table and continued to kiss me before pulling the peasant shirt over my head.

"Do you remember," he started, stripping his T-shirt off, "when we were in my study, and I fucked your ass for the first time?"

I felt my face blush as he pushed my knees apart and stood between them, his grin evil and his eyes dancing while he unbuttoned my shorts and pulled the zipper down.

I leaned in close. He thought he was embarrassing me, did he? Taking his hair in my hands, I tugged, turning his head to the side and licking his ear. "I remember I liked it. But who says I'm giving you permission to fuck my ass again?"

One hand raked up my back, pulled the tie out of my messy bun, and gripped a handful of hair.

"I need to ask permission?" he asked, closing his mouth over mine.

This kiss had a hunger to it.

"Don't you remember what I said you'd do the next time I wanted to fuck your ass?"

I shook my head, although I remembered perfectly. My hands moved to explore his chest. "Refresh my memory."

"Something about you bending over my desk and spreading yourself open. Something about begging me to do it."

"You think I'll beg you to fuck me?" I chuckled

and slid my fingernails down his back to push my hands into his shorts and cup his tight ass.

"I do," he said, tugging my shorts off and dipping his head down. "I think I'll have you begging to be fucked in no time."

"Do you?" I asked as I leaned back.

He gave me a cocky grin and slid the crotch of my panties aside. Sparing one glance at my pussy, he returned his eyes to mine.

"Judging from this dripping cunt, yes."

He dove in, making me suck in a sharp breath, only taking breaks to taunt me.

"I think I'll make you wait too."

He tickled my clit.

"Make you bend over and spread yourself open while I watch. Hell, maybe I'll make a couple more steaks while you're begging."

I pushed his head into my pussy. "You talk too much."

Fuck, he could work his tongue. He could make me come in a minute or an hour, depending on how evil he felt. And today, Satan himself feasted on me.

"You're killing me," I finally said, refusing to beg, to ask him to make me come, but trying to drag his mouth back to me.

"Stay," he said, straightening. "Just like that, legs wide. And hold your panties aside. I want to see your cunt."

"I hate you," I said to his back but pulled the

string of my panties aside, feeling all the more exposed for it.

"You love me," he answered, disappearing into the house.

I stayed as I was, liking it, out in the open, exposed for him. The backyard was completely private, but it thrilled me to think someone could walk around the house at any moment and find me like this.

He was back a few moments later, and I saw what he carried with him. A tube of lube.

"Good girl."

He was happy to see that I was still in position. He lifted me to stand, turned me around, and pushed me to bend over before sliding my panties down to midthigh and stopping.

"What are you doing?" I asked, glancing back at him as he stepped away.

"Reach back and spread your ass open."

"I won't beg you," I said and slid my hands back to my ass and did what he wanted. The expression on his face was worth my own embarrassment. I slipped the panties off to spread my legs wider.

"Fuck."

"What?" I taunted, wanting him but wanting him to be the one to beg. "You want?"

He rubbed himself over his jeans and approached me. He unzipped his jeans, took out his cock, and stroked it.

"You okay there, Salvatore?" I asked, arching my back and wiggling my hips before sliding a finger inside myself, then smearing the moisture up and around my back hole.

With a groan, he slid into my pussy. I put my hands back on the table when he gripped my hips, his eyes going dark as he watched himself fuck me.

It felt so fucking good, him slowly sliding in and out of me, thinking of him seeing me as I opened for him making me wetter.

But then he stopped moving, kept his cock in my pussy, and picked up the lube.

I groaned, and he grinned, uncapping it and squeezing out a generous amount before rubbing it onto me. That was when he started to move again, his cock in my cunt, his fingers in my ass.

"This is not fair," I managed.

"Just ask for it, and I'll give it to you good and hard just like you like it."

"Fuck you."

He withdrew his cock and rubbed it through my folds instead, his fingers still working in my ass.

"I won't," I grunted, fisting my hands. "I..."

He leaned over me and tickled my ear with this tongue. "Just say please. Just once."

"Never!"

"Feels good and tight, Lucia. You're ready for a good, hard, ass fucking. You want it. I just need the word,"

"You'll never let me forget it."

"Think of it, of me pounding into that tight little hole. Think of how sensitive it is, how you're already so close." He pulled his cock away from my clit and withdrew his fingers. "But if you don't want it—"

"Please!"

"Please, what?" he whispered, cock ready at my ass.

"Please fuck my ass."

I swear I heard him smile.

"I told you you'd do it."

He kissed my cheek before straightening. He pulled apart my ass cheeks with one hand, smeared lube on his length with the other. How I loved watching him grip his cock. I could just look at that all day long. He grinned and slid the other hand beneath me.

"And you call me dirty."

I arched my back. "Fuck me already."

"Up on your elbows. It's going to be hard and fast."

I braced myself but couldn't have been ready for that.

"Good girls get rewarded, Lucia, remember that?"

"Fuck, yes!" His fingers worked my clit roughly while his cock thrust in and out, movements deep, slow at first but increasing in pace as I came, my first orgasm making me cry out, making him thicken inside me until, on the heels of my second orgasm, he thrust one final time and fell over my back, his cock throbbing as he came. He breathed hard against my ear and bit the edge of it just a little too hard, but that nip drew one final, smaller shudder from me.

We clung to each other, neither of us speaking as our breathing slowed. I don't think either of us took our time together for granted. I knew I never would, and I knew it would never be enough.

We showered afterward before sitting down to eat. I plated the steaks and carried the dish over to the table where Salvatore had just put two beers down. I took a seat across from him.

"You're really going to eat two steaks now?"

I nodded, ravenous, unsure how to tell him, happy myself but uncertain how he'd feel. We'd only been living together for half a year if I didn't count the time in New Jersey.

He watched me for a long minute, sipping his beer while I devoured the food. He pushed my untouched beer toward me. I met his gaze but popped another bite of meat into my mouth instead of going for the beer.

"Lucia?"

He could always read me like a book.

"I'm pregnant."

SALVATORE'S EPILOGUE
THREE MONTHS AFTER THAT

I married Lucia on the beach in our backyard. Lucia walking toward me barefoot, her belly swollen, wearing a simple, flowing white dress bound by golden thread just beneath her breasts and a crown of flowers in her hair, was probably the most beautiful thing I'd ever seen.

I'd never been so happy in my life.

We wrote our own vows, and she blamed hormones when she wept throughout the ceremony. Luke and Isabella were our witnesses and Effie our flower girl. That was all. No other guests apart from the priest who married us. Afterward, we barbecued and swam and talked about baby names and about Isabella and Luke moving closer. Effie spoke more to her little cousin inside Lucia's belly than to anyone else. She may have been as excited as Lucia and I were.

They spent the night and drove back home the next afternoon. We didn't have a honeymoon. There was nowhere either of us wanted to be but here. Together.

"We have everything," she said as we lay on lounge chairs, watching the night sky.

We did, and neither of us took a moment of it for granted.

"Will you tell your father?" she asked.

"In time."

"What's on your mind?"

I looked over at her and tugged the thin blanket over her shoulder. She'd filled out a little with the pregnancy, and she couldn't be more beautiful to me.

"Dominic. I'm worried."

"He'll turn up. He has a lot to process, and probably feels awful for what he did."

"He'd know by now that I'm fine. He'd know where we live. He just disappeared, and that worries me."

She touched my hand and brought it to her belly. I faced her to kiss her lips and rub the warm mound.

"He'll turn up when he's ready. Give him space."

"What if he's…hurt himself?"

"He's not the type. It's far more effective to torture yourself while living, Salvatore. You and your brother both—guilt is like a second skin to you. It's like you have to learn how to live, how to breathe, without it. You're learning, but you've got a good teacher," she finished with a wink.

"How did I end up so lucky?"

"You signed a contract, remember?"

She rolled onto her side, her back to me, and I pulled her in, holding her tight.

"Smart-ass."

"Don't forget pigheaded."

"Oh, no, you prove that on a daily basis."

She jabbed her elbow into my gut.

"Apart from my brother, my life couldn't be more perfect. It scares me a little." It scared me more than a little. "What if... I've done bad things, Lucia. I don't know if I deserve all of this."

"You've done good things too, Salvatore. You deserve all of this and more. We're making up for lost time, you and I. It's time for us to be happy and carefree and walk in the sun with sand between our toes. It's past due, in fact."

She squeezed my hand, pulled it up to her heart.

"Don't be scared of losing this. Just be happy and grateful. That's what I've learned. I think that's what we're supposed to learn. It's so simple, but we make it all so complicated."

"My oracle."

"I am wiser than you, that's true."

"And not at all arrogant." I heard her smile.

"Good night, husband."

"Good night, wife." I kissed her neck and held

her as she fell asleep, her body relaxing, her breathing soft and even. I looked up at the night sky, at all the stars, and listened to the sound of the ocean, knowing I held everything that mattered right here in my arms. Knowing she was right about Dominic, that he needed space, that he needed to figure this out for himself. She was also right about the guilt. I was very good at wrapping it over my shoulders, weighing myself down with it. Maybe I needed to learn that some of that didn't belong to me.

Lucia was wise and strong. I'd given her what I'd promised, a peaceful life, happiness. And while doing so, I had given the same to myself.

I may not be able to save my brother, but maybe it wasn't up to me to save him.

I squeezed Lucia tighter and closed my eyes, nuzzling my nose in her hair. Life was both crazy and beautiful, and out of the ugliness and hate, we'd made love. I would not forget to cherish that, to cherish her, forever.

WHAT TO READ NEXT
DOMINIC: A DARK MAFIA ROMANCE EXCERPT

Dominic

Fear has a distinct smell, something that belongs only to it. Pungent. Acidic. And at the same time, sweet. Alluring, even.

Or maybe only sweet and alluring to a sick fuck like me. Either way, the girl huddled in the corner had it coming off her in waves.

I pulled the skull mask down to cover my face. The room was dark, but I could tell she was awake. Even if she held her breath and didn't move a single muscle, I'd know. It was the scent. That fear. It gave them away every single time.

And I liked it. It was like an adrenaline rush, the anticipation of what was to come.

I liked fucking with them.

I closed the door behind me, blocking off the

little bit of light I'd allowed into the small, dark, and rank bedroom. She'd been brought here yesterday to this remote cabin in the woods. So fucking cliché. Cabin in the woods. But that's what it was. That's where I did my best work. The room contained a queen-size bed equipped with restraints, a bedside table, and a locked chest holding any equipment I needed. The attached bathroom had had its door removed before my arrival. Only the bare essentials were there: a toilet, sink, and a shower/bathtub. The bathtub was truly a luxury. Or it became one at some point during the training period.

The windows of both the bedroom and the bathroom had been boarded up long ago, and only slivers of light penetrated through the slats of wood. Both rooms were always cold. Not freezing. I wasn't heartless. Well...I had as much heart as any monster could have. I just kept the rooms at about sixty degrees. Just cool enough that it wouldn't do any damage but it wouldn't be quite comfortable.

I walked over to the crouched form on the floor. She stank. I wondered how long they'd had her. If they'd washed her during that time.

I wondered what else they'd done to her, considering the rule of no fucking on this one. My various employers didn't usually give that order. They didn't give a crap who fucked the girls before auction. It's what they were there for. But this time, Leo—the liaison between the buyer and me—had made certain I understood this particular restriction.

I shoved the thought of rape aside. I didn't do that. Whatever else I did to them, I didn't do that. Some tiny little piece of my fucked-up brain held on to that, as if I were somehow honorable for it.

Honor?

Fuck.

I had no delusions on that note. Honor was a thing that had never belonged to me. Not then, not when I was Dominic Benedetti, son of a mafia king. So close, so fucking goddamned close to having it all. And it certainly didn't belong to me now. Not now that I knew who I was. Who I *really* was.

More thoughts to shove away, shove so far down they couldn't choke me anymore. Instead they sat like cement, like fucking concrete bricks in my gut.

I stepped purposefully toward the girl, my boots heavy and loud on the old and decrepit wood.

"Wakey, wakey."

Available in all stores. Buy Now!

THANK YOU

Thanks for reading Salvatore: a Dark Mafia Romance. I hope you enjoyed it and would consider leaving a review at the store where you purchased the book.

Want to be the first to hear about sales and new releases? You can sign up for my Newsletter Here!

Like my FB Author Page to keep updated on news and giveaways!

I have a FB Fan Group where I share exclusive teasers and interact with readers. It's called The Knight Spot. If you'd like to join, click here!

ALSO BY NATASHA KNIGHT

To Have and To Hold Duet
With This Ring
I Thee Take

The Society Trilogy
Requiem of the Soul
Reparation of Sin
Resurrection of the Heart

Dark Legacy Trilogy
Taken (Dark Legacy, Book 1)
Torn (Dark Legacy, Book 2)
Twisted (Dark Legacy, Book 3)

Unholy Union Duet

Unholy Union
Unholy Intent

Collateral Damage Duet

Collateral: an Arranged Marriage Mafia Romance
Damage: an Arranged Marriage Mafia Romance

Ties that Bind Duet

Mine

His

MacLeod Brothers

Devil's Bargain

Benedetti Mafia World

Salvatore: a Dark Mafia Romance

Dominic: a Dark Mafia Romance

Sergio: a Dark Mafia Romance

The Benedetti Brothers Box Set (Contains Salvatore, Dominic and Sergio)

Killian: a Dark Mafia Romance

Giovanni: a Dark Mafia Romance

The Amado Brothers

Dishonorable

Disgraced

Unhinged

Standalone Dark Romance

Descent

Deviant

Beautiful Liar

Retribution

Theirs To Take

Captive, Mine

Alpha

Given to the Savage

Taken by the Beast

Claimed by the Beast

Captive's Desire

Protective Custody

Amy's Strict Doctor

Taming Emma

Taming Megan

Taming Naia

Reclaiming Sophie

The Firefighter's Girl

Dangerous Defiance

Her Rogue Knight

Taught To Kneel

Tamed: the Roark Brothers Trilogy

ABOUT NATASHA KNIGHT

Natasha Knight is the *USA Today* Bestselling author of Romantic Suspense and Dark Romance Novels. She has sold over half a million books and is translated into six languages. She currently lives in The Netherlands with her husband and two daughters and when she's not writing, she's walking in the woods listening to a book, sitting in a corner reading or off exploring the world as often as she can get away.

Write Natasha here: natasha@natasha-knight.com

Click here to sign up for my newsletter to receive new release news and updates!

www.natasha-knight.com

Printed in Great Britain
by Amazon